DICK STORNAWAY

OR,

A Hero in Spite of His Foes.

———◦◦◦◦◦◦◦———

By E. H. BURRAGE.

———◦◦◦◦◦◦◦———

SPLENDIDLY ILLUSTRATED.

"BEST FOR BOYS" PUBLISHING CO., 17, GOUGH SQ., FLEET ST., E.C.

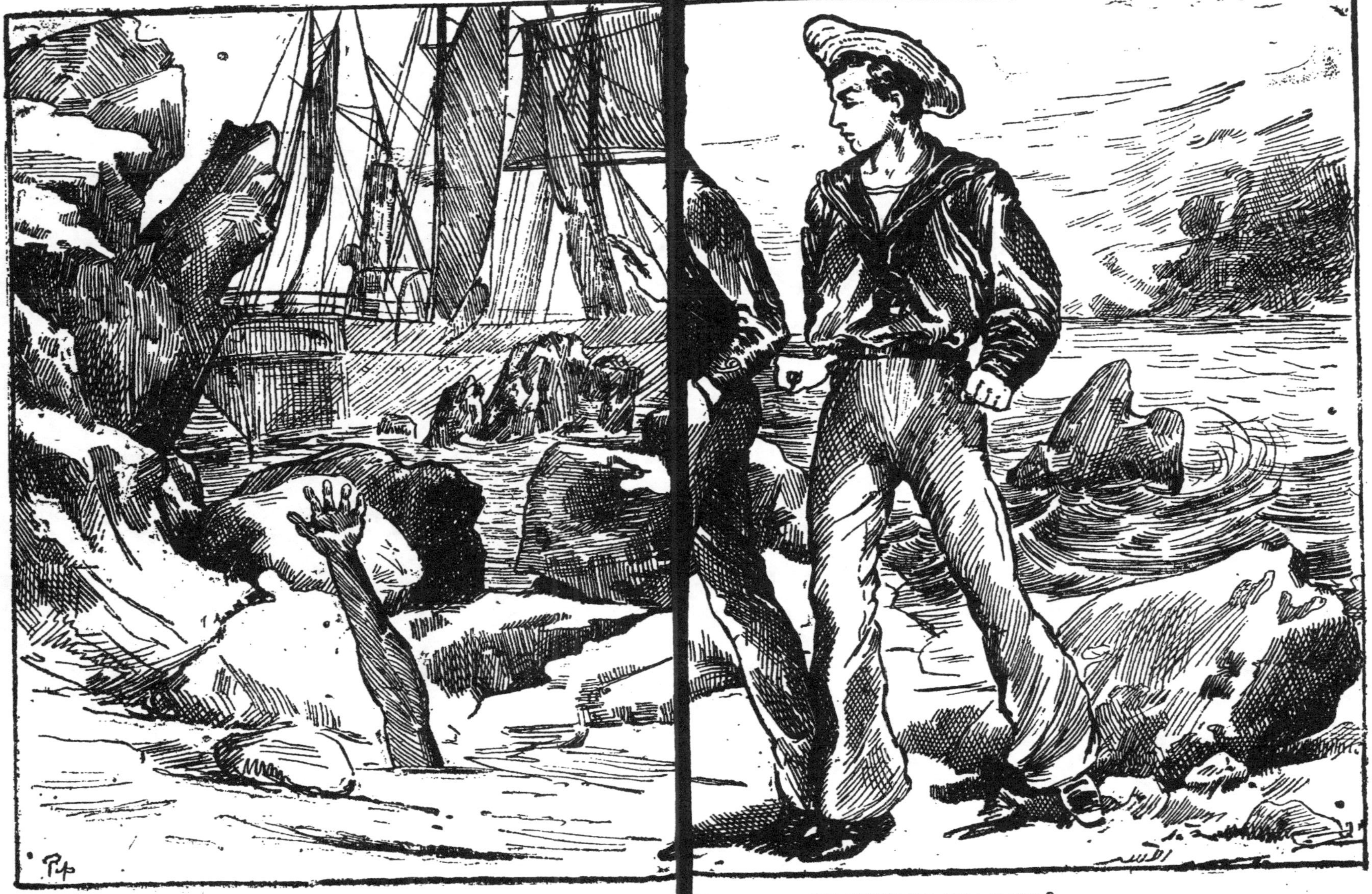

DICK DISCOVERS A STRANGE SIGHT: WHAT LIES BENEATH THE HAND?

DICK STORNAWAY;

Or,

A Hero in Spite of His Foes.

By E. HARCOURT BURRAGE,

AUTHOR OF

" Handsome Harry" and " Cheerful Ching Ching."

CHAPTER I.

"TOO HANDSOME BY HALF"—UNREASONING HATE— BLACK HEARTS AND WHITE HANDS.

"I HATE the fellow. From the moment he came on board I felt he came here to be—well! I don't know exactly what. He isn't an enemy, for an officer doesn't recognise an ordinary seaman. But—there—hang it all, I can't explain it. All I know is that I HATE him."

The speaker was the Honourable Gorton Fontenoy, heir to the recognised Earldom of Staunton, and about as plain a looking aristocrat as could be found in the great circle of the "upper ten."

He was acting as third lieutenant of Her Majesty's

cruiser the "Cyclops," although still a midshipman at present engaged in looking out for slavers off the coast of Africa.

The person he addressed was Hanson Seaforth, senior midshipman, a good looking but somewhat effeminate fellow, in appearance at least. They were standing aft by the side of the vessel, apart from the others on deck, and Gorton Fontenoy spoke in an undertone.

His companion answered him in a slow drawling way.

"You get excited about nothing, my dear boy," he said. "I never see anything wrong about this Dick Stornaway. He's only a lad, you know, although he's a fine fellow."

"A fine fellow be bothered," said Gorton Fontenoy, impatiently, "as for being a mere boy, he's as old as you are."

"Eighteen last birthday," drawled Hanson Seaforth. "It's a great age. I think I shall soon be grey."

Although he spoke in this strain he did not seem to be much affected by the contemplation of his "great age."

His way of speaking might be termed lazy and there was a sleepy look in his handsome eyes that reminded an observer of one not yet fully awakened from slumber.

"He was no sailor when he came on board," said Hanson, "and he's not a bit like the rough lot he has to mix with. They are rough, but ready, and a lot of good fellows."

"Oh! that's like you, sticking up for common people."

"Don't stick up for anybody, only say what I think. Man's a man if he acts like a man, you know."

Gorton Fontenoy shrugged his square thick-set shoulders impatiently.

"You have no family pride," he said.

"Family pride don't count for much," said Hanson, without changing his tone; "never filled empty pockets yet. My governor's got a lot of it, but it doesn't pay his tradesmen, nor does it satisfy the lot of useless servants he keeps about him."

"Really, Hanson, I am sorry to hear you speak against your father in that way."

"On my word I am not saying anything against the governor; only pitching into family pride. Governor's a good fellow, but pig-headed—didn't make his head, so can't help that. Family pride's bosh, and he ought to sit on it—as I do. Perhaps I sit on it because I like sitting about. It's easy work."

"Here comes the beggar," said Gorton Fontenoy. "Now just see how he carries himself. Hang it—I'd like to take the starch out of him."

"No starch," murmured Hanson, who, by the way, was known among the sailors as ' Young Lazy Bones, Esquire.' "Family pride and starch same thing. All Stornaway's got is a lot of GO in him. Wish I had some of it."

The object of these remarks went by as they were speaking.

He was a tall and exceedingly handsome lad of eighteen or so; possibly he might have been a year older or younger.

The dress of an ordinary seaman, always becoming, sat well upon him, and he added grace to it by his easy elastic movements.

As he passed by he cast a quick glance at Gorton Fontenoy, and there certainly was some meaning in the look, although it was not in any way offensive.

But the lieutenant, who, by the way, was about twenty years of age, promptly resented it.

"Stornaway!" he said sharply.

Dick turned and saluted, and in his very salute there was something that gave him a dignity Gorton Fontenoy did not possess.

"Sir," he said.

"If you are insolent I shall report you," said the lieutenant angrily.

"Yes, sir," returned Dick quietly, "but I do not mean to be insolent; I hope I never am."

"That very reply is insolence," said Gorton Fontenoy. "Go to your duty. I shall report you."

Dick saluted again, and unmoved as far as his exterior went, walked forward.

Hanson Seaforth might have been a wax figure for all the notice he apparently took of the little scene, and when Dick was gone he indulged in a yawn.

"Now, what do you think of that?" asked Gorton Fontenoy.

"Of what, my dear fellow?" asked Hanson.

"Of his impudence."

"Didn't see it."

"But you heard it."

"No."

"Do you mean to say that you didn't hear what he said?" demanded Gorton Fontenoy.

"Oh, yes! heard him right enough," replied Seaforth, "but couldn't see or hear insolence."

"You wouldn't see it," said Gorton Fontenoy, with a considerable amount of acidity in his voice.

"Would rather not say what I saw," said Seaforth. as he began to slowly move away.

"Then you did see something?" eagerly demanded the lieutenant.

"Oh, yes! but would rather not say what it was."

"But I really wish to know."

"Tell you if you like, then," said Seaforth. "My dear fellow, you made an *ass* of yourself."

There was not the least change in his voice as he expressed this somewhat emphatic opinion of his companion's conduct.

He gave it out in his sleepy, drawling way as he might have uttered something commonplace.

But it hit home.

As Seaforth, yawning, lounged away, the face of Gorton Fontenoy changed slowly, first to white and then to a faint green.

His small eyes flashed with evil fire, and his hands closed tightly as if he had all he could do to restrain himself.

"Confound you, Seaforth," he muttered, "I will one day be even with you for this. You have taken the part of this Dick Stornaway from the first, and for all your sleepy way of doing it I can see that you have put yourself between him and me. Mind I don't break *you* one day."

Hanson Seaforth, indifferent to the effect of his words, strolled aft, when he suddenly came upon Captain Harrison, the commander of the "Cyclops," just emerging from below.

Seaforth had his hands in his pockets, and the captain fixed his eyes upon them.

" Beg pardon, sir," said Seaforth, as he withdrew them.

"I have told you before, Mr. Seaforth," said the Captain, "that you set a bad example by going about in that slovenly way."

" Sun very hot, sir," he murmured, " hands get so dreadful tanned."

His hands, it may be said, were long and as delicate as those of a woman. They were also very white, as if he had never used them in his life.

Captain Harrison was stern for a moment, but as Seaforth did not appear to think that he had done or said anything unusual, the expression of his face changed to its normal appearance of good temper.

The commander of the "Cyclops" was a kind man in the main, but he was a great stickler for duty, and anything like shirking work or showing the white feather he never overlooked.

"Mr. Seaforth," he said, "I do not know exactly what to make of you. You do your duty in your way and I cannot complain of you in that respect. What else you may be fit for I shall see when we get to the serious work I think lies before us. Let me tell you, however, that it is not *woman's work*, and white, delicate hands are not the claws for it."

He passed on, and Seaforth having saluted went below to the middies' berth.

It was not his watch, and he had nothing to do. The only other occupant of the cabin was a middy, of fifteen, who was lying on a locker asleep.

" Not woman's work, and white hands not fit for it," murmured Seaforth, as he looked at his tapering fingers. "Well, I suppose if I have to do the work I had *better begin to brown them.?* I wish I could take them off and hang them out a bit. It's a bore. Not woman's work. Who said it was? Am I a woman? Don't think so. Wake up there, Ned."

The boy lying on the locker slowly opened his eyes half way, and stared sleepily at Seaforth.

"Get up, you lazy little beggar," drawled Seaforth. "What do you mean by idling there?"

"It's so beastly hot," replied the boy, as he slowly struggled into a sitting position, "and I do like you talking to anyone about being lazy. Why, snails are racehorses to you."

Seaforth looked at him in his dreamy way for fully half a minute before speaking. At last he drawled out:

"Were you ever slippered?" he asked.

"No," replied the boy.

"Then you will be if ever you compare me to a snail again," said Seaforth. "Idleness is the root of all evil. It is good to be active and happy. The idler of to-day is likely to be hanged to-morrow or at some other period of his life time. Avoid cheek as you would a bottle of poison. Ned Dawson, you will oblige me by taking these precepts to heart, and to utilise the passing moments, in an industrial sense, by getting me a bottle of lemonade?"

"I don't see why I should," grumbled Ned.

"I am afraid your mental vision is not what it ought to be," said Seaforth. "Are you going to do it?".

Still serene in his manner, there was, however, something in him that induced Ned Dawson to do as he was told, and from that locker on which he had been lying he brought out a bottle of lemonade and a tumbler.

As he removed the wire, and the cork popped, the cry of the look-out faintly floated in through the open porthole.

"Something in sight," said Seaforth, as he took up the glass, "go and see what it is, Ned. Remember if you are active and obliging you can be good and happy without riches."

"Oh! blow your precepts," said Ned, "it isn't fair to run a fellow off his legs such a beastly hot day as this."

Fair or unfair he went, and was soon back with the following information:

"Land in sight, and two Arab dhows racing for the shore."

"All sail is crowded on," the boy added, "and we shall overhaul them."

"In that case there may be work to do," said Seaforth. "I may flesh my maiden sword. Not work for women. Pity I haven't time to brown my hands. Well! never mind. I'll see what a pair of white ones can do."

CHAPTER II.

CHASING THE DHOWS — VOLUNTEERS WANTED — WHERE IS DICK STORNAWAY?—THE CUTTING OUT.

IT was about noon, and the sun was right overhead. The shadows of the men as they moved about on deck were almost nil. The heat came down upon all like fiery rain.

Hanson Seaforth on returning to the deck had a look round, and far away saw the land just getting defined.

Between the "Cyclops" and the shore were two white specks, which were the Arab dhows, laden in all probability with some hapless savages captured to be sold as slaves.

They were making for a river, which, if they could reach it, would be a haven of safety. The object of the Captain of the "Cyclops" was to cut them off from that place of refuge, and drive them into a bay a few miles to the north.

There they might succeed in getting into shallow water, but the boats could cut them out and capture or kill the crew.

The wind favoured the "Cyclops."

It was freshening up, and coming from a quarter which gave the cruiser the first advantage of it. The two dhows were, as yet, only favoured with a very light wind.

Forward stood the seamen of the watch, with Dick Stornaway in their midst.

He was very quiet, and a little pale.   While others softly conversed on the prospect of a fight, he remained silent.

Presently one of the men, named Muzzle, an old salt with rather an unpleasant sort of face, turned to Dick and said :

"You've never had a brush with the Arabs, have you ? "

"No, nor anybody else," Dick answered.

"Ah, then that accounts for your looking so white, my lad," said Muzzle.

"I generally lose colour if I am excited," returned Dick, "but that does not show I am afraid."

"Most people looks on it in that way," sneered Muzzle.

"Well, I am not afraid," answered Dick.

"If you are told off for the cutting out, in course you will fight ? "

Dick did not answer him, but one of the other men said :

"Can't you keep your tongue between your teeth, Muzzle ?   The lad's one of the right sort."

"That's what YOU say," returned Muzzle, "but I don't think he's got a heart in him."

"Have you ? "

"As much as I want."

"Don't quarrel about me," interposed Dick, "if I show the white feather I must take the consequences."

Half an hour later it was known to all who were watching events that the dhows had been cut off from the river of refuge, and must take themselves into the bay

It was known as Safety Bay, and possessed the advantage or disadvantage of having a very narrow entrance with a sand bar.

At low tide ships of deep draught could not enter it.   It was almost low tide then.

The dhows would therefore have to be cut out, and

this being foreseen arrangements for the work were at once begun.

Captain Harrison did not treat it as a heavy task. He considered that two boats and about thirty men would suffice and speedily carry it out.

To Gorton Fontenoy he gave the command of the first boat and was debating in his mind whom he should entrust with the second boat when Hanson Seaforth lounged up.

" Beg pardon, sir," he said, saluting," but may I see what I am fit for, by taking the second boat ?"

Captain Harrison was surprised. He would rather have expected the sleeping middy to have cried off.

" Don't forget, Mr. Seaforth," he said, " that it may be stiff work. Sometimes these Arab fellows fight like devils."

" I hope they will," said Seaforth, lazily. " One doesn't like to be considered a WOMAN, sir."

" You shall command the second boat," the Captain said.

Volunteers were called for, and, as usual on board British vessels, about three times the number required came forward.

The two commanders then proceeded to pick their men.

One of the first Seaforth chose was Dick Stornaway, which made Gorton Fontenoy very wroth.

" Still determined to run him against me," he muttered.

Then he beckoned Muzzle, who came over to his side with the air of an old favourite.

The two dhows had by this time reached the mouth of the bay, where a line of moderate-sized breakers proclaimed the presence of the bar.

Over this the " Cyclops," as stated. could not go. But she sailed right up to it, and was then brought to.

Although order was strictly maintained, there were some signs of bustle and excitement as the two boats were lowered.

This was about a quarter of an hour after the selection made from the volunteers.

Armed with cutlass and revolver the sailors tumbled into the boats, and the two in command took their places,

Then in a moment it was discovered that a man was missing from each.

Gorton Fontenoy wanted Muzzle and Hanson Seaforth was looking for Dick Stornaway.

Their names were called out and Muzzle speedily responded by appearing at the side.

" Where have you been, you lubber ? " cried the captain angrily.

" Beg pardon, sir," replied Muzzle, " it was hot, and I went below to get a drink of water."

" Get in with you ! "

Muzzle dropped into his place.

" Stornaway ! "

This was the second time Dick had been called for, and he did not respond.

" Stornaway—Stornaway ! "

" Skulking somewhere," said Muzzle.

" Take another man in his place, Mr. Seaforth," said Captain Harrison.

" I should like to have him if I could," replied Seaforth.

" But the expedition can't wait for one man," was the answer.

Seaforth, of course, yielded, and another volunteer dropped into the boat. The eyes of Gorton Fontenoy flashed with malicious joy.

" Give way," he cried to the crew.

" I should like to be the first there," said Seaforth sleepily to his men.

He looked back two or three times, evidently troubled by the non-appearance of Dick Stornaway, but could see nothing of him.

On deck there was a number of men, including the other officers, watching the boats.

The bows had got into the bay and run as close in shore as the retreating tide permitted, but although they drew only a few feet there was a wide stretch of water between them and the beach.

They were boats about fifty feet long, narrow, built for speed. Over their sides peered a number of dark faces, looking the darker for the white turbans above them.

Arms glittered in the sun, and it was clear the Arabs meant to fight.

The two boats of the "Cyclops" got safely across the bar and having reached the smooth water the men began to race for the place of honour in the coming fight.

"Don't pull yourselves to pieces, men," said Gorton Fontenoy, "you will want some of it left for the attack."

"Go ahead, men," cried Seaforth.

"Take the dhow on the left," sang out Gorton Fontenoy, "you will find that handiest."

"And the biggest of the two," muttered one of the men.

It was the larger craft, and showed more men on her deck. There was also a small swivel gun in her bows, and nothing of the sort was visible in the other.

Seaforth was well contented. Gun or no gun that was the dhow he had fixed upon, and as his men pulled with all their might the boat that ought in naval etiquette to have been second was a good first.

When within about fifty yards of the dhow, the swivel gun was fired.

It had been loaded with a lot of small missiles that spread about the water and around the boat.

Two or three of the crew were hit with something, but what it was they did not know or care.

No great injury resulted.

The boat dashed up, the bow man sprang up and hooked on. Then it swung round, and Hanson Seaforth, in a moment, was over the side.

He was literally the first on board.

A few seconds sufficed for the men to follow, and then began a desperate hand to hand fight with the Arabs, who were about forty in number.

It was one of their "devilish" days, and they fought as savage men fight for their lives.

Hanson Seaforth, in a calm way, walked into the

thick of them and speedily showed the stuff he was made of.

Suddenly his apathy was gone.

The white hand closed with a strong grip on his sword, and with lightning like thrust, cut and parry, he struck terror into the hearts of the swarthy foes.

His men needed no example but his bearing inspired them with additional daring, and like the rush of some irresistible machine they forced the Arabs into a heap and speedily decimated them.

A few leaped over the side and swam for the shore, but the majority had fallen.

The dead were still, the wounded lay sullenly on deck, refusing all aid from the "infidel."

Some of the fierce fanatics held their wounds open to let the lifeblood flow freely.

They were defeated, they had fallen in fight, and they wanted to die so as to join the blest believers in paradise.

"Let 'em be, sir," said one of the men to Seaforth, as he made an effort to bind up the wounded head of an Arab, who spat at him in return. "You can't either knock sense into 'em or show 'em a kindness. They'd rather be let alone."

Meanwhile the other dhow had been attacked and the fighting was still going on. The seamen were as gallant as those of the second boat, but their leader did not so readily enter into the fight.

He did not show the white feather, but he was not *eager*, as one of the men put it, so the work was slower.

But they were victorious. They had fewer Arabs to deal with and the destruction that had attended one crew was reserved for the other.

A small number of the Arabs also made for the shore and about a dozen in all escaped.

Now came the second part of the task which would have to be performed with great care.

Under the decks of the dhows were the slaves whose howls during the fight had not been heeded, but now fell with unpleasant emphasis on the ears of their rescuers.

They seemed to know what the riot above them meant and howled like chained dogs which hear a canine fight going on outside the yard.

These men had been captured at some place along the coast, for the dhows were sailing from it when first seen and had put back again.

The slaves, when set free, would, in a sense, be within hail of their homes.

The hatches were raised, and there was seen below a seething, raving mass of dark-skinned humanity bound together by strong ropes, so knotted and placed as to defy the biting powers of the captives to sever them.

The foremost were handed up, their bonds cut, and signs made for them to get ashore.

With yells of joy they leaped into the sea, and uttering strange cries, waded to land.

There was quite a procession from each dhow.

Four hundred despairing wretches were thus given their freedom.

About two score had gained it another way.

They had been stifled in the hold and lay there in every attitude expressive of dire suffering.

The fight was over, the majority of the Arabs were dead: only three or four of the wounded still survived, and they were as doggedly determined as the rest to die.

Gorton Fontenoy gave orders for both the slave craft to be towed into deep water.

There, according to his instructions, he would see them dismasted, scuttled, and sunk.

The attacking party had half-a-dozen wounded to care for, and these being carefully placed in the bow of the boats, the dhows were taken in tow.

There was nothing on board that could be turned into prize money.

"Just two dirty shells," said one sailor to another, "and nothin' more."

Gorton Fontenoy did not congratulate Seaforth on his success, or the gallant way in which he had behaved, and the other did not show that he thought anything of it.

Immediately after the fight, he relapsed into his original sleepy state.

"Not a ruffled feather about him," said one of Gorton Fontenoy's men, aloud, "Mister Seaforth's a cool'un."

"Silence there," cried Gorton, angrily.

"All right, sir," muttered the sailor, inaudibly, "if he's cool, you're hot, but you might ha' showed a little more pepper in fighting.

The dhows were towed out into deep water, just without the bar, and the wounded Arabs on board being by that time all dead, the scuttling was swiftly performed.

Before the two "Cyclops" boats had been hauled into their places, the foul vessels engaged in the most villainous trade on earth had gone under the restless rippling sea.

CHAPTER III.

AFTER THE FIGHT—THE FINDING OF DICK—BRANDED WITH SHAME—SEAFORTH TO THE FRONT.

WHEN the boats returned, the first person Hanson Seaforth looked for was Dick Stornaway.

He had been strangely troubled by the non-appearance of his hero, and when not engaged in the fight his mind had been occupied with it.

What was the cause of it?

Dick was not an ordinary sailor, or of the class of which the usual able seamen spring; but that was the reason why he took an interest in him.

He liked Dick because he was such a manly fellow, and it may here be said that the majority of the seamen had the same feeling towards him.

They could see that he had, in the matter of education, been more fortunate than any on board, but he never gave himself any airs, or assumed any superiority.

Not a word did he ever say about himself previous to his coming on board the "Cyclops."

He did not strike any of the men as being a runaway from home, for he was always cheerful and made himself one of them.

But he had terribly lost caste that morning by his non-appearance to accompany the attacking party.

During the fight all had been on deck. Discipline as to the watch was for the time relaxed and there was a little crowd on the forecastle.

Captain Harrison, his first lieutenant, and second lieutenant were there, also the petty officers.

For the time Dick had been utterly forgotten.

But on the return of the victors their thoughts turned to him again.

Hanson Seaforth, after being complimented by the captain on his gallant conduct in action, asked after Dick, and the reply was a shrug of the shoulders.

"I haven't seen the fellow," was the reply, "but now I will look him up. Desertion, as it practically is, cannot be left unpunished."

Gorton Fontenoy stood by hoping also to be congratulated, but all he got was a general word.

"The men under you," said Captain Harrison, "fought well, and I shall report it favourably to the authorities at home."

"Hang that Seaforth," muttered Fontenoy, "he has taken the wind right out of my sails, but I'll lower his colours before he is many weeks older."

At that moment Muzzle presented himself before Captain Harrison, who was moving away, and saluted

"I axes your pardon, humbly, captain," he said, "but that ere Stornaway——"

"Well," said the captain.

"He's a lying by the door of the store-room drunk or asleep, sir."

"Show me where he is," said the captain, with a face like a thunder-cloud.

The captain and Muzzle went off, and Fontenoy, after a moment's hesitation, followed.

The leery old salt led the way below, and ushered the captain into the store-room.

There, sure enough, lay Dick, with his head upon a coil of rope, sleeping soundly and snoring.

"Rouse the coward up," said the captain.

This was not to be done in a moment. Muzzle gave

DICK CALMLY SET FIRE TO THE FONTENOY FLED FOR HIS LIFE.

him a hearty shaking in vain.

"Get a bucket of water," said the Captain.

Muzzle, with wonderful alacrity, ran upstairs, and speedily returned with a bucket of salt water.

Close behind him, in his usual leisurely manner, came Hanson Seaforth.

Muzzle, with all the violence necessary, and a little more it may be said, dashed water into Dick's face.

The shock it gave aroused the youth and springing up he stared wildly about him.

"Where am I?" he asked.

"Stornaway," said the captain, sternly, "you may well ask that question."

Dick turned his eyes towards him, and in a confused way saluted.

"I——I—don't quite understand it, sir," he said.

"I do," was the answer, "you are a coward, you have been skulking."

Dick's face flushed violently, and then became deadly pale.

The memory of things that recently happened flashed upon him.

"I don't know how I came to fall asleep, sir," he said, "just now my head is in a whirl, I hope to be forgiven, I am ready to go."

"Where?"

"To help to cut out the slavers."

"Now," said the captain, "when you know it is all over."

"All over, sir," exclaimed Dick Stornaway, terribly agitated.

"Yes," was the answer, "the work has been done, while you have been lying skulking here."

"If you please, sir," said Muzzle, "the store room is unlocked."

"That makes matters worse," said the captain, "let me look at it. As I suspected, the lock has been forced back. You coward; first you came here to get up a little Dutch courage, and to do it you have committed a robbery. I shall place you under arrest."

"For Heaven's sake, sir, don't do that," cried Dick,

"I am innocent."

"Innocent?"

"Yes, sir, try me any way you like, I am not a coward, and have never, all the time I have been on board the 'Cyclops,' tasted a drop of strong liquor."

"That is why it overcame you," said the captain, "Mr. Fontenoy, you will take charge of the prisoner until I can hold a court martial upon him."

"Sir," said Dick, with a wild light in his eyes, "I have not done this thing, I swear it."

"Naturally you would. May I ask what brought you down below?"

"I came for a drink of water, sir. The day is very hot and I did not want to go into action thirsty."

"So you broke into the store room and drank the first thing that came to hand."

"I have not touched anything but the water. I noticed that was very peculiar——"

"And where did you get it from?"

"There was a jugful in the mess room and I took some from that."

"Out of which, sir, I'd drunk the moment before," said Muzzle.

"Yes, I saw you there as I came in," returned Dick. "I don't say it was the water, all I know is, that I drank some of it and then a sort of haze came before my eyes. I staggered from the room and I remember no more."

"A very pretty story," said Captain Harrison, "but it will not save you. You will be tried for robbery and desertion from your post."

"Again I implore you, sir, not to do this," said Dick, "if you only knew——"

He stopped short, and put his hand to his brow.

"Knew what?" asked the captain.

"Nothing, sir," replied Dick quietly, "it does not matter. I only say that I am innocent of this charge."

"You will have to prove it," was the dry response. "Mr. Fontenoy, you will see that he is properly placed under arrest."

So saying, Captain Harrison, with an angry face, went

up the companion.

Hanson Seaforth, who had been quietly surveying the various actors in the scene, now stepped forward and said :

" Stornaway, do not give up. I, for one, believe you to be innocent."

" Thank you—thank you," replied Dick. " You have been kind to me more than once. Why, I don't know. Believe me, I am grateful."

" I don't know why you put yourself out of the way, Seaforth, in this matter," said Fontenoy ; " but let me tell you it is a serious thing."

" How ?" asked Seaforth.

" You virtually give your superior officer the lie," said Fontenoy.

" Do I ? Not aware of it," was the cool rejoinder.

" You give it to me, and I am your superior officer."

" Oh ! you are referring to yourself," said Seaforth. " I don't see how it is giving you the lie, because I can't call to mind that you made the charge. Was Muzzle your deputy accuser ? "

An angry flush spread over Fontenoy's face, but he made no answer.

Turning to Muzzle, he said :

" Go on deck with the prisoner ; I will follow ; he must be put in irons."

" Really—really !" exclaimed Seaforth.

" Do you DARE to interfere with me doing my duty ? " demanded Fontenoy.

" As for daring — I dare do anything perhaps," replied Seaforth, " but I am not going to play into your hands by interfering further—all right—do as you please with him."

" And one day you will surely repent it," said Dick.

" Do you threaten me ? " demanded Fontenoy.

" No," said Dick, " I only warn you. I am innocent of willingly shirking my duty, *and you know it.*"

" I ? "

" Yes, but how you know it I am unable to say. I have seen it in your face. You do know it.' In a dim way I see the villainous trick that has been played upon me, and one day I may be able to *prove it*."

"Go on. How dare you persistently argue with me?" said Fontenoy.

"Ay, that's what most people would like to know," growled Muzzle.

"Perhaps you DO know," calmly suggested Hanson Seaforth.

"I shall be obliged to report you," said Fontenoy, violently.

"For what?" asked Seaforth, quietly.

"Oh, for—well, you have no right to suggest that Muzzle knows anything about it."

"Then let Muzzle take action. Isn't it unusual for an officer to take the line you are doing?"

Gorton Fontenoy bit his lip and motioned for Muzzle to proceed.

Dick, with his arms folded, and his head erect, walked proudly up the companion to the deck.

The story of his real or supposed delinquency had got there before him, and as he appeared a slight hissing was heard.

"Silence," said Seaforth, who was immediately behind the prisoner, "You are not his judges."

They were silent then, and Dick, with a proud light in his eyes, went forward, followed by Fontenoy and Seaforth.

The boatswain was summoned, and instructions given for placing Dick in irons.

This was done in the sight of the crew, many of whom, by the expression of their faces, sympathised with him, but did not openly say so because they dare not with the officers present.

But their sympathy did not extend to a belief in his innocence. They were only charitable to him.

"He's very young," said one, softly. "I know how I felt when I first went into action. The lad wants seasoning."

When Dick, with his manacles, was taken away, Gorton Fontenoy walked aft with Seaforth by his side.

"Satisfied now, of course," said the latter.

"Seaforth," said Fontenoy turning upon him. "why

do you persistently take the part of this fellow ?"

"I take it now," was the answer, "because I think he is the victim of a villainous trick, and I hope to help to prove it. Fontenoy, it is bad enough to make an ass of oneself, but when it comes to roguery——"

"Seaforth."

"All right, old fellow. Report me if you like—oh ! hang your looks ! I'm not afraid of you. All I can say is—*that I would not be a chum of a man like Muzzle*—and if I wanted a tool I would not have a two-edged one. That's all I have to say—at present."

CHAPTER IV.

DICK IN CONFINEMENT — HE FINDS A FRIEND—MUZZLE GETS A STAGGERER—THE SEDIMENT AT THE BOTTOM OF THE JUG.

THE "Cyclops" steered away from the scene of the recent exploit, bearing north, where it was expected some other slave-dealers would be fallen in with.

In addition there was a certain African chief, one Tokoa Fay, king of the Wanpa Tribe, who had judiciously put himself under the protection of the Britisher, and was now in need of assistance.

Tokoa Fay had sent word that he was threatened with an attack from foes, who had surrounded him on all sides, and the "Cyclops" was on the way to his assistance when she fell in with the two dhows.

As a matter of public duty, Captain Harrison was obliged to deal with these at once, and having done so he proceeded on his mission.

With regard to Dick Stornaway, the captain of the "Cyclops" was not exactly satisfied with the affair.

He had often observed Dick at his work, and considered him to be a very smart young fellow.

He was quick, energetic, fearless in going aloft, and in every way a smart sailor.

Therefore did his apparently cowardly act seem unaccountable.

But the fact remained.

Dick had volunteered for a dangerous duty, and at the last moment had not appeared to perform it.

Then there was the breaking open of the store-room, for picking a lock is in law breaking open, and the stupid, sodden sleep in which he had been found.

"Well, everything is very dark against him," the captain said, "and if he cannot explain it, he must be punished."

The whole of that day Dick was confined in the hold, in irons.

His proud, handsome face was very white, and the agony he endured was shown in the frequent quivering of his lips. Occasionally a few words would burst from him.

"Branded a *coward*. Despised, dishonoured, and whom am I to thank for it?"

He could make nothing of it. No clue to the origin of that sudden sleep could he obtain beyond the fact that Muzzle had been drinking out of the same jug a few minutes before him.

And what did that prove?

Nothing, absolutely nothing.

The day passed in wearying reflection and the evening brought a visitor. It was Muzzle with some ship's biscuit and a tin mug of cocoa.

The face of the old salt was on the grin, and having put the biscuit and the drink within reach of the prisoner he took up a position before him as if studying some very pleasing picture.

"You've brought your pigs to a nice market, young man," he said at last.

"I would rather not have anything to say to you," Dick replied.

"In course you wouldn't," sneered Muzzle, "but you can't stop my saying anything to you."

"If I were to make a complaint of your conduct to Captain Harrison, he ——"

"Oh! you won't do that," interrupted Muzzle. "I know you're one of them sneaking chaps as wouldn't do this or that just to set yourself above other people."

"Pray do not waste your time here," said Dick.

"The moment you came aboard." said Muzzle, stooping down and leering in his face, "I took a dislike to you. *You ain't one of us.*"

"What do you mean by that?" asked Dick scornfully.

"You ain't one of us common chaps," said Muzzle.

"Common," said Dick, "no man is common if he is honest. You are common enough, you dog, you tool. I know I cannot prove it, but I am sure that I owe my present position to you."

"Maybe—maybe," said Muzzle banteringly. "I don't admit it, mind you. The moment you came aboard I says to myself, 'He's a chap that will go wrong,' and t'others said the same."

"By others you mean—what does it matter?" cried Dick, impatiently, "get away, man."

"I'll go in my own time," said Muzzle savagely, "just when I like."

"I think you had better go now," drawled somebody behind him.

It was Hanson Seaforth, who had come up in his leisurely way without being heard.

He looked as sleepy as ever and had an eyeglass in his eye, a thing he rarely wore, but when he did fix it he was usually in an extra apathetic condition.

"Axin' your pardon, sir," said Muzzle, saluting, "but I'm appointed over the prisoner."

"Who appointed you?" asked Seaforth.

"Mr. Fontenoy, sir."

"Then I remove you. Have you the key of these irons?"

"Yes, sir."

"Take them off."

Muzzle stared at Seaforth in dismay.

"Take 'em off?" he said.

"Is it usual for a seaman to hesitate when he gets an order?" asked Seaforth, "take them off, I say."

"I hope, sir, as I'm doing my duty," mumbled Muzzle, as he felt in his pocket, "but Mr. Fontenoy was so premptery 'bout my keeping the prisoner safe."

"If you say another word to me," said Seaforth

in leisured tones, "I will report you for insolence.

Muzzle gave in then, and said not another word.

In obedience to the command he received, he unlocked the irons and Dick shook them off.

"Carry them away," said Seaforth to Muzzle, "and you need not return. I will arrange for another man to wait upon Stornaway."

"He didn't say the 'prisoner,'" muttered Muzzle as he crept out of the hold, "why on earth do he take the part of the beggar ?"

Seaforth did not say anything until Muzzle had disappeared. Then he turned to Dick and said :

"You need not thank me for doing this. It is not much. As I said from the first, I believe you to be innocent. I'll lay a hundred to one that you were drugged."

"But how can it be proved?" asked Dick. "You know, sir——"

"Stornaway," said Seaforth, "you need not 'sir' me in private. I don't want to pry into your affairs, but I can see that you were not brought up to the life you lead."

Dick made no answer for a moment or two. Then he said :

"No, I was not."

"As I suspected," answered Seaforth ; "you have run away from home."

"No."

"Quarrelled with your father ?"

"I have none to quarrel with."

"Friends then ?"

Dick shook his head.

"No," he said, "I came on board the "Cyclops" so as to get to the Antipodes. You know she was ordered to Melbourne, and then at the last moment that order was countermanded, and she was sent on here."

"And why do you want to go to Melbourne?" asked Seaforth.

"I simply want to find——" Dick stopped. "It would hardly interest you, and I am afraid if you knew my story you would laugh."

"You shall tell me it another time," said Seaforth, serenely. "I am not at all curious, and you must want your supper. You will understand that you are still a prisoner."

Dick's countenance fell.

"I—I was in hopes," he said, "that the charge had been withdrawn—that the *mistake* had been discovered——"

"You are on your parole to be of good behaviour," said Seaforth. "I have staked my own honour in the matter, which, of course, doesn't count for much."

"I cannot find words to thank you," said Dick. "Why do you do all this for me?"

"All this is nothing," said Seaforth, as he dropped his eyeglass; "nothing—do it for any fellow—don't thank me for *amusing* myself. I must do something on board to keep alive. Good evening."

He sauntered away a few steps, then stopped and looked over his shoulder.

"By the way," he said, "I got hold of the jug you drank out of."

"Yes?" said Dick, eagerly.

"A little water was left in it," returned Seaforth, "at the bottom there was a sediment—captain got it bottled up—going to have it analysed as soon as we get into port. Looks suspicious anyway. Don't worry —you'll get out of this."

Waving his hand as much as to say, "Don't say another word to me, my good fellow. I haven't the strength to bear it," he sauntered up the steps and disappeared, leaving Dick with the star of hope rising before his gladdened eyes.

Meanwhile Muzzle, who acted occasionally as servant to the junior officers' mess-room, had gone in search of Gorton Fontenoy, whom he found alone walking slowly up and down.

He turned on Muzzle as if he had been a dog, and asked him "what the devil he wanted there."

"I've come to say as Mr. Seaforth's been interfering again," replied Muzzle.

"That's no news," replied Fontenoy.

"So it's all true," said Muzzle, sitting down with the air of a confidential friend. "You've been chucked."

"Get up with you," said Fontenoy; "suppose Seaforth or anyone came in—what would they think?"

"The truth," grinned Muzzle, "that you and I—are friends, like."

Gorton Fontenoy palpably winced, and some hot words rose to his lips, but with an effort he restrained himself.

"You are playing a fool's game, Muzzle," he said. "Remember this—you can prove nothing against others although much can be proved against you."

"What can be proved?"

"Captain Harrison has got the water that was left in the jug. He's bottled and sealed it to have it analysed."

"What's that?"

"He will give it to a professor of chemistry who will find out *what was put into the water*."

Muzzle's face turned green, save the tip of his nose, which remained a rusty red.

"How did he get hold on it?" he asked, in a cracked voice.

"Seaforth gave it to him. Why didn't you empty the jug after he drank?"

"There wasn't time."

"You are a miserable messer," snarled Fontenoy, "and mind you, I won't bear any of the blame."

"You'll have to do it," snarled Muzzle, "one drop, both drop. If I goes to prison, so do you. Blessed if you ain't got me for life."

"Well, Muzzle," said Fontenoy, "we ought not to quarrel, that would be the most foolish game of all. Nothing has been proved yet, and if we can only find out where the bottle is kept——"

He stopped and looked at Muzzle, who softly murmered, "Ay, ay, sir."

"And if that bottle should disappear."

"Ay, ay, sir."

"Nothing could be proved."

"I follow you, sir."

"And then we might turn our attention to Seaforth, who's been prying into what don't concern him."

"He's as good as a dead 'un," said Muzzle, fiercely, "there's hundreds o' ways of getting rid of a officer."

"Yes," said Fontenoy, looking round carefully, and dropping his voice to a whisper, "say it's his watch—and a dark night—men have gone overboard——"

"Yes, sir, and he's no great weight."

"Or ashore on some of these islands," continued Fontenoy, "a man might be stabbed, or cut down and left in some hole, where nobody would find him."

"With half a chance I'll do it."

"And with *him* dead, and no proof, Muzzle, this Stornaway will get kicked out of the ship. Oh! the game is not over yet. We hold all the trump cards. Don't fear."

"You puts a new heart in me, sir," said Muzzle, "and if you've got such a thing as a drop o' sperit I'll drink to our better luck."

"There's a bottle in that locker," said Fontenoy, "take what you want, and get away sharp. Just now it won't do for us to be found talking together."

Muzzle went to the locker pointed out and took out a bottle and a glass.

The former contained brandy, and having helped himself to a double dose he disappeared.

"All is not lost yet," muttered Fontenoy, "but what a miserable fool to *leave* any of it remaining. It MAY spoil all, and if I see exposure coming, I'll put you to rest, friend Muzzle, *somehow*. That brandy bottle may be *your* trap, and if you should be found dead, why what more natural than that you who drugged a fellow seaman to ruin him should commit *suicide*."

In a moment the face of this young, but sinful, man was lit up with exultation. Then it suddenly darkened.

"But where am I going? Why do I do all this?" he muttered, "for nothing tangible. The very echo of a fear, and yet it grows stronger What is this I am ever hearing sounding in my ears: 'Ruin, dishonour, and why am I *haunted* by this Dick Stornaway? What is he? Who is he that I should trouble about him as I have done?"

He was violently agitated, and walked quickly up and down the limited area of the room about a dozen times. Then suddenly stopped and spoke again.

"And what did my father say when I last left home, 'Remember this. In the world there is one who MAY be your bane and our ruin.' What did he mean by that, and why should he say that the secret had better remain with him? Who is that one I have to fear? Can it be Dick Stornaway? And if so, by what accident or design have we been brought here together?"

To none of these mental problems could he find an answer, and after some minutes of wild communing with himself he turned to his locker and took out the brandy bottle.

With trembling hands he filled the small glass and emptied it once, twice, and thrice—then replaced the fiery dangerous liquor, and with a step somewhat unsteady went up the companion to the deck.

CHAPTER V.

KING TOKOA FAY—HIS CHEERFUL LITTLE WAYS—
THE ADVANCE OF THE TRIBES—DICK'S DARING
FEAT.

KING Tokoa Fay was King of the Wanpa Tribe, and the tribe were not only peaceful and numerous, but uncommonly lazy.

The example of idleness was set them by the monarch who passed most of his time under a big umbrella, the shade of which was very grateful to him

To teach his people the value of self denial he generally had a number of his chiefs and people seated around him in circles without umbrellas to protect them from the burning sun. They oiled their heads and greased their faces and bodies as a means of protection from the scorching luminary, which is a very wise thing to do, but for all that they frizzled, and fried and perspired in a degree that would have settled any living owner of a white skin.

They were dutiful subjects and did not complain.

If they had he would have done his duty as a monarch and chopped off their heads.

Tokoa Fay did not allow any of his people to argue with him.

The only people who indeed dare so were those who came well armed and strong enough to smash his big umbrella and bowl him off his royal seat.

Some years before the opening of our story he had been introduced to the Britishers in this fashion :

A cruiser anchored off his coast and sent a boat's crew ashore for water and fruit.

His Majesty, then in the zenith of his fame, said none should be given.

Had he spoken English at the time he would have said : "I'll see you blowed first," but as he was then ignorant of the language he desired his chiefs to give battle by way of answer.

A lot of arrows were let fly at the boat and a sailor was killed.

Promptly a number of men were sent ashore, and before the sun set that night half the chiefs had been knocked on the head, and the rest had fled with the people to the woods.

King Tokoa Fay being too fat or too lazy to run was taken prisoner, and one of the tars having laid hands on the sacred umbrella banged about his majesty until all the cane ribs were broken.

As soon as he got his breath again, his majesty sued for peace.

He also expressed a desire to be taken under British protection, and offered to make his kingdom a water and fruit station for our cruisers for ever.

He likewise asked for his umbrella to be mended.

Everything was done to his satisfaction, and the cruiser, having got what it wanted, went away, leaving an old tar behind to teach Tokoa Fay the English tongue."

The name of this old sailor was Jimmy Tartub, and

he taught Tokoa Fay English as HE knew it, and very nice English it was.

Now certain tribes inland heard of Tokoa Fay having become friends with the Great White Queen, of whom they had heard, and knew that she was a lady who would not stand any nonsense.

They were also informed, through some of the Wanpa people, that the White Queen had sent to Tokoa Fay one of her best "medicine men," who, of course, was no other than Jimmy Tartub.

All sorts of wonderful tales were recorded of him, the particulars of which need not be entered into here.

Suffice it to say that these tribes wanted to get hold of Tartub, so that they might have the benefit of his miraculous powers, and for that purpose they prepared for war.

To stop them in their nefarious proceedings was the object of the " Cyclops."

Tokoa Fay, as a monarch, was nobody, but it was just as well to have his country as a health station for the cruisers.

So the belligerent tribes were to be taught a lesson, and *instructed* to let him alone.

One morning His Majesty sat under his umbrella upon the beach, with his frizzling subjects around him.

There was a sound of distant drum beating on both sides of him, for the foe was advancing.

By the side of Tokoa Fay sat Jimmy Tartub — a grizzled old tar with a leery eye. He was calmly smoking a short pipe, and puffing the smoke right under His Majesty's nose, to Tokoa Fay's visible discomfiture.

"They're coming along, Tokey, old man," he said, " and if the ' Cyclops ' don't turn up soon you'll have to fight or cut it."

" Me no fight," said the monarch simply. " Damery, villains."

" Then you must run," said Jimmy. "Here—stop— what's this? A sail in the horizon — hurrah — they're coming ! "

Jimmy jumped up, took a long look to seaward and then shouted again.

"Come! old Foozleum," he said, banging the fat and helpless Tokoa Fay on the back. "In half-an-hour she'll be here."

"Shivy me timbers," said Tokoa. "Good."

It was the "Cyclops" approaching, and presently she drew in and anchored a mile or so off the shore.

Old Jimmy got up and did a part of the British hornpipe, and then dug the monarch in his ribs.

"Saved, old Beefy," he said.

"Good," said Tokoa Fay, coughing, "but no gib me so mooch punch."

"All right," said Jimmy Tartub; "but they are only just in time. Look right and left, you old jelly fish."

Tokoa did so, and in the distance on either side of him beheld a body of dark skinned men.

These were the warlike tribes advancing.

None of his subjects dare turn their heads or even their eyes to see either the ship or the foe. "Eyes front" was their condition when in the presence of the great king.

No boat was lowered from the "Cyclops," much to Jimmy Tartub's disgust.

"They just come to look on and see us fight it out," he said. "Well, it's all right as far as I'm consarned. They'll not kill me, being a precious sort of harticle. Will they, old beeswax?"

Tokoa Fay smiled and seemed quite proud of the number of titles bestowed upon him.

He had little upon him in the way of actual dress, his suit of clothes being confined to a red cloth around his loins, but he had ornaments galore.

In his nose were two big brass rings; others were in his ears, and around his neck, wrists, and ankles he wore many strings of varied colour beads.

The dress of his chiefs was of the same sweet simplicity, with fewer beads, and two thirds of his subjects wore the cloth alone.

"What's up aboard?" asked Jim. "Oh, I see, going

to give 'em a scare."

As he spoke a gun was fired on board the " Cyclops,"
and a shell went screaming away to the right.

It struck the sands and buried itself without exploding.

This was followed by a second that burst in the air
just before it reached the ground.

The effect was all that could be desired.

As if blown into the air by the shell the advancing
tribe broke up and disappeared, leaving nothing but a
lot of little drums which they had been beating behind
them.

Attention was now turned to the other side, and the
first shell, aimed like the other in advance of the
approaching foe, caused them to halt.

A rapid consultation followed, ending in their retreat,
pretty rapid, but orderly, and to the sound of their
exhilarating martial music.

" They've postponed the job," said Jimmy Tartub,
" and now here comes a boat."

Captain Harrison did not deem it necessary to come
ashore in person.

He sent Mr. Moore, the first lieutenant, who was accompanied by Fontenoy, Seaforth, and a number of
men in the longboat.

Among the latter were Muzzle and Dick Stornaway.

Dick had not been tried, nor would he be tried until
the contents of that bottle had been analyzed. Meanwhile Captain Harrison had allowed him to resume his
ordinary duties.

But Dick's lot was far from a happy one.

Muzzle had told his yarn, but Dick scorned to
relate his, for the present, at all events, and the con-
sequence was that the stigma of cowardice still rested
upon him.

Seaforth and the first lieutenant had been told off to
interview the King, and Fontenoy was desired to go
up the beach, and, if possible, recover the unexploded
shell.

He was permitted to take half-a-dozen men with
him, and among them he selected Muzzle and Dick.

When the boat touched the beach the first lieutenant sprang out, and, with Seaforth by his side, strolled towards that mighty monarch, Tokoa Fay.

He received them with royal gravity, and Jimmy Tartub, who had not forgotten his sailor duties, stood up and saluted.

The chiefs and people sat like statues, never moving a muscle.

Bows were exchanged, and Tokoa Fay motioned the two emissaries to advance.

" Come under dis blessed umbella," he said.

" Thanks, no," replied the first lieutenant, " we do not mind the sun."

" His Majesty is rather HIGH," murmured Seaforth, "I wonder what sort of cart grease he uses for his hair ? "

" They ile him all over every morning, sir," explained Jimmy Tartub, " half-a-dozen of his women folk does it and he do lay out on 'em with his tongue, most frightful."

Leaving the lieutenant and the leisurely Seaforth to carry out their visit of courtesy we will follow Fontenoy and the men he had taken with him.

He had made a deliberate selection of Dick for the purpose of insulting and annoying him.

When they drew near the spot where the shell had fallen he desired him to look about.

" And don't shirk this job as you did the other," he said to Dick.

" I did not willingly shirk it," replied Dick.

" Silence, or I will report you," cried Fontenoy, "how dare you turn your tongue at me ? "

" Mr. Fontenoy," said Dick firmly, " I am not a dog, and unless you address me in a more becoming way I will not obey your orders."

" Look about for that shell," said Fontenoy angrily.

Dick, with a disdainful face, began his task.

To disobey the command would be to play into the hands of his enemy and that in common prudence he would not do.

But he was resolved to teach Fontenoy a lesson that

day, even if he lost his life in the doing.

His quick eyes had already discovered where the shell had plunged into the soft sandy beach and with angry resolute steps he strode towards it.

The shell had not travelled far and he began to kick aside the sand with his foot.

"Steady there, you fool," cried Fontenoy, "you might explode it."

"What care I?" replied Dick looking back, "if you are afraid of it I am not."

The shell had struck the earth almost horizontally and did not lie deep. He soon laid it bare—a nine inch shell, with a single fuse.

By some means it had escaped ignition and Dick raising it in his hands, walked backed to Fontenoy with it.

Muzzle stood by his side and the other seamen, who also were near.

"Hand that over to me," said Muzzle.

"In one moment," replied Dick, "see here."

Holding out the shell in his left hand he quickly produced a match from his pocket, rubbed it against the side of the shell, and set it alight.

Then he calmly set fire to the fuse.

CHAPTER VI.

WHO IS THE COWARD NOW?—DICK'S RASHNESS— FLIGHT—VOLUNTEERS TO SEEK HIM.

"You fool!" yelled Fontenoy as he fell back. Then wheeled round and fled for his life.

"You blarmed ass!" roared Muzzle, as he staggered back and fell all in a heap.

The other men, petrified by the daring act, began to sheer off.

"Who is a coward now?" cried Dick.

Then, with an unmoved face, he laid the burning shell upon the ground and walked quietly away.

Muzzle, in mortal terror of his life, lay as flat as a flounder on the beach yelling "Murder?"

Fontenoy and the other men had already got out of danger.

Bang !

The shell had exploded and a great mass of sand was tossed about on every side.

Dick heard the whirr of a piece of the shell as it flew past his head, but he neither started nor moved an atom quicker.

After going a few more paces he turned round and looked for Muzzle.

He had disappeared for the moment but where he had been a little hillock of sand was being broken up.

After a few seconds Muzzle, half choked, emerged from the mass and began to yell louder than ever.

Fontenoy had now stopped also.

"Seize him !" he cried, "arrest the murderous brute ! "

Dick stood his ground glaring fiercely at the men, who now, in obedience to orders, were rushing towards him.

Muzzle, with drawn cutlass, was the first to get near him.

He aimed a wild blow at Dick, who dodged it, and then hit him fairly between the eyes, bowling him over as if he had been a tailor's dummy.

Snatching the cutlass from the hand of the staggered Muzzle, Dick turned and faced Fontenoy and the men.

"Don't try to take me," he cried, " I won't be taken, and will sell my life dearly."

"Arrest him," cried Fontenoy, white to his very lips.

"Why not do it yourself, coward ? " cried Dick, making a dash at him.

Fontenoy once more turned and fled, and Dick, with a laugh of derision, ran after him.

The men stared at each other as if in doubt of what they ought to do.

Before they could decide, Dick had turned sharply to the left and was now running for a wood that stood about a furlong from the sea.

" He's cut and run," said one of the seaman, "and

blessed if I don't think he's right, for drawing a sword on your superior officer ain't a joke."

Fontenoy did not stop or look back until he was drawing near the circle of King Tokoa Fay.

The circle still remained in its statuesque state of duty, but the king himself, Jimmy Tartub, and the two officers had seen all that had taken place, and with the exception of Seaforth, exhibited signs of excitement.

"Why! the fellow IS dangerous," said the first lieutenant, "he is mad."

"I don't think so, sir," replied Seaforth, "it was a cool trick, anyhow."

Fontenoy came panting up, trembling with anger and fear.

"You saw that fellow make an attack upon my life, sir," he said.

"I saw something unusual going on," was the reply, "what possessed him to set light to the fuse of that shell?"

"He meant to murder us all, sir," said Muzzle, who now came up, "he said he would do it."

"And now he's deserted," said Fontenoy.

"He must be brought back. Take half-a-dozen of the men and go after him."

"That would be of no use, sir," returned Fontenoy; "it is an enormous forest."

The first lieutenant turned an enquiring eye on Jimmy Tartub.

"It is so, sir," he replied.   "It's miles through, but there's tracks as these Wanpa people knows on."

"Could they find him?"

"I reckon so, sir," said Jimmy Tartub. "Here—I'll see to it—they know me and I knows them.   You go aboard, sir, and I'll have him back afore morning."

"And your own foes, or rather the foes of Tokoa Fay —what of them?" asked the first lieutenant.

"Well, they won't show their noses for the next six months; then we'll hear more on 'em, and you'll have to come and purtect His Majesty again."

"Dat so," said Tokoa Fay, "giggermeifitaint."

"What did he say?" asked the first lieutenant.

A soft embarrassed smile spread over the face of Tartub.

"It's a kind o' broken English he's picked up, sir," he said ; "ain't it, ole Twentystun ?"

The king nodded and grinned. He was as proud of his English as he was of his titles.

Hanson Seaforth said a few words to the lieutenant in an undertone, who replied :

"Yes — I don't see why you should not go, if you——"

The jealous ears of Gorton Fontenoy caught the answer and divined the meaning of it.

"I should think," he said, "that the natives could get on better alone."

"Your thoughts, Mr. Fontenoy," said the first lieutenant coldly, "do not, as a rule, influence your superior officers. We will return on board, as I desire to consult Captain Harrison."

"Can I remain here, sir ?" asked Seaforth.

"Certainly," was the answer, " as I understand it, the pursuit of the deserter will begin at once."

"Sartinly," said Jimmy Tartub, " Old Hippopotamus will have to get on without me for a few hours, d'ye hear ?"

"Me sleep," said the compliant monarch, "shiber-my-topsels, dat what I do."

The first lieutenant called the men together, and with Fontenoy returned to the boat.

And still those grim circles of slaves, the chiefs and chosen people of Wanpa, never stirred nor seemingly looked at the strangers.

After they were gone, Jimmy Tartub looked curiously at Seaforth and said :

"Hadn't you better change your mind, sir ?"

"Why ?" asked Seaforth.

"We may get in among a rough lot," was the answer, "I'm all right, because I'm supposed to be a medicine man, able to do what I like with the moon and stars and sich like, but if they get hold of you, heaven only knows what they won't do."

"For all that," said Seaforth, "I will go. The

deserter must be captured, and brought back to his ship."

"Then come on," said Tartub. "I say, old ebony bag," addressed to the monarch, "pick out a dozen chiefs, and fifty men for scout work. Them as can look at a stone, and tell at a glance if a man has sat down on it a month off."

"If they can do that," said Seaforth, "they are very clever,"

"They can do summat pretty near it," replied Tartub hitching up his trousers, "and they'll track him down as sure as he's a bolter. Living or dead, they'll have him."

CHAPTER VII.

DEPARTURE TO THE WOODS—A SHARK—HANSON SEAFORTH'S RETURN — DISHONOUR FOR THE HONOURABLE.

ALL but Hanson Seaforth returned to the "Cyclops," leaving him to accompany Jimmy Tartub and his party of natives to search for Dick.

Gorton Fontenoy was in a joyful state although he exhibited none of it to those with him.

Everything had played in his hands.

If Dick had designed to do all he could to please his foe he could not have arranged matters in a form more agreeable to Fontenoy.

The daring act of lighting the shell could be easily construed into an attempt upon the life of his officer and his fellow seamen. Then he had deliberately attacked Fontenoy and finally fled into the woods.

Flight might reasonably be construed into evidence of guilt. The world is ready enough to judge a man by such a movement, especially after he has broken some law, if only a social one.

"The fellow is a murderous ruffian as well as a coward," said Fontenoy, as he took his seat in the boat, "and we are certainly well rid of him."

"I don't know," said the first lieutenant, "so much about his being a coward, Mr. Fontenoy. It wanted a little nerve to do that shell trick."

"He's a bad lot, anyway," said Muzzle.

"Silence," said the lieutenant sternly, "how dare you speak? Be quiet."

"I only said, sir——"

"Hold your tongue."

Muzzle collapsed, feeling deeply mortified, especially when he saw the suppressed grins on the faces of the other sailors, among whom he was no great favourite.

"Old Muzzle" was given to lording it over them a bit, and it was no secret that he relied on Gorton Fontenoy to protect him from trouble.

He had indeed boasted that he would never be punished, not while he was on board the "Cyclops."

That day the declaration was destined to be falsified, for on his return to the "Cyclops" he was reported by the first lieutenant for insubordination and had his tobacco and grog stopped for fourteen days.

This was a bitter pill to swallow, but there it was, and he bitterly cursed the indirect cause of it all —Dick Stornaway.

The conduct of our hero did not meet with the approval of Captain Harrison.

On the contrary, he being a strict diciplinarian, was very angry about the lighting of the shell to begin with.

"He had no right to waste Her Majesty's property," he said, "without reckoning the loss of life that might have taken place."

For his absolutely mutinous conduct in attacking and threatening his officer there was of course no defence.

"I fear he has been goaded to it," said the first lieutenant.

"That is not accounted for in the naval criminal code," said the captain; "an ordinary seaman has no right to allow himself to be goaded into insubordination."

Fontenoy gave his version of the affair, and taking advantage of the captain's temporary anger he openly avowed that he believed Seaforth had gone with Jimmy Tartub and the natives so as to secure Dick's escape.

"By what right do you say that?" asked Captain Harrison.

"He makes the fellow his friend," replied Fontenoy.

"An officer and a seaman friends! It is impossible!"

"Incredible as it may seem," said Fontenoy, with marvellous effrontery, "it is true, sir, and Seaforth will come back without the fellow."

"If he does," said Captain Harrison, "I shall demand a full explanation from him."

Thus all went well, and without having recourse to overt acts that might have had inconvenient results, Fontenoy was securing a victory over those he hated.

If Seaforth came back without Dick, a prisoner, he would get into trouble.

If he brought Dick back with him, the punishment of the rebellious young seaman would be swift and sure.

Meanwhile, Seaforth and Jimmy Tartub had made what little preparations that was needed to search the wood.

Fifty of the natives, armed with spears and bows, were drawn up under Tartub's command, evidently much against King Tokoa Fay's will.

He did not want to be left without his great medicine man.

"What for why you go?" he said. "Stowmytoplights, what de good?"

"I'm bound for to go," replied Jimmy Tartub, "seein' it is the command of the great White Queen."

"Me go too, den," said Tokoa Fay.

"Seein' as we've got to travel more than a mile an hour," said Jimmy, "I think you had better stop here. You're all right under your rumerella."

Tokoa Fay sniffed, and two pearly tears rolled down his cheek.

"De Famshays and de Caramas come and eat me up," he said.

"Blessed if they musn't have rum taste to do it," said Jimmy. "Now I'm off. You've got the "Cyclops" here, and all you've got to do is to holler if you sees a Famshay¦ or a Carama coming, and then fold up your rumerella and get inside of it."

"All ready, sir," he said to Seaforth.

"Why should not his majesty go?" drawled Seaforth.

"Why, sir, he's a human snail. We should not find that young chap in ten years—not as I pertikly wants to, but——"

He stopped, and looked at Seaforth, who returned his gaze steadily.

They slowly both began to smile.

"All right," said Jimmy Tartub, "I see there ain't no hurry in this 'ere job. His Majesty shall go. Now, old injy-rubber, you are all right. You shall be one of us. But you'll have to walk, and leave your rumerella behind you."

Tokoa Fay groaned.

"Me no walk," he said.

"All right," said Jimmy; "then stop at home."

"Me walk," cried Tokoa Fay. "Splicedemaintop, me ready."

And so they set out with his Majesty, who rolled over the ground at a pace that compelled others to crawl.

But the pace suited Seaforth, who had always liked lounging when he could indulge in it, and Jimmy Tartub also took things easily when he could.

As for the native followers, the men with the keen eye and infallible scent, they went the pace that was desired or no pace at all, just as their monarch willed.

They had outwardly no separate wishes of their own. They were walking machines.

During that day nothing more was seen of the party.

The natives left behind showed the delight they felt at the absence of their ruler by bathing in the sea, rolling about like porpoises, and screaming.

Suddenly an end was put to their fun.

The men on board the "Cyclops" who had been watching them, saw a couple of the well-known fins of the shark peep above the waves and dart along in the direction of one man who was swimming out beyound the rest.

He too saw the fins and turned back.

He swam with a vigour and at a pace that was amazing, but he was no match for the pirate of the deep.

Swiftly it bore down upon him.

He turned at the last moment and battled for his life, but in a few seconds all was over.

The fins disappeared, and the seaman knew that the monster had turned upon its back to get a bite at its prey.

Then the wild-eyed native uttered a cry, not likely to be forgotten for many a day by those who heard it, and disappeared.

The other natives who had already scuttled back to the beach saw the last act of the tragedy, and sent forth a chorus of responsive yells.

All was over.

No more bathing, and they took to rolling on the beach, and capering and leaping about like a lot of wild animals.

They were letting off the steam bottled while his majesty was present.

Nothing was seen of the search party that day, but soon after sunset a native canoe appeared at the side of the "Cyclops."

In it were two natives and Hanson Seaforth.

He came over the side with his leisurely manner, and the frail bark—a mere shell—in which he had returned, darted back to the beach.

The first lieutenant was in charge, and to him Seaforth went to make his report.

"Returned aboard, sir," he said.

"So I see, Mr. Seaforth. Has Stornaway been taken?"

"No. sir."

"Any information concerning him ?"

"None."

"Is there likely to be any soon, to-night or to-morrow ?"

"I do not think so."

"Seaforth," said the first lieutenant, "I am sorry to hear this. I hope you have done your duty."

"I am sure I have, sir," replied Seaforth.

"Yes; but to whom ?"

Seaforth was silent.

"Captain Harrison is below," said the first lieutenant, "you had better go down to him and make your report."

"Very well, sir."

Seaforth went below and knocked at the cabin door.

"Come in," said a stern voice.

He entered, and found the captain alone.

"Come to make a report," he said.

"Well ! "

"We have not found the escaped man, sir."

"I did not expect it, Mr. Seaforth," was the answer. "I have been thinking over the whole business of to-day, and I am sure that you have connived at his escape."

Not a word did Seaforth offer by way of denial.

With a calm face and quiet eyes resting on the captain he awaited the denunciation he knew was coming.

"You took that obese wretch with you to hinder the pursuit," continued Captain Harrison. "I watched you closely through my glass, and although, of course, I could hear nothing, I could guess pretty well what passed between you and Tartub."

"Yes, sir,'" said Seaforth.

"I ask you, Seaforth, if you can answer for what you have done ?"

"From your point of view a very serious thing, sir."

"It is; you have made yourself accessory to the escape of a man who is a mutineer. Stornaway threatened his superior officer. Nay, more. But I need not go into details with you. You know all that took place."

"Stornaway has been injured," said Seaforth, "I am sure he has, and, smarting under a sense of wrong, he may have done something that ———"

"Seaforth, it is not for you to judge the matter or to act upon sentiment. In doing our duty as seamen we have often to sink our private feelings. If Stornaway was innocent of one thing he has been guilty of another, that is sufficient to condemn him. You have done wrong."

"As an officer, yes, sir," said Seaforth.

"And you knew you were doing wrong."

"Yes."

"Whilst admiring your candour I cannot condone your offence," said Captain Harrison. "Pending your trial by court-martial, which I cannot take upon myself to hold, but must leave to the Admiral, I suspend you from duty. You may go."

Seaforth quietly saluted, and left the cabin.

He knew what his fate would be.

As sure as he was living he would be disgraced and dismissed his ship.

As the captain said, sentiment was not a thing that could be allowed to interfere with Naval duty.

Entering the midshipman's berth, Gorton Fontenoy was there, making memorandum in a small pocket book, with the aid of a swing lamp.

He looked up at Seaforth as he entered, and smiled.

"So you've come back alone," he said.

"Beg pardon," returned Seaforth.

"I said that you had come back alone."

"What of that?"

"Why everything, for you, I should say," was the answer, "there's been a lot of talk about it during the day. Nobody believes you meant to catch the blackguard."

"What blackguard?" asked Seaforth.

"Why, that fellow Stornaway."

"He's no blackguard, but you are one."

Seaforth gave this reply without so much as a visible ripple in voice or manner.. But the sting of it was as keen as need be.

"A blackguard," repeated Seaforth, "why, hang you, what do you mean by insulting MY FRIEND by calling him such a name? You miserable hound."

Then Seaforth, with a quick movement, leant across the table, and, with his finger and thumb, laid hold of Fontenoy's nose.

The grip he put on was a deadly one, and luckily for the victim of it, he made it short.

"There," he said, "let that end the matter. Don't you speak to me again until I give you leave."

"Seaforth," said Fontenoy, speaking in gasps, "do you know what you've done?"

"Rather," was the cool reply, "and would do it again, if you say another word to me."

"I swear," said Fontenoy, backing towards the door, "that one day I will have your life for this. You hear, *your life.*"

"All right," replied Seaforth, "talk of that sort is very cheap."

"Already," hissed Fontenoy, "you are *disgraced.* you will be dismissed the service. Ah, I have you there, the court martial will not be long in coming."

"Go away," said Seaforth.

"In a minute," said Fontenoy, "it won't be long in coming, then you will be dismissed the service. What you think of it will not much matter. Probably with that accursed coolness of yours, you will make light of it. But your father has some pride left, what will HE think of it? Ha, ha, the last of the Seaforths branded, disgraced, KICKED out of the navy. Ha, ha, how will that fit in with the old man's family pride?"

Fontenoy laughed again and disappeared, leaving Seaforth standing quite still as if he had been suddenly frozen.

"My father!" he said softly, after a long pause, "my father! Oh! I had forgotten him. What will *he* think of it? It will KILL him. All through this affair

I have only thought of myself."

Then he sat down and covered his face with his hands.

With all his personal indifference to family pride he respected it in his father, who was proud of his name and descent and at all times would have preferred death to dishonour.

CHAPTER VIII.

DICK IN THE WOODS—MORNING ON THE CLIFF— IN THE HANDS OF SAVAGES—WHAT WILL BE HIS FATE?

DICK when he fled into the woods was burning with a sense of almost unendurable wrong.

It was only by the exercise of a powerful will that he had succeeded in warding off the temptation to punish Gorton Fontenoy in such a manner that he would never be able to show his teeth again.

In other words Dick was tempted to kill him.

Now in his heart there was none of the murderer. Dick Stornaway was as far as possible removed from being blood-thirsty. He was no ruffian but simply as others are.

When roused by great wrongs he was somewhat beside him, and who in his place would not have felt all the bitterness that a sense of wrong can create?

He had never sought the enmity of Gorton Fontenoy.

On the contrary, he had good reasons to keep at peace with him, and as far as he could on board the " Cyclops " he had held aloof from him.

But the instinctive enmity of Fontenoy was not to be held off.

The lives of these two young men were linked together, and the good fortune of one must be the misfortune of the other, although it was felt in an undefined way only by Fontenoy.

Dick had a clearer idea why they should hate each other, but he kept his secret, and for the present we must keep it for him.

Into the wood he plunged, and once in its shade turned to look behind him.

DICK STORNAWAY BRINGS ROY TO HIS BEARINGS.

The pursuit of him was feeble, and with a sarcastic smile on his face he started at a walk into the density of the forest.

"I must lose myself," he muttered, "for years, it may be, and be forgotten. Then I can in another name carry out my purpose."

He knew he had been rash, but he was not sorry.

Life on board the "Cyclops" had been getting unendurable, and for a long while ahead there did not seem any prospect of being released from it.

Now at last he was free.

It is true that his freedom was of a nature that many would have fought shy of, but Dick had a stout heart, and was not assailed by common fears.

He had read of travellers living years in unknown lands, and among strange people, not only unharmed but respected, and sometimes reverenced.

He thought of Jimmy Tartub and his history as he had heard it from the crew, and asked himself:

"If he can be made a hero of, why should I fear for my life?"

He strolled leisurely on, now and then pausing to listen for sounds of pursuit.

But all was still.

Around him were many strange trees, of which he had never heard or read. Some grew tall and straight while others twisted about in all sorts of fantastic forms.

There were broad leaves, short leaves, long and narrow, and on the summit of some of the trees he could see different sorts of fruit hanging, all strange to him, but looking very tempting to the eye.

He kept on for two good hours, bearing, as well as he could guess, in a semi-circle, his object being to get back to the sea-shore, out of sight and hearing of those on board the "Cyclops."

By and bye he came to a space of half-an-acre or so, where no trees grew, but in their place there was a net-work of plants, something like our pumpkin, growing over each other, and lifting up their broad cup-like leaves to catch the health-giving sun by day and dew by night.

These plants were covered with huge fruit. Dick cut out a piece from one of them and tried it. It was as palatable as a melon.

He ate sparingly, in case it should not be really edible, and found it refreshing. Then, with one of the big gourd-like things under his arm for future use, he tramped on.

The undergrowth in the forest was a source of hindrance to him, but only in places was it very dense.

These latter places he had to go round, and that put him somewhat out of his reckoning.

Hour after hour passed, and he was still in the gloom of the forest.

More than once during the day he had heard the sounds made by some beast shifting inside those denser portions of the wood, but nothing formidable came into view.

He was not attacked, nor did he see anything worth attacking.

So far all was well by day, but he knew it might be different at night, and he hoped ere then to be free of the forest.

Bearing slowly and steadily to the left, he, at last, attained his object.

Just as the sun was slipping into the sea he emerged from the wood.

As he stepped out he had just time to see that he had reached rising ground, and that ahead of him was a cliff which gradually shelved down to the level beach for a mile to the left.

And far away he saw the " Cyclops," lying, a mere speck upon the sea.

One moment he saw it, and then the sun went down.

As he had felt no ill effects from the fruit he had eaten, he decided to make an evening meal of what he had with him, and walked towards the cliff, finally sitting down within a few feet of the verge of it.

He did not fear being seen, for night was coming on

very fast, and darkness set in ere he had finished his evening meal.

He rightly judged that he was now in as safe a place as any to pass the night. The wild beasts of the forest would have no object in coming to where he was.

They did not find their prey upon the cliffs, nor would they come to drink salt water. On emerging from their lairs they would go inland.

So fairly assured of his safety Dick lay down, and being wearied out soon fell asleep.

As a moon would rise about nine o'clock, he covered his face with his jacket, knowing what a strange influence the orb of night will sometimes exercise on those who sleep in her rays.

It was a precaution all wise travellers take, and no sailor who has been round the world cares to lie down to sleep in the moonlight.

Not a sound did Dick hear all night, but early in the morning he was awakened by an exclamation uttered by someone near him.

In a moment he was aroused and upon his feet, sword in hand, ready to repel any attack made upon him.

As he sprang up, a tall, hideous looking savage ran back to a group of his friends who it seemed had been holding aloof while their companion advanced to see what it was that lay so still and quiet on the edge of the cliff.

Dick, having his face covered up, looked a mere bundle, and it was when the savage drew back the garment and saw a white face under it, that he uttered the exclamation which aroused our hero.

The moment Dick was on his feet, they raised their spears and uttered a series of horrible yells.

Dick took in his own position, and saw that it was far from enviable.

Behind him was the cliff going a hundred and fifty feet sheer down to a hard, pebbly beach.

Before him were at least four score savages, nearly naked, with ornaments of wood and bone in their noses and ears, to add to their natural hideousness.

The main body, however, kept well in the rear, and only a small body was near him.

"I've got to frighten them somehow," thought Dick, "for I can't fight the lot."

He had his sword drawn, and with the object in view, flourished it threateningly.

They answered him by coming slowly forward like a cat about to pounce on a single mouse.

Dick did not care to play the waiting game.

By sheer force of numbers they could bear him over the precipice, so quickly making up his mind he dashed into the thick of them.

They opened out, and the next moment he stumbled and fell.

A stone unseen had tripped him up, and he fell with sufficient force to confuse him for the time.

Before he could recover himself, they were upon him.

In an instant his arms were secured, and several strong leather thongs were passed round his body and legs.

They did not bind him painfully tight, but the knots were so well tied that he was a helpless prisoner.

Then they raised him up and held him aloft, giving him a command of the scene around him.

All the savages now swarmed about him, capering and brandishing their arms, and uttering cries that sounded very appalling.

Naturally, Dick gave himself up for lost, and when his bearers slowly began to march towards the edge of the cliff, he braced himself for a fall which could only end in every bone in his body being smashed.

But it did not seem to be their object to hurl him over.

The crowd opened out, and fell back while his bearers advanced to the very edge, and coolly marched along it at the imminent risk of going over with him.

However, they kept their feet as securely as cats upon a parapet, and then turned inland again.

And now they bore away by the wood, keeping just without, tramping steadily along, still holding him aloft, and without exhibiting the least sign of fatigue.

Behind, came the mob of savages, and as Dick was carried head first, he could see them capering with exultant joy.

Their wide mouths were for the most part opened to the full extent, exhibiting double rows of teeth such as no dentist but Nature could supply, white, even and strong.

The ornaments in their ears and noses, and about their arms and legs, rattled like castinets, and the way they brandished their arms put their comrades in peril.

But nobody was hurt.

On they went for about two miles, then Dick heard the sounds of another body of men ahead shouting, and, as he judged, capering also.

He called to mind what he had read about sacrifices performed by savages, and heartily wished now that they had tossed him over the cliff.

That at least would have ended everything.

His bearers halted, and he was put upon his feet with reverential tenderness, carefully as some people handle their own valuable china.

Before him was an African potentate, as fat or fatter than Tokoa Fay, seated under an umbrella double the size that redoubtable monarch could boast of.

Behind him sat a number of other fat persons, who at a glance could be seen to be women, all in a state of wonderment and grinning delight.

We may as well introduce the monarch to our readers at once.

It was Tu-tu, the king of the Fanshays, and the ladies behind him were his wives.

Tu-tu was evidently struggling with his inner man to keep calm, but he too was swathed in delight.

A grin of a spasmodic nature distorted his royal countenance.

In apparel he could boast of the simplicity that marked the attire of Tokoa Fay, and the ornaments were much of the same nature.

Such a yelling and clattering of weapons Dick had

never heard before.

"What does it all mean?" thought Dick.

He cast a quick glance round, expecting to see some preparations to inflict torture upon him, but there was nothing of the sort in view.

After a few minutes of the clattering and shouting, Tutu held up his right hand.

The noise instantly ceased,

Another sign from the monarch led to the thongs that bound him being removed as if by magic. His sword and everything else had of course been previously taken from him.

Tu-tu sat upon a huge log, out of which a seat had been laboriously chopped so as to give it the resemblance of an arm chair.

It was wide enough for two, and Tu-tu, having obligingly shifted up, he invited Dick to sit down.

Then it flashed upon Dick that he had not fallen among enemies but friends.

He recalled what he had heard of Jimmy Tartub, and the hero that the Wampa monarch made of him. Was it not possible that a similar fate was in store for him?

It seemed so ridiculous that he could have laughed outright, but was afraid he would outrage the feelings of Tu-tu, so composing his face he sat down beside the monarch under the umbrella.

As he did so the screeching and howling begun again, and the Fanshays—numbering at least a thousand—began to dance, running in and out so as to make a Scotch reel multiplied by a hundred.

Dick had not had any real solid food for twenty-four hours, and the excitement of the morning having taxed him, he felt somewhat bewildered and faint at the sight of so much running to and fro.

Happily it did not last very long.

Tu-tu rose up, and in a moment all were still.

Then the monarch turned to his many wives and roared out something which brought them all to their feet.

Then, for the first time Dick, who had turned his

head to look at them, saw, a short distance away, an African village, composed of about two hundred huts, built of rough logs, and thatched with dried grass.

Towards them the women waddled, Tu-tu shouting out orders to them that had the effect of making them endeavour to break into a run.

One of the huts was very large, and into this they disappeared.

After a short delay they reappeared, bearing wooden bowls containing milk, and huge palm leaves filled with fruit and some sort of corn cake.

There was enough brought to satisfy the appetite of a hundred hungry men.

They came up to the umbrella, in single file, the foremost offering Dick milk, and he drank to the palpable gratification of Tu-tu, who did the same.

The fruit was offered, and after that the bread, so that Dick, ere long, was satisfied as far as his appetite was concerned.

After the monarch and Dick had had their fill, the wives squatted down and speedily disposed of what remained, while the rest of the tribe looked on with longing eyes.

A sign from the king sent them racing away to their huts to get their morning meal, and Dick was left alone with the king and his wives.

Now if he desired it he had an opportunity to make a run for freedom.

But a moment's reflection showed him the folly of it.

He was unarmed and in a strange country, and if he succeeded in getting away he would probably starve or become a prey to some wild beast.

"I am among kindly people, or kindly to me," he thought, "and here for the present I will remain."

Tu-tu was hardly able to take his eyes off him.

He looked him up and down like one who has at last got hold of some great work of art for which he has been thirsting for many years. Every now and then he would gingerly handle his arms or stroke him down the back uttering short guttural sounds of delight.

Suddenly he said, " Good, medicine man, better."

" You speak English," said Dick.

" Good, medicine man," said Tu-tu again.

It was all the English the king of the Fanshays knew at present.

To dwell on all that followed during the next days might be tedious, nor have we the space for it.

Dick, like Jimmy Tartub, had fallen upon good quarters in the savage sense of the word.

He was attended upon with a reverence that threatened to soon grow wearisome.

A great part of the day he was expected to sit under the umbrella with his majesty, and at night he had a hut all to himself with a bed of grass that was comfortable enough, but not exactly an Englishman's idea of a resting place.

All night long that hut was close guarded.

Not to keep him a prisoner, for Tu-tu took it for granted that he was happy, but to shield him from the possible purloining efforts of some envious tribe.

Every morning he was allowed to bath in the sea, natives armed with spears making a ring round him to protect him from the sharks. In the evening he was regaled with exhibitions of feats of agility by the tribe.

Excepting the king and his wives, they were an active athletic people. The ordinary women and children took their part in the sports, distinguishing themselves greatly.

The men wrestled, but Dick, who knew something of the art, saw that they were not well versed in it. So one evening, he had been with them six days, he challenged one of their big men.

Tu-tu, who was picking up little bits of English from Dick, was against it and said :

" No, no, strong, too so."

But Dick laughed, and insisted, and all he said being law, he went out, and in two seconds had thrown that savage with a back heel trip, and laid him on his back in a state of mind to which chaos was order.

If anything were wanted to complete the admiration from the Fanshays that trick did it.

The people roared with delight, and Tu-tu, laying aside his dignity, capered like an elephant.

To the fallen one was meted out the usual thing that comes to the defeated.

The men derided him, and when he got upon his feet a lot of women fell upon him, got him down, and gave him a good hearty SPANKING.

Dick burst into a roar of laughter, and he turned to the King to bid him signal to the women that the defeated one had suffered enough, when his eye fell upon a form that was slowly approaching.

It was that of an Englishman, and he wore the uniform of a Naval officer. In his right hand he carried a drawn sword.

CHAPTER IX.

THE MEETING ON THE SEA SHORE—DICK IS NEAR DOING SERIOUS MISCHIEF.

DICK was not long in coming to a conclusion about the officer, who was altogether too young in appearance to be one of the senior officers, and it was not Seaforth or Ned Dawson.

It was Gorton Fontenoy.

What was he doing there alone?

Dick could not give him credit for daring to come there by himself in search of him, but it might be so, and here was an opportunity Dick had wished for.

He wanted to meet his enemy on equal terms, but he had no sword. The Fanshays had removed his weapons, and had not thought proper to return them.

They too had seen Fontenoy, and Tu-tu's eyes glistened.

Having got hold of one treasure, in the form of Dick, he was anxious to get another.

With TWO white medicine men he would be impregnable, of course.

Dick saw what was in the king's mind, and signalled to him that he would go down and capture the other white man, but he wished to go alone.

Tu-tu looked doubtful.

But Dick knew his power, and was imperative.

"I go away," he said. "Fly up in the air. Leave you."

Tu-tu was alarmed, and bowed his head in token of submission.

The great strong white man who had thrown the Fanshay chief wrestler could do as he pleased.

So Dick hurried off, and by keeping well back in the cliff, succeeded in getting in the rear of Fontenoy, who was strolling carelessly along at a snail's pace.

Just there on the beach the sand had been thrown up into little hillocks, probably by the action of a storm, and below one of these hillocks lay a boat with Muzzle and several seamen in her.

She had been dispatched from the "Cyclops" in one direction to search the coast for Dick, and another boat had been sent the other way. Captain Harrison judged that Dick would not in any case go far from the sea.

The cliff shelved down to where Fontenoy was moving about, and along the slope there grew clumps of palms which enabled Dick to get down without being observed.

The soft sand deadened his ootsteps, and his presence was not suspected until he had seized Fontenoy by the shoulders, turned him round, and wrenched the sword from his grasp.

"Don't stir or make a noise, Mr. Fontenoy," said Dick, "if you have any of your friends near."

Fontenoy was completely taken by surprise.

He had no idea of finding Dick or a desire to do so, but was simply pretending to search for him.

Therefore when he came thus suddenly upon him, it was like a spirit rising from the ground.

"Do—on't kill me!" he stammered.

"I am no murderer," replied Dick, as he cast the sword aside, "nor do I desire to harm you in any way *now*. By-and-bye, when the end comes, one of us may have to go."

"Who are you?" demanded Fontenoy; "you do not speak like an ordinary seaman. Is your name Stornaway?"

"What matters, *at present* ?" returned Dick.   "It will not be always so, I hope.   What are you doing here ?"

"I am sent in search of you"

"Indeed, then you are not alone ?"

Dick had not seen either the boat or the men owing to the sand-bank, but he suspected that some of the " Cyclops " men were not far away.

A cunning twinkle in Fontenoy's eyes was a good omen, although it was not the only one given.

"I have some men with me," Fontenoy said, "but they are a long way off."

As he spoke he involuntarily glanced in the direction where they were lying.   Dick smiled.

"A lie," he said, "comes as natural to you as drawing breath.   Your men are *there*.   Now, make no attempt to fly to them for I am swifter of foot than you are.   All I want from you is truthful answers to two or three questions.   First: What is thought of me by Captain Harrison ?"

"What any naval commander would think of a common sailor striking an officer," Fontenoy replied.

"Suppose I returned to my ship," said Dick, "what would be my punishment ?"

"You would be put in irons, taken to the admiral's station, and there tried."

"And my punishment ?"

"At least two years' imprisonment.

"I see," said Dick, "that you would rather I did not return."

"Do you think I wish to spare you ?"

"No," answered Dick, "but you are afraid of me, and I may frankly tell you that you have good reason to."

"Fear you !" sneered Fontenoy.

"Not as a naval officer, but in things apart from the ship," said Dick.   "Have you no other fears ?"

Gorton Fontenoy looked keenly at Dick, scanning his features with an eager intent.

"Look close," said Dick, "did you never see me before I joined the ' Cyclops ' ?"

"I can't say," replied Fontenoy.

"You never did," replied Dick, "but is there no picture that will recall me to you?"

Gorton Fontenoy leaped back a pace, startled and amazed.

"I know now," he said; "you——"

"Dare to utter the word," cried Dick.

"I can think it," said Fontenoy. "Bah! you to play the hero. You, the son of——"

Dick sprang upon him, and seized him by the throat. Fontenoy sank upon his knees.

"Dare to whisper an insult to her," cried Dick, "and I will kill you, you dog."

"Spare me," gasped Fontenoy, "I have always been taught that——"

"A straw for your teaching," cried Dick, furiously. "When I think of what was done in the years gone by I am almost beside myself."

At this moment Muzzle, getting weary of waiting, peeped over the hillock to see what Fontenoy was doing, and to his utter and complete amazement saw Dick shaking Fontenoy as a good terrier does a rat.

He snatched up his cutlass, lying on the sand, and called on the other men to follow him.

"Where?" they asked.

"There," he cried, "hurry, or there'll be murder done."

The men got up, lazily, and looking in the direction he pointed, saw Dick and Fontenoy. Apparently they were not much moved thereby.

Two put their hands into their pockets, and two more turned faces towards the sea.

"Ain't you a coming?" cried Muzzle.

"In a minute," they replied, "it's only a couple of youngsters having a tussle."

"It's that Stornaway," said Muzzle.

"Not that," said one of the men, with a grin, "it ooks like Mister Seaforth. You go, and when you've got up there and made sure, just holler for help."

Muzzle, with a curse, hurried forward cutlass in hand.

He understood the apparent blindness of the men. They favoured Dick, and were averse to bearing a hand in taking him back to the ship.

Before Muzzle could come up, Dick had thrown Fontenoy panting on the sand, and picked up his sword.

"I cannot kill you," he said, "but I can degrade you. Go back to your ship with a broken sword."

So saying he snapped it across his knee, and was about to cast the pieces down, when he saw Muzzle advancing.

With half a sword Dick rushed towards him, and Muzzle, not overburdened with bravery, turned tail.

"Help! Help!" he roared.

Then the sailors roared with laughter, and made a feint as if coming to his rescue.

But they were very slow in picking up their weapons from the sand. Dick did not pursue Muzzle far, but halted, and having thrown down the broken sword, began a leisurely retreat up the cliff.

Fontenoy was now upon his feet again, running towards the boat and calling on the men to capture Dick.

The men, as before, seemed in no hurry to act, and all pursuit was stopped by the advance of the Fanshays in war-like order.

They had come along stealthily half the way and then began to sing and yell. The verge of the cliff swarmed with them and the foremost warriors rushed down towards Dick.

They surrounded him, and so far he was safe, for Gorton Fontenoy made no effort to attack the savages.

He leaped into the boat and gave his men orders to push off, and pulled hard out to sea.

"In course he is not afeared," muttered one of the men, and the others chuckled.

"Silence, there!" said Muzzle.

"All right, Muzzle," said Fontenoy, "I command here. Quick, men! Why don't you pull?"

The Fanshays had came right down to the beach and were expending a few of their spears and arrows at the retreating boat.

"A skewer skeers him," muttered the bow oarsman, and the next man laughed aloud.

"Brown," said Fontenoy, "I shall report you for insolence."

"Axing your pardon, sir," said Brown, "but mayn't I laugh at the fools of savages?"

"If you *are* laughing at them," returned Fontenoy, "but——" he paused, and then added savagely, "Give way, will you—oh!"

A half-spent arrow had struck him in the back, piercing his clothes and just penetrating the skin.

The wound was not a serious one, more ludicrous than painful, but Fontenoy made the most of it.

He fell off the seat upon his side, and Muzzle pulled the arrow out.

It came out without much effort, and the point was not even tinged with blood.

The sailors began to fairly swell with silent laughter and had to pull hard to prevent themselves from exploding.

Fontenoy got up sullenly and resumed his seat.

He could see that the men were thoroughly enjoying themselves, but what could he say or do?

He knew what a yarn they would make of it on the return to the "Cyclops."

It was humiliating and exasperating.

"And I owe it all to that beggar," he muttered. "If I had known who he was a fortnight ago I would have given him a *longer sleep*. Pull there! will you? and no chattering. Silence, fore and aft."

CHAPTER X.

PRISONERS OF WAR—ANOTHER ARRIVAL—TARTUB'S OPINION OF SEAFORTH.

WHATEVER may have been the nature of the report made by Gorton Fontenoy on his return to the "Cyclops" it did not lead to closer search for Dick.

Several days passed and he saw no signs of any of his old associates.

The Fanshays continued to hold him in reverence, and Tu-tu got on with his English, and also took to exercise by the advice of Dick, and shook off some of his obesity.

It was a pleasant life for an idle man to lead, but it was not the purpose of our hero to remain there.

After a time he hoped that some passing ship would stop there, and take him off—that is—if the Fanshays would let him go.

With regard to these fervent admirers the position was rather embarrassing.

Dick was not fond of adulation, and he sighed for the companionship of white men. His desire was destined to be gratified in a most unexpected way.

One morning a party of Fanshays who had been hunting in the wood returned with two prisoners in the form of the persons of Jimmy Tartub and Tokoa Fay.

Jimmy looked as if he had been having rather a rough time of it, and Tokoa Fay was in the condition of a camel after a long desert journey. He had lost all his fat.

The meeting with Dick was a surprise to Jimmy Tartub, who had no idea of meeting with a white man.

They were strangers to each other, but confidences were soon exchanged and their relative positions understood.

Jimmy was a thorough old salt and a keen fellow in his way. He saw that Dick was of the class from which men before the mast are not usually drawn, and fell quite naturally into the positon of a follower.

"We've had a high old time of it in the wood, sir," he said—"me and that blarmed fool, Tokoa Fay, having lost ourselves, and what we've lived on would not keep a porker. He'd got fat to work on, and I hadn't, but I've survived, and here we are."

Tu-tu was in the seventh heaven of delight.

He had got another white medicine man, and Tokoa Fay was his captive.

Without a king the Wanga tribe would go to pieces.

He was not so kind to Tokoa Fay as he might have been, for he shut him up in one of the huts in the village and spent half-a-dozen hours in deriding him through a hole in the wall before he gave him anything to eat.

Dick was not aware of this proceeding, or he would have said a good word for the humiliated monarch who bore his fall with meekness.

The next day the "Cyclops" was seen cruising along the coast and occasionally firing a blank gun.

The Fanshays' village was not visible from the sea, and the natives, by Dick's desire, lay close, and as dumb as mice when there's a score of cats around they remained for hours.

"Somebody's lost or left ashore," said Jimmy Tartub, as the gun boomed for the fifth time, ; "if it's a hofficer they will go on wasting powder for hours, but if it's a or'nary seaman they won't do much more on it."

As the gun continued at intervals to boon, it was settled that it was an officer, and Dick wondered who it could be.

Was it Fontenoy?

If so, by what chance had he been left upon that shore?

But speculation was useless for the present, and for hours they listened to the occasional sound of the gun.

Towards evening the firing ceased, and the "Cyclops" was seen bearing out to sea.

"They've given him up, whoever he is," said Jimmy Tartub.

"And who he is we must find out," said Dick, "or rather our friends must."

Half-a-dozen words with Tu-tu sufficed.

Dick's word was law, and at his suggestion the smartest scouts of the tribe were sent forth to find the missing man or men.

Night came on, and the tribe as usual retired shortly after the sun.

Early to bed and early to rise was their practice.

Jimmy Tartub and Dick Stornaway remained awake for a long time talking together.

They had the largest hut in the village for their

accommodation, and such comforts as the Fanshays could provide.

Both agreed that it would be impossible for them to live there for ever.

Dick said very little about his private affairs, but he gave Jimmy to understand that he had an important mission to fulfil.

"Not for myself alone," he said, "although success will bring me all that a man need ask for in this world, but to remove a stain from the name of one I love dearly."

"Wherever you go, sir," said Tartub, "I goes too with you willin' and whatever you does I'll d it. But I think, sir, that when we goes we ought to take poor old Tokoa Fay with us. He's been unkimmon kind to me, and if we leave him with Tu-tu, his life won't be ALL bread, beans and bacon."

"At present," said Dick, "I do not see what we can do, but something is sure to turn up. Good-night, Tartub."

"Good-night, sir."

Dick did not sleep for awhile, he had so much to think of, but when he did, he slept soundly. He was awakened by a voice outside:

"Thanks, I'm sure, Tartub. You are a good fellow I'm all right, I assure you."

Dick could only think that he was dreaming, for the voice was familiar to him, and of all others within a thousand miles the one he most wished to hear.

He got up with all speed, and hurried to the door, and then he saw Hanson Seaforth, seated on a rough sort of stool, and Jimmy Tartub binding up a wound in his leg. A number of the Fanshays stood by, looking on with absorbed interest.

"How are you, Dick?" said Seaforth, as quietly as one friend would greet another in the ordinary way, "glad to see you."

"You here?" was all Dick could say.

"Yes," replied Seaforth, "I got beastly tired of the 'Cyclops' and thought I would have a run ashore. That will do, Tartub, my good fellow. Got a scratch in the wood from some sort of wild cat, or something; we were having a bit of a tussle together when your people came up. Much obliged to them, I'm sure, especially as they were satisfied with the brass buttons from an old coat."

"Mr. Seaforth's deserted, sir," said Tartub, with a grin.

"Never!" exclaimed Dick, "impossible."

"Fact," replied Seaforth, "came ashore in the night —swam—couldn't bring my chest—so strapped a few odd things in a bundle on my back."

"I am sorry to hear this," said Dick, earnestly, "excuse me, but I hope you will not think me a fool, but I fear you have done this for my sake."

"No," said Seaforth, "I don't know that I've done it for anybody's sake; fact is, Captain Harrison and I did not agree, I thought we had better part company."

"It won't do," said Dick, shaking his head.

"No," said Seaforth, raising his eyes, "then I will try another game by-and-bye. Meanwhile, if you don't mind, I'll turn in somewhere and get forty winks."

It was yet early, the sun not having risen half-an-hour, and Tokoa Fay was still at rest.

He did not rise so early as his subjects, and in that matter was very much like the rulers of the more civilized world.

Dick showed Seaforth where he could lie down, and that phlegmatic young man, stretching himself upon the simple couch of leaves, covered with skins of various animals, went to sleep like a child.

Closing the door Dick walked apart with Jimmy Tartub.

"What does it mean?" asked Dick.

"I don't know, sir," replied Tartub. "He'll tell us if he likes, and if he don't like he won't. He's a cool 'un. I don't know as ever I see a cooler."

"He was my friend on board the 'Cyclops,'" said Dick, "and I fear he has got into trouble through me."

"Don't you bother about that, sir," said Tartub, consolingly. "Whatever he's got into he'll get out of. He's the sort to do it. So mighty cool! Why, ice is *red hot* to him. I don't know as iver I see a party so—so—don't-carish. He's got a gashly wound in his leg that would make some people howl, but do he howl? Not he! He looks at it, an' he says: 'Rather a neat scratch, ain't it?' That's what he says, and yawns—yawns, sir! Blessed if he ain't cool enough to make this bilin' climate FEEL CHILLY."

CHAPTER XI.

TU-TU'S CANOE—THE SIGNAL OF DISTRESS—FLIGHT —NOT SUCH A FOOL AS HE LOOKED—PERIL AT SEA.

THE Fanshays were smart men on the sea. Hidden in a small bay they had quite a little fleet of canoes built in various sizes to carry from one person up to fifty.

They were for the most part frail structures that would take very little to upset them, and only the skilled canoists could hope to keep afloat in them.

Tu-tu when he went out took care of his royal person by using a bark canoe, forty feet long, and seven feet wide.

It was constructed to carry a sail made of fine long grass, dexterously woven, and in case of no wind there were a dozen paddles.

In this boat all our friends were keenly interested, as it offered them the means of escape from their amiable captors.

Tu-tu at their request exhibited its sailing powers, and the way it skipped over the sea in a moderate breeze was very wonderful.

It was not what one would call a safe sea boat, but all were prepared to run a certain amount of risk.

Before depriving Tu-tu of his boat, they decided to wait a week to see if any vessel came by, and Jimmy Tartub hung out a strip of cloth on a solitary tall tree as a signal of distress.

When Tu-tu asked what it was, Tartub told him it was a lucky thing to do, and while it was there the Fanshay people would be great and prosperous.

Tu-tu said nothing in reply, but his small eyes twinkled as if the idea tickled him.

Tokoa Fay was not kept in durance vile.

Tu-tu set him free, and made a body servant of him, ordering him about in a style that helped to keep him in a lean and active condition.

Meanwhile Tu-tu resumed his life of ease and got fatter than ever.

He got so fat that his eyes became creases, and his waddle was as Tartub said: "The sailing of a Dutch lugger with only a jury mast and four square feet of canvas."

There was a group of islands about twenty miles at sea, and at one of them trading vessels often touched for water and fruit.

The inhabitants were few in number, and very peaceful.

To that island our adventurers settled they would go. That is, if they could get away, and wind and weather permitted.

One thing alone troubled them.

They did not like to rob Tu-tu of his boat.

So one day Dick asked him what he would sell it for if anyone wanted to buy it.

Tu-tu promptly said that he would take twenty brass buttons, as his people could make another boat, but not a single button.

Dick said he would buy it from him, and between them they got the buttons together somewhat inconveniencing their attire, but a few bits of string put matters right. So the boat became Dick's, and Tu-tu was apparently delighted.

He strung the buttons on a piece of twisted grass, and put them round his neck, wearing them with all the pride a civilized lady would adorn herself with a necklace of diamonds.

Thus far all things were settled, and it only remained for them to decide how and when to get away.

"It won't do to hurry," said Seaforth; "because I've an idea that Tu-tu is not such a fool as he looks.

Under his fat he has a lot of talent."

Dick laughed, and said it was just as well to be careful.

"We will wait another week," he said.

Before the week was out Tu-tu unexpectedly declared that he meant to make war against an inland king, who was reported to have an umbrella bigger than his.

Jimmy Tartub, who occasionally wandered into the regions of romance, thereupon declared that he knew that king, and had seen that umbrella.

"It's two or three feet bigger than yourn, Tu-tu," he said, "and got a lot o' ornamental work about it that this 'ere hasn't."

Tu-tu then said that he would have that umbrella, and conduct the war in person.

"Couldn't have happened better," said Jimmy Tartub.

"Perhaps not," said Seaforth, in his quiet way.

Warlike preparations of the Fanshays were soon made, and the very next evening was chosen for the start.

He did not propose to take Tokoa Fay or any of his captives with him.

Accordingly, after sun-down, and after sundry rites, which we need not enter into here, Tutu started at the head of his men, waddling off at a pace they did not expect from him.

He left about a score of his tribe, and the women and children behind him.

After he was gone Tokoa Fay was taken into the confidence of the adventurers, and he was delighted.

"Good," he said.

He was told to be down by the bay just before sunrise, and as usual everybody retired early.

The friends did not all sleep, but kept watch and watch until about three in the morning, when Tartr said it was time to start.

The stars were still shining brightly, and gentle breeze blowing aslant off the land.

All in the village was quiet.

Carrying their shoes in their hands they stole out, and without a sound got clear of the place. It was only half a mile to the bay, and ten minutes brought them to the spot where Tokoa Fay had arrived a few minutes before them.

All the canoes were drawn up out of the reach of the tide except the big one which lay close in shore, securely tethered to a stake driven into the sand.

The mast stood up naked in the starlight, and the sail lay in a huddled heap in the bows.

As there was little wind in the bay owing to the high land behind it, they elected to paddle out to sea and there hoist.

They slipped in, and with Dick and Tartub paddling glided over the quiet water.

All was still on land.

Not the slightest sign of their absence being discovered reached their ears.

Not a word was uttered by any of them.

Silence was imperative until they reached the open sea.

They reckoned they could make the run to the group of islands in two hours, and Jimmy Tartub knew the bearings well. He was the chief navigator of the fragile craft.

Half an hour's paddling brought them to the mouth of the bay, and on shipping their paddles they got ready to hoist the sail.

We must keep this cockle-shell trimmed," said Tartub, "for she's got no keel and is about as ricketty as a sarsepan-lid. Mister Dick, will you keep her head afore the wind while I run up this ere bit o' hay canvas."

Dick steered with a paddle, and kept the canoe in the position required, while Jimmy Tartub cautiously crept forward on his hands and knees to get at the sail.

It was attached to the mast by a long rope made of strips of hide, and there were two stays fixed to the side of the canoe.

These stays could be hauled in to let out on

either side, according to the way they wished to work the craft.

Tartub began to haul up, and had hauled it about half-way, when he let go and down it came with a run.

"Look out there," cried Dick, "or you will have us over."

"Over," said Tartub, breathlessly, "I'm blessed if I ain't been turned right over."

"What's the matter?" asked Seaforth.

"I'm blessed," said Tartub, "if we aint got a live hanimal of some sort under this ere sail."

"Nonsense," said Dick.

"Well! I see it move," replied Tartub.

"Haul up and let us see what it is," said Seaforth.

Tartub tilted his hat on one side and began to scratch his head.

"It's summat big," he said, "a darn crittur from the wood that dropped in here to have a nap."

"Come back," said Seaforth. "I'll raise the sail. We must have it up. Paddling twenty miles won't do."

Jimmy Tartub came cautiously back, breathing hard, for he was very much excited. Tokoa Fay stared wildly at him.

"Bad you look," he said.

"Well! as I said," replied Tartub, "it's give me a turn, in and out, mostly in, and I aint given to squirm, neither. Take care, Mr. Seaforth."

"All right," was the calm reply.

Seaforth laid hold of the sail rope and calmly pulled it up.

When the sail was clear of the boat, a figure of considerable rotundity was seen to struggle into a sitting position.

"How are you?" said Seaforth, coolly.

"Me come, no stop, you go," was the reply.

It was Tu-tu.

The cunning monarch had somehow fathomed their design and made himself one of the party.

He might be glad of possessing a few brass buttons

but he was not going to be taken in by them.

The first impulse of Dick and Tartub was to roar with laughter, while Tokoa Fay stared at the figure of the rival monarch dimly seen in the starlight as if his doom at all events was sealed.

"No—go—you not stay," said Tu-tu again.

"You will have to go with us now," said Tartub.

"Can't he be put ashore?" asked Dick. "Tu-tu, what is to become of your people if you are taken away from them?"

"People—be blow!" replied Tu-tu. "Me tire—see more now—sit—sit under umbrella all day—all tire—me go."

"Why not?" said Seaforth, "it isn't everybody who has the chance of going to sea with two kings."

"Me happy now," said Tu-tu, squatting down and folding his hands across his ample chest.

"It's a go, isn't it?" said Tartub.

Dick did not reply.

He was wondering what he should do with these two monarchs when he got to the civilized countries he hoped to reach.

However, there they were and not to be got rid of, and of course he would have to keep them for the present.

Seaforth took it all as a matter of course.

He came back to his seat beside Dick and quietly settled down.

"She goes well," he said, alluding to the craft, which was literally flying over the sea.

"Splendidly," replied Dick, who had his countryman's love of the sea; "but hang it all, Seaforth! I never expected this."

"I expected something," returned Seaforth, "but what it was I could not tell. I thought it would have been worse. If you don't want to keep his majesty you can send him back with the boat and let him keep the buttons by way of fare, I dare say he will be contented."

"I say, young Tu-tu," said Jimmy Tartub, squatting down in front of the obese monarch:

"Me hear," he replied.

"How did you get away from your army?"

"Me no go away, dey go."

"Run off."

"Me say—Tu-tu tired—dey go—me go down and sleep in canoe. Me know you come."

"How in the tarnation did you find it out?"

"What for you buy canoe?" asked Tu-tu, with a child-like simplicity.

"Oh, you're no chicken," said Tartub, "what say you, Tokoa Fay?"

Tokoa Fay did not answer for awhile, but finally he said slowly:

"He a land lubby, great cuss.

"Me put you out canoe," said Tokoa Fay.

"You don't fight here," said Tartub, "there ain't room, but it is a go."

Merrily spun the canoe along, and in a little while the sun came up, not with a clear sky as it had done for weeks, but with a dark line of cloud just above it.

Both Tokoa Fay and Tu-tu looked at it for some little time, and then the former said:

"Go back, storm dere."

"We can't do that," replied Dick.

"Well, den," said Tokoa, severely, "canoe turn ober, big sea, big noise in sky."

It was not a good look out, but go back Dick would not. Nor were either Seaforth or Tartub disposed to do.

Each, in his way, watched the cloud with interest.

It spread swiftly to the right and left, and then began to break at the edges.

Several patches detached themselves, and then rapidly rose up in the sky.

As they advanced out they grew in size, absolutely grew, gathering the elements of a tropical storm as they came.

The cloud also spread downward, obscuring the sun.

A moaning was heard in the distance, which Tartub knew was the noise of the advancing storm.

"It will be a cyclone, sir," he said to Dick.

"We must go on," was the reply.

"We simply can't get back with a head wind," added Seaforth, "let her race."

And the canoe WAS racing.

Had it been a thing of life, knowing the advancing peril, it could not have done more to carry them to a place of safety.

About three quarters of an hour had now elapsed since they left the bay, and more than half the distance between the mainland and the islands was covered.

Jimmy Tartub directed the steering with his strained eyes fixed on the horizon with a hope of getting a speedy glimpse of the haven of safety.

But ahead and all around them the misty clouds were gathering.

Daylight had come, but not the clear sunshine they had recently been accustomed to. Overhead the clouds in dark patches were racing.

There were two currents above, for the clouds were going in two directions; one lot travelling slowly, and the other careering wildly on its course.

"I think I see the island, sir," said Jimmy Tartub, pointing ahead.

He could not make sure, nor indeed could anyone in the boat, for the horizon everywhere was each moment growing darker.

The mainland was out of sight.

They were encircled by the sea.

The waves began to increase in size, and here and there appeared the white caps that showed the increasing power of the wind.

On, like a well-spurred horse sped the canoe.

Ten minutes later Tartub cried out:

"I see the islands now. Hurrah!"

Yes, there was no doubt of it.

They lay, far away, like huge animals floating on the sea—six miles away, at least.

Poof!

It was a short sharp gust of wind that struck the sail, and made the canoe lean over dangerously.

A short guttural expression escaped Tokoa Fay.

"You medicine man," he said to Tartub. "Stop storm."

"I ain't got the right sort of medicine for that with me," replied Tartub. "I think, Mr. Seaforth, that we might lower the sail a bit."

"Just so," returned Seaforth, serenely, "we shall be able to do without it by-and-bye."

"Had you not better get ready to let it go," suggested Dick.

"That's a seaman's idea and a good one," answered Seaforth.

He and Tartub accordingly loosened the stays and held them in their hands.

The strain on the sail made a tough job of it.

An exclamation from Dick drew all eyes in his direction. He was pointing to windward.

About two miles away was a ship coming along under closely reefed canvas.

It was a familiar craft to all, and Seaforth said quietly:

"Our friend the 'Cyclops.' She's come back for something or somebody. Well, she's got all she can do to take care of herself."

Whether the canoe was seen or not they could not tell, but she was bearing down upon them, and bringing with her an increasing breeze.

Poof—poof!

Two gusts, one after the other, bent the canoe over, and all on board instinctively bent to windward.

The movement saved the craft from being upset; as it was she shipped several gallons of water.

"A few more like that," said Tartub, "and we must swim. It's no use keeping her right before the wind, Mr. Seaforth; we shan't make the islands if we do."

"We may not make them anyway," said Seaforth. "Ha! our friends see us."

CHAPTER XII.

THE FURY OF THE STORM—A BLINDING MIST—ON THE LONE ISLAND—A NIGHT OF HORROR.

A GUN was fired on board the "Cyclops" as a signal for the canoe to lay to. It was, of course, only blank that was discharged.

No heed was paid to it, and a second gun was speedily fired. This time it had a shot that sped along ahead, ripped open the tops of several waves, and sending up a column of water as it made its final plunge.

"Look at the fools!" cried Tartub, "putting on more canvas. Do they know what is coming?"

"They only think who is going," said Seaforth. "They have made out who we are."

As he spoke a tremendous gust struck the canoe.

The sail was torn away, and the stays were drawn through the hands of those who held them with terrific velocity, literally burning and blistering their palms.

Seaforth took no notice of it any more than he had recently done to a wound which, by-the-bye, was still occasionally painful.

Jimmy Tartub clapped his palm to his mouth, and licked it vigorously.

Tokoa Fay and Tu-tu were now crouching down in the bottom of the canoe, quietly awaiting their impending fate.

The sail, wrenched from the mast, was seen to rise and twist and turn in the air like a wisp of paper, until it fell into the sea, a third of a mile away.

But still the canoe kept on.

Its pace was materially lessened, but it had wind and tide in its favour, and the islands were now not more than two miles away.

"That one to the left is the one we want," roared Tartub, "but we must take the first that comes. Look at the 'Cyclops.'"

Dick did not turn his head, for he had to watch every wave so as to steer right and avoid being swamped, but Seaforth looked and saw that the extra canvas put had been torn away, and with the mizen topmast hung in a tangled mass to leeward.

A number of the seamen were aloft, cutting away the wreck.

"If they don't be very careful," ne said, "the 'Cyclops' will get into trouble. She's driving down upon the islands."

"Something's wrong with her rudder," roared Tar-tub, "she's drifting."

"It's a race between us for life or *death*," said Seaforth; "now it is simply a question of who shall first be wrecked."

He was as cool as ever, and there was no exhibition of fear on the part of any on board the frail craft.

Tu-tu and Tokoa Fay relied entirely on the three "white" medicine men to carry them safely through the storm.

After Seaforth spoke not a word more was said. If any remark had been made the increasing roar of the storm would have drowned it.

Dick still did his best to steer the canoe safe over the heavier seas, but an oar is a poor substitute for a rudder, and now and then the craft narrowly escaped broadsiding too. Had it done so, over it would have gone, and then the end for all would have arrived.

How it kept afloat in the now raging sea was a mystery, but keep afloat it did until they could see the undulating shore close at hand.

All eyes had been turned in that direction, and the "Cyclops" had temporarily been forgotten. Seaforth, now for a moment, looked seaward in search of her, but could see nothing but what looked like a great white wall driving towards the canoe.

It was a mixture of cloud and sea spray rushing before the climax of the storm.

He knew then that the light canoe would be tossed about like a straw, swamped, and perhaps completely crumpled up by the fury of the elements.

One chance remained.

Land was near, and if——Whirr! The white wall was upon them, and immediately everything was blotted out from their sight.

Dick, in the stern of the canoe, felt the paddle torn from his grasp, and himself tossed out of his seat.

There was the turmoil of seething water in his ears, and he fought for breath and for life.

Although an excellent swimmer, he found the art of little service at that awful moment.

Whither the wind and water took him, there he had to go.

Enveloped in the mist, he could see nothing, hear nothing, and had no idea what had become of his companions.

It was all like a horrible dream, a veritable night mare, such as we have when we fight for breath in our sleep, and awake to find the dew of agony on our brows.

What is this he is violently dashed against? The shore.

He clutched at it, and found the soil torn from his grasp by a receding wave that carried him back.

But only half way, for another wave comes and carries him forward again, higher up, right inland among palm trees that must have been growing very near the sea.

He is thrown against one, and clasps it with his bruised and aching arms.

Back go the waters, to meet with yet another huge wave, that tears Dick away from his anchorage and carries him further into the pine grove.

Another trunk he grasps with enfeebled arms feeling that the end is near

Something like a sob of despair escapes him, but he plucks up his heart and prepares to die.

"The end can come but once," he said, and with a prayer on his lips, humbly awaits another rush of the angry sea.

It comes, all too swiftly, and he makes no attempt

DICK STORNAWAY IS TRAPPED BY HIS UNRELENTING FOE.

to hold on against its power, but lets go, and is carried onward.

He can see nothing, only hear the mad contention of the elements. Suddenly he is dashed against a huge stone, and a thousand fires dance before his eyes.

But only for a moment, and then come darkness and oblivion.

        *   *   *   *   *   *

"He'll come out of it right and regular, for he ain't been breathing like a man who's done for. Now if you just look at him, you'll see that he's got a natral appearance, and——"

It was the voice of Jimmy Tartub that fell upon Dicks ears, and opening his eyes, he saw the old salt and Seaforth kneeling one on either side of him.

Dick was lying on soft, sandy soil, his head pillowed on Tartub's jacket, and over his head—can it be?—yes, it is—a gorgeous umbrella.

Outside its circle he could see the sun was shining, and a little distance away Tu-tu and Tokoa Fay going through a series of antics, which were probably of a religious nature, intended to propitiate their idols, and help to restore the sick medicine man.

The moment Dick opened his eyes both Jimmy Tartub and Seaforth uttered an exclamation of joy.

The latter had lost all his air of drawling indifference, and in its place was a buoyancy which Dick had never seen before.

"Hurrah!" he cried. "Dick, old fellow, I had almost given you up. How do you feel? Nothing worse than shaky I hope."

"I feel a bit confused," replied Dick. "How long have I been here?"

"The sun's gone down," replied Jimmy Tartub, and Dick knew that he must have lain many hours in an unconscious state.

"You are not to talk much," said Seaforth, briskly. "That cannot be good for you, and you must have some fruit or something to eat."

"One thing I want to know," said Dick, looking upward. "This umbrella; isn't it Tu-tu's?"

"'Yes,' Seaforth answered.

"Then we have been taken back to the old place. No—that—can't be—I——"

"He had it stowed at the bottom of the canoe," said Jimmy Tartub, "and in course it got chucked ashore with the rest on us. We come ashore all in a heap, clinging to each other. Didn't we, Mister Seaforth?"

"I am afraid that our arrival was of a most undignified description," Seaforth answered, "but being bunched may have done something towards saving us. I believe that the nigger's heads got all the hard knocks. They acted as sort of buffers. But how I am gabbling on. You keep quiet, Dick."

And off he rushed going straight for Tokoa Fay, whose propitiatory services he cut short by pushing Tokoa Fay into the arms of his rival, and bidding them look alive and get something to eat.

Now, between Tokoa Fay and Tu-tu, no love of course was lost, and not even the joy at having escaped a watery grave had softened their instinctive enmity.

Therefore, when Tu-tu felt the rush of Tokoa Fay he concluded that it was a case of deliberate assault, and resented it with all the energy his obesity permitted.

Seaforth soon interrupted the wild clawing and scratching which ensued by dragging away Tokoa Fay by his limited apparel. Having put him on his feet he gave him a mild, admonishing kick, and then called on Tokoa Fay to rise.

"The chief medicine man," he said gravely, "has come back to the sunshine. Go, you two chuckle-heads, and get him something to eat. You know what is good and what isn't. Be smart."

"Blessmereyes," said Tokoa Fay, "good white man, all live. Me get fruit. You stop here, you Tu-tu, who you, jamfool?"

"What you?" demanded Tu-tu, "you no king wifout rumbrella. Yah!"

"Me gib him smash one day," said Tokoa Fay, significantly.

"If you do," said Seaforth, "I'll smash you. Get

away with you. White medicine man want good fruit."

Tokoa Fay then ran off to a line of wood behind him, and Seaforth returned to Dick.

It then transpired that in their anxiety about Dick, none of them had tasted food throughout the day.

Indeed, they had not left him since they discovered him lying senseless among a fringe of palm trees that grew near the sea, and by which he was now lying.

"You had a good two hours to yourself, Dick," said Seaforth, ruefully, "for it took us all that time to shake ourselves up."

"Hadn't you been shaken enough already?" asked Dick, with a faint smile.

"In one way, yes," said Seaforth, "you never saw such a lot of addleheads as we looked, when we found ourselves mixed upon the beach away there to the left. After all I believe it was Tu-tu's fat carcase that saved us. He floated like a dead whale, and acted on land as a feather bed against castle wall."

"The storm was over when we came round," said Jimmy Tartub, taking up the thread of the story, "it must have shut as suddenly, like a—like a umbrella," he added, as his eyes fell upon Tu-tu's property. "Anyway, it was gone when I got round and could look about me."

"I see how it is," said Dick, "you have suffered as much as I, perhaps more, but you make light of it. Now I can look after myself."

"You just keep still," said Tartub," "we's all right. Look here, I'll give you a bit of the British hornpipe."

Jimmy Tartub favoured him with the opening of the national dance, but it was rather a groggy performance, and he soon gave in.

"It is all right, you see," he said, "nobody's hurt but you, and we've got to look arter you."

Tokoa Fay was now seen running towards them with his arms full of cocoanuts and a species of melon.

The milk of the former was a splendid cooling drink, and its flesh was sufficient food for the time; the melons also were good.

Refreshed and invigorated, Dick was able to get upon his feet and walk to and fro, leaning on Seaforth's arm.

Jimmy Tartub proceeded to make arrangements for the night.

' You, too," he said to Tokoa Fay and Tu-tu, "have got to obey orders and give a helping hand when you are wanted to."

"Me king," said Tu-tu, "simply only sit under umbrella."

"You can sit under your umbrella when I tell you," said Tartub, "and not afore. You've a lot of supuffluous flesh in you that's got to be taken off. So run along and get some wood. We shall want a fire, if it's only to keep off them musketers. Be sharp now, and don't you go running your head agin a real live medicine man by shamming lameness."

" He a bery lazy beast," said Tokoa Fay, "all fat, no work."

"Don't you cut in when you're not wanted," said Tartub. " I don't remember iver seeing you do more'n you could help, and it's no thanks to yourself that the fat's taken off your bones. Work is good for kings as well as common folks; and, by gum, I means to keep you two Royal pussenges a goin'."

Meanwhile Seaforth and Dick, as they sauntered slowly to and fro, talked of their position.

Seaforth had been told by Tu-tu that they were thrown upon an island of which he knew nothing.

It had never been visited by his people, as an evil spirit was reported to reside there.

It was, according to Tu-tu, by far the largest island of the group.

"And what are our chances of getting away?" asked Dick.

Seaforth shrugged his shoulders, and in his old easy-going way said:

"That we shall know more about in a day or two when we have had time to look about us. The canoe has been turned into matchwood, and with no better weapons than our pocket-knives we can do very little in the way of shipbuilding."

. "Well, it won't do to despair."

"Despair, Dick ! Not a bit of it. Rather early to do that. If it comes to eating each other we have in Tokoa Fay provisions for a month."

"Oh, don't mention that," said Dick, laughing.

"But it MAY come to that," said Seaforth, gravely. "Melons and cocoanuts are undoubtedly filling, but they hardly satisfy the carnivorous appetite of man."

"I wonder what has become of the 'Cyclops,'" said Dick.

"Ah, the 'Cyclops,'" replied Seaforth, as if that vessel had been suddenly recalled to his mind, "I should say it is all U P with her.

"Wrecked ? "

"Not as we are, but gone down with all hands. She never withstood the cyclone with that tangled rigging hanging about her for the terrific winds to play upon. I don't see that there is any chance of her being afloat."

Dick became very thoughtful, and as they walked slowly to and fro Seaforth heard him mutter more than once :

"I wanted him to live—to live."

At last Seaforth said :

" It seems to me, Dick, that you and Fontenoy are mixed up in matters outside the 'Cyclops.' It isn't my business, of course, but I'm naturally of a prying and a curious disposition——"

"I will tell you everything Seaforth," interposed Dick, "but not to-night. And I shall do so with the selfish idea of having your friendly help and counsel in the future. The story I have to tell you is a strange one."

"I am getting used to strange things," returned Seaforth, " so that is all right. One thing more that is strange will not disturb me. There goes the sun, and Tartub is getting up a fire. We may want it, if I mistake not; the dews are heavy here, and the sky is not the warmest of overcoats."

CHAPTER XIII.

EXPLORING THE ISLAND—WHAT THEY SAW ACROSS THE BELT OF SEA.

THE adventurers slept in the open with a huge fire burning, for, as yet, they knew nothing of what might be in the forest.

Once in the night, Dick, who lay awake a great deal, thought he heard the roar of some wild beast, but nothing came to disturb them.

Tokoa Fay and Tu-tu, in turn, replenished the fire, being commanded by Jimmy Tartub to do so under certain pains and penalties which he would inflict upon them if they failed to do their duty.

It was not bodily pain he threatened them with, but the punishment arising from " medicine spells " he would weave for their benefit if they were disobedient.

" I aint done much in that way yet," he told Tokoa Fay, " but when I do begin I'm a gummer at it, so just mind your books, will you ? "

What he was going to do to them he did not state, and this mysterious reservation probably added to the potency of the threat.

Whether it did or not the two monarchs were assiduous in their duties as stokers, and kept the fire going through the night.

Had they known what was soon to be discovered Tokoa Fay and Tu-tu would have been relieved of that duty. No fire would have been lighted.

They were all awake betimes, and Tu-tu's umbrella was put up for Dick's benefit, but he would have none of it.

" I am as right as any of you," he said, " what are you going to do ? "

" There's a bit of a hill yonder," replied Tartub, " and me and Mister Seaforth thought of getting up it to have a look round."

" I fear that would be too much for me,' replied

Dick, laughing, " you had better go alone, and I will have a lazy day."

" You can have them 'ere monarchs to look arter you," said Tartub.

" One will be enough," replied Dick. " Tu-tu will do. He is my man, you know."

" I don't know as we wants either on 'em," said Tartub. " What do you say, Mister Seaforth ? "

" We will take Tokoa Fay," replied Seaforth, "as light porter in case we come across any provisions Dick I fruit is all you will get to-day."

" Why not send old Tu-tu along the shore ? " suggested Jimmy Tartub, " he might find summat toothsome."

" That's not a bad idea," said Seaforth.

So Tu-tu was told off to see what he could find on the shore, receiving instructions that were rather needless, not to go too far away, for his ponderous majesty was not so fond of perambulating about.

" Me sit under my umbrella," he said, plaintively, " dat bess for Tu-tu."

" You ain't got to sit under it until I gives you orders," said Jimmy Tartub, " and don't you do it unless you wants me to weave a spell agin you."

" Oh, no, not dat," said Tu-tu, clasping his fat hands.

" You just obey orders then," said the old salt, looking at him sternly.

He and Seaforth took leave of Dick, who was very weak, weaker than he cared to admit, and with Tu-tu behind them, started for a huge hill, about three miles inland.

From the summit of it they would undoubtedly get a view of the sea and surrounding islands, and " take their bearings," as sailors say.

" By the way, Tartub," said Seaforth, as they walked briskly across a plain literally covered with beautiful wild flowers, " what sort of spell is this you are going to weave ? "

" I don't know, replied Tartub, " I don't even know what a spell is, but it seems to kinder ketch these monarchs up and keep 'em going. I used to give it to Tokoa Fay, afore you come. I allus told him," lowering his voice, "that it was too horrible to talk on."

"Well, Tartub," said Seaforth, serenely, "you are not the only person who makes use of vague threats with success."

"It's the mystery of it that does the trick," said Tartub, "if I threatened to chop their fingers or toes off, they'd laugh at me, most likely, but weavin' a spell they don't get at, and so I has 'em under my thumb."

They crossed the plain and came to rising ground. The way then became more rugged and barren, but here and there were patches of verdure or flowers, and groups of trees all the way up the huge hill side.

It was rough work, for the sun was hot, and half-a-dozen times they had to sit down and rest.

It was fatiguing work anyway, and neither of them had by any means got over the fatigue arising from their rough experience of the day before.

"It's a good job Mister Stornaway didn't come," said Tartub, as they stopped on a shelf of rock, and lay down panting.

Tokoa Fay had struggled up about a hundred yards in the rear.

The King of the Wanpa people was pretty well blown, and but for the fear of having a spell thrown at him, would, undoubtedly, have turned up the job."

But he had to keep on, and as the other two settled into a reclining position on the rock they watched him for awhile as he crawled towards them.

At last Seaforth turned his face towards the sea.

Before him lay a magnificent panorama of water and islands, one of the latter so close in upon his own that only a narrow belt of sea divided them.

An exclamation burst from Seaforth's lips.

"What's the matter, sir?" asked Tartub

"Look over there," cried Seaforth.

Tartub looked, it may be said, with all his eyes, for in the narrow water bay, and on the shore of the adjacent island, lay the "Cyclops," high and dry.

She had been thrown up upon her side, so that she was utterly and hopelessly lost, as far as future sea-going was concerned.

But the crew, apparently, had experienced no great loss.

There they were, busy, about ten erecting tents and taking out provisions, looking like huge ants upon the sand.

"Who could have thought of this?" exclaimed Seaforth, breathlessly.

He knew the danger that threatened, but did not for a moment think of himself.

It was on Dick that his mind turned.

"Tartub," he said, "we shall have to shift our quarters, and put as much of the island as we can between ourselves and our old friends."

"Mayhap they won't cross over," suggested Tartub.

"They are sure to do so," said Seaforth, "remember the fire we lighted up last night. Of course they saw that, and as fire means men on the island, they will inevitably cross over to see who it is."

"If they have a boat, sir, I don't see one," said Tartub.

"I can see two, and one they are tinkering at, there, by the bow of the 'Cyclops;' and see, there they have another, and are running it down to the water. Tartub, they will cross over. Stornoway will be taken by surprise. Oh, it is a fearful misfortune."

"We must get back," said Tartub, rising stiffly; "it's no use thinking of resting now."

"Not a bit of it," replied Seaforth, struggling to his feet. "It's a double misfortune to us. Get back, Tokoa Fay."

"What you see?" asked Tokoa, looking up, "Shivermytopsels, me berry tired."

"We must get back, tired or not," said Seaforth.

They set out on their way down, but the rough road and steep incline made it terribly hard work.

Going down hill for a time is easy, but a long spell of it makes it harder than climbing up.

Every experienced mountaineer knows this.

Seaforth and Tartub soon began to experience the pains of a swift descent.

The calves of their legs ached horribly, and seemed to swell as if they would burst.

Their breath came short and thick.

"We must stop again," said Seaforth, in despair.

"All right, sir," said Tartub hopefully, "take it easy. It's no use hurrying. They may not drop on the spot where he is, and it may take 'em time to get there."

"I hope so," was all Seaforth said.

But the perspiration of fear stood on his brow.

He, who could be so calm in time of peril to himself, could suffer terribly when there was a prospect of danger to others.

Of such sterling stuff are true men made.

They soon started again, and after much suffering reached level ground once more.

It was easier going then, but their progress was anything but quick.

At last they came in sight of the spot where they had left Dick. He was nowhere to be seen.

He, and Tu-tu, and the umbrella had completely disappeared.

CHAPTER XIV.

DICK TAKEN PRISONER—CAPTAIN HARRISON PUTS FONTENOY RIGHT—WITH THE SHIPWRECKED CREW.

DICK, on being left alone by his friends, sat for a time, thinking over recent events, and endeavouring to map out some line of action for the future.

His meditations were interrupted by the return of Tu-tu, who had not been absent more than half an hour.

"No fish—no nuffin," he said.

"Have you looked for any?" asked Dick.

"Me look—all eye," replied Tu-tu. "Nuffin on de shore. Me see berrer if me sit under rumberella and watch for dem."

"You can take it," said Dick, rising.

He was not then in the humour to be bothered with Tu-tu, and having an idea that the sable monarch was unhappy without his umbrella, he gave it up to him.

Tu-tu took his umbrella, and went away to the beach, where he fixed it up, and sat down under it to watch for fish.

This duty he performed apparently with his eyes shut and snoring.

Leaving him there we will return to Dick, who soon began to find time hang heavy on his hands.

He still felt weak, and exercise in the heat of the sun soon began to tell upon him.

He was glad ere long to retire to the shade of a tree and lie down.

There—as it was with Tu-tu under his umbrella—he soon fell asleep. From dreams of his past life he was aroused by hearing a voice say :

"That's right; bind his hands, Muzzle. We don't want any more trouble with him than we can help."

He opened his eyes and strove to rise, but found himself unable to do so.

His first idea was that he was suffering from nightmare, but it vanished in a moment.

Bending over him, with a malicious leer upon it, was the face of Muzzle, and close by stood Gorton Fontenoy.

Two seamen were holding him to the ground, and Muzzle was binding his wrists together with a piece of rope.

By what strange mischance they had found him, he knew not, but in an instant he saw he must be reticent about his friends.

"So you've escaped wrecking," said Fontenoy, "where are the others ? "

"Where you are not able to annoy them," replied Dick, quietly.

"So," said Fontenoy, with a smile of satisfaction, "that beggar Seaforth's drowned."

"There you are," said Muzzle, "all right and tight, young fellow, get up."

Dick saw no use in disobeying. He was rather anxious to get away from the spot, in case Seaforth or any other members of the party returned.

"We didn't come on here in vain, sir," said Muzzle, with another grin, "it was kind o' you to light that 'ere fire, Stornaway, and so let us know where you was. We've been mighty anxious about you aboard the 'Cyclops.'"

"Fall in there," said Fontenoy, "guard the prisoner. If you lose him this time there will be no grog for a month for any of you."

He drew his cutlass, and the others did the same.

With Muzzle on one side, Fontenoy on the other, and the two men in the rear, Dick was marched away.

He was silent and depressed, for he had not the physical strength to stand up boldly against his position.

Fontenoy saw that he walked with some difficulty.

"Hurry up there," he said to the men, "there is no time to lose."

"What's the hurry, sir?" asked Muzzle.

"Silence—how dare you?" cried Fontenoy flushing angrily.

"The hurry is—that he sees I am in a weak condition," said Dick quietly, "and like the miserable coward he is he does his best to add to my discomfort. Fontenoy, you are a cur!"

Fontenoy made no reply, but he doggedly kept up the same pace, which was verging on a trot.

Dick could barely keep up from the first, and it soon began to tell upon him.

The heat of the sun was very great, and perspiration poured from every pore in his face. At last he began to reel, and would have fallen but for Muzzle, who grasped his arm.

"Steady it is," muttered one of the men in the rear.

"Keep on," said Fontenoy, "he is shamming, and it isn't the first time. Perhaps he wants to go to *sleep*."

"I am suffering from injuries I received when I was cast ashore," said Dick. "You are a miserable hound. Take your hands off me, Muzzle. I do not want your help."

With an effort he raised himself up and walked on, head erect and eyes flashing with scorn. Fontenoy made another remark or two about "shamming," but Dick did not answer him.

Fortunately for Dick, the boat 1 is captors came in was not far away. When he reached it he felt himself gi ing way. A strange and terrible feeling of utter helplessr ess came over him.

He had just strength to get into the boat, and then he sank down unconscious.

"It's right done for him, sir," said one of the men.

"Give way," said Fontenoy, brutally, "what matters if such a scoundrel is dead ?"

"He won't die," grinned Muzzle, "such as him are saved for the hanging."

The men bent to their oars, and the narrow belt of sea water—it was not more than a third of a mile wide —was soon crossed.

The boat grounded on the beach close to where the "Cyclops" lay like some huge creature stranded on the sands.

Captain Harrison and the first and second lieutenants were there to meet the boat.

At a little distance were some of the men looking curiously on. The fact of there being an addition to the party had been noted.

"Who have you there ?" asked Captain Harrison.

"Stornaway, sir," replied Fontenoy.

A slight shade passed over the captain's face.

"Why doesn't he come out of the boat?" he said.

"Well! he's given way to fear, sir," replied Fontenoy. "Our finding him upset his nerves."

"Help him out then," said Captain Harrison.

The two men lifted up Dick and brought him ashore. The look of utter exhaustion upon his pale face was not to be mistaken.

"Why the man is half dead," said Captain Harrison, "and what is he tied up in this way for ? Really Mr. Fontenoy, with four of you there was no occasion for this."

"He is violent and dangerous, sir," pleaded Fontenoy.

"He looks so now," said the captain coldly, "lay him here under the lee of the ship, and get me a little brandy from my cabin."

"I'm hanged if HE isn't going to be the beggar's friend," muttered Fontenoy.

But Captain Harrison, although a humane man, never let his private feelings interfere with his sense of duty.

Whatever he might think of Dick's original guilt there was one thing which could not be overlooked.

He had struck an officer and deserted.

The question of how far his acts had been due to provocation was not for him to decide at the time

Nor was Fontenoy on his trial.

He was no favourite with the captain, as our readers have seen, but he was still an officer of the "Cyclops," and entitled to all the advantages of his position.

Therefore, when Dick had been restored with brandy, and was able to be conversed with, Captain Harrison told him that he was a prisoner.

"We are wrecked here, Stornaway," he said, "and may have to remain on this island for some time. Now, if you are willing to give your word of honour that you will make no attempt to escape I will allow you to associate with the rest of the crew."

But that Dick would not do,

"I shall escape if I can, sir," he said, "not because I wish to shirk the consequences of what I have done, but because my duty to another calls me far away from here."

"I think you are wrong," the captain said, "not in doing that duty, but in not accepting the offer of temporary freedom."

"Believe me, sir," said Dick, in a voice husky with emotion, "I am grateful, but I cannot accept your kind offer. I shall get away if I can."

"And where will you go to, Stornaway?"

"I hardly know, sir; but I can tell you where I want to go, sir."

"And where is that?"

"To Melbourne."

"Have you ever been there before?"

"No, sir."

"Then what in the name of goodness do you want

there? Have you friends in the place?

"No, sir."

"Foes then?"

"No, sir."

"Do you know anybody there?"

"Not a soul."

"Stornaway," said Captain Harrison, "you are a mysterious fellow. Who and what are you?"

"Nothing now," replied Dick sadly, "but I may be somebody by-and-bye."

During this conversation everybody else had withdrawn in respect for their captain. He now signalled for the first lieutenant to advance.

"Stornaway will not give his parole," he said, "and you must keep him a prisoner. See that he does not escape."

The lieutenant, who looked amazed at the idea of a common sailor being offered his parole, said nothing until the captain was gone, and then he asked Dick to follow him.

"Don't hurry," he said; "there is plenty of time."

The amazement of the lieutenant spread to the others when it was known what the captain had done.

"Offered him his parole," muttered Gorton Fontenoy. "What does it all mean?"

He felt very uneasy, especially as neither he nor Muzzle had been able as yet to find out where the bottle containing the drugged water had been hidden.

The captain had succeeded in putting it away where no prying eyes could find it.

Confining Dick on board the "Cyclops" was not a possibility.

The good ship lay so much over that all her cabins and holds were at an acute angle, like dice set on the point of the square.

Nobody could walk about her, and it was not by any means an easy task to get at her stores, for all the doors had been more or less jammed together.

The only thing that could be done was to place him in one of the tents and keep a close watch over him.

This was done, and relieve watches were appointed to see that he did not get away.

In these watches neither Muzzle nor Fontenoy were allowed to share.

Both these worthies had cause to feel uneasiness and a consultation between them was a necessity.

But how were they to get it?

A close confab where they were was not possible, unless they were prepared to run the risk of being marked and suspected.

That Fontenoy did not dare to do.

But his cunning came to his aid, and he proposed to Captain Harrison that he should return to the other island and make further exploration in it.

"For what purpose?" asked the captain.

"Well, sir, we may find something that will be of use to us."

"You can go, but be back by sunset," was the curt reply.

"How many men shall I take with me, sir?"

"As few as you can. One ought to be enough."

"Very well, sir."

He did not dare to suggest Muzzle, for fear Captain Harrison might say "No;" so he quietly gave his satellite a hint, and a little later on they got away, apparently unheeded.

But a watchful eye was upon them.

Captain Harrison and the first lieutenant both saw them depart, and the former said:

"Fontenoy and Muzzle seem to be rather attached to each other."

"A sort of modern Nelson and Hardy," said the lieutenant.

"Not quite the same," said Captain Harrison.

It was not the first time the intimacy between Muzzle and Fontenoy was commented on.

Not that there is anything new in a seaman being attached to an officer, for that can be observed on board two-thirds of the ships of the navy.

But it was seen that the tie between them was neither admiration nor affection.

Muzzle, too, was wont to refer to it among the men in a boastful spirit as a thing that Fontenoy could not break.

In a vague way he had let them know that the link which united him to Fontenoy was an iron one.

"No good either of 'em," was the general opinion.

They were seen to land on the other side, draw the boat up a bit, and tie it to a big stone sticking in the sand.

Then with cutlasses drawn, as if on a dangerous expedition, they went inland.

Neither of them thought there was any peril in it, nor did the observers think of danger, but there was more to be feared than any one for a moment suspected.

Hour after hour went by and they did not return.

Now, the attention of all was drawn towards them, and many a pair of eyes were fixed on the boat, a mere toy in the distance, which was lying tenantless on the shore.

The sun was low, and night at hand. If anything had happened to them, it was too late to go to their rescue.

"What are they doing?" asked the captain.

"It is possible they have deserted," replied Lieutenant Brown.

"No, I think not," returned the captain.

The sun went down, and night came.

Over the sky above, the darkness spread like a curtain drawn by a strong hand. The stars came out in myriads.

Still there was no sign of them.

"Shall we light a fire on the beach, sir," asked Ned Dawson, who had been idling about all day, and just returned to learn about the capture of Dick and the absence of the other two.

Ned did not suggest it exactly for Fontenoy's benefit. He did it because he had the love of a youngster for a bonfire.

"It is not a bad idea," replied the captain carelessly.

This was permission enough for Ned, and he went to

work. With the assistance of half-a-dozen men he soon had a huge fire roaring.

It amused Ned, but it did not act as a guide to the missing men. Up to midnight the fire was kept going and then gradually allowed to sink down to a heap of red-hot ashes.

Whether they were popular or not the continued absence of the missing men gave rise to great anxiety.

What did their continued absence mean?

Had they fallen into the hands of man or beast—or had they wandered in a wood and lost their way?

The latter was hardly probable, because the island was not of vast extent, and being sailors, they knew how to guide themselves—taking the sun by day and the stars by night.

Nor could the question of desertion be entertained.

They had taken no provisions with them, no arms except their cutlasses, and not even a change of clothing.

No, the general opinion was that they had fallen into the hands of savages on the island.

The night ended, and daylight came. All were awake and every eye was turned towards the spot where the boat had been lying the night before.

They could not see it.

"It is not full day yet," said one of the men.

They waited a little longer, and the sun came up. Full daylight had arrived.

Then there was no longer any doubt about it.

The boat was gone.

CHAPTER XV.

NED DAWSON WANTS TO KNOW SOMETHING AND DICK CONFIDES IN HIM—A DAY'S SEARCHING.

DICK had passed a somewhat restless night, but having got a few hours' sleep he was better and stronger in the morning.

He had heard something of the commotion going on and seen the reflection of the fire through the canvas of the tent, but knew nothing definite about the matter.

The tent where he was held a prisoner was a small one, the property of the captain.

It was pitched about fifty yards from the " Cyclops," inland and away from the men's quarters, the original idea being that it should be used by the officers to sleep in.

But it having been turned into a temporary prison for Dick they had found other quarters.

Dick knew that a very close watch was kept upon him.

During the time he was awake he could hear the quiet footsteps of two armed sentries outside passing round and round the tent in opposite courses, so that they passed each other every few seconds.

He could not have raised the canvas an inch or so without being seen.

Sailors are accustomed to watch by night, and have well trained eyes. They are also very faithful in the performance of their duties, and Dick knew that any attempt to escape would be futile.

It would also lead to his being put in irons, and at present he had unfettered limbs.

The bonds put on his wrist by Muzzle had been removed by Captain Harrison when he lay in a fainting condition, and no suggestion had been made for their replacement.

Dick had slept on a plain leather arm chair, and the night was warm enough to make covering dispensable.

On awakening he sat up and listened once more to the soft gliding to-and-fro of the nimble-footed sentry.

Suddenly the entrance to the tent was opened a little way, and Ned Dawson glided in.

He had his hands in his pockets, and looked like a casual visitor just strolled in to say good-morning.

" I say, Stornaway," he said, " this is a bad job."

" Is it ? " replied Dick.   " Well, I will make the best of it."

" Of course you will, and enjoy it," returned Ned.

" Would you enjoy it if you were in my place ? "

" Rather." ✦

"It is a matter of taste," said Dick calmly, " but I would rather not be here."

" I am not talking about you," said Ned ; " haven't you heard about your two friends—Fontenoy and that beggar Muzzle ? "

" No."

" Hang it ! I thought somebody would be sure to have told you. As they haven't I will."

Ned then told him of the continued absence of the pair, watching Dick's face while he was spinning his yarn, as closely as the dull light in the closed tent permitted.

" Odd, isn't it ? " he said, when he had finished.

" It is really nothing to me," replied Dick.

" No, but can't you guess what has become of them ? " asked Ned.

" Guessing is nothing."

" No it is not, unless you are in a position to know. Come, Stornaway, you can trust me. I'm a friend."

Dick looked at the boy and smiled.

He had a frank, honest appearance that made his rather plain face quite pleasant to look at.

Ned had not made much of a mark on board the ship, and hitherto Dick had taken very little notice of him. Now he saw that there was something about the boy he liked, and would probably like better as time rolled on.

" What good would come of my confiding in you ? " he asked.

" A lot," replied Ned. " The fact is, I never believed in that job when you were supposed to shirk a brush with the slavers. It didn't seem likely you would do it. I'm very fond of Seaforth, too. He hasn't always given me a rosy time of it, but I am sure he did what was for the best. Nobody likes brushing up, but it does them good."

" Well, you must have been sorry to hear that he was drowned," said Dick.

" Do YOU say he was drowned ? " asked Ned.

"I, no, what need was there for me to do so?" said Dick, "Fontenoy brought back the news with him, did he not?"

"He made a guess," said Ned, with a sarcastic smile, "and like a fool, got on the wrong tack. Seaforth's alive, isn't he?"

Dick sat silent. He could not lie, and he did not feel that he ought to say too much to Ned, at present.

Had it been his own affairs only, he would have cheerfully confided in him, but Seaforth's life and liberty were another matter.

"You had better trust me with *everything*," said Ned, "the other boat will start soon, with a dozen men to survey the island, and search for them. If you tell me where Seaforth is, I will do my best not to capture him."

"Are you going to command the expedition?" exclaimed Dick.

"Not openly," replied Ned. "Groves, the second lieutenant takes charge of it, and I go with him. Of course he will look to me for advice."

Dick smiled.

"Anyway," said Ned, as a grin expanded over his face, "I can gammon him. Groves is a good fellow, and a beggar to fight if he's wanted to, but he doesn't think much for himself. Now, you had better give me the tip, and I'll see that nothing happens to Seaforth."

"Perhaps he can take care of himself," said Dick.

"Then he is alive?" said Ned, with a joyous laugh. "All right. You needn't be humpy because you let the cat out of the bag. I'm square."

"I believe you are," said Dick.

"Then tell me how and where you left him," said Ned.

Dick saw no reason for further concealment and he told Ned of the miraculous escape of the canoe party and how it was he happened to be discovered alone.

"I'm glad you have told me," said Ned, "now I know exactly what to do. I can put dust into Groves's eyes and lead him in every direction but the right one. You trust to me."

"When do you start?" asked Dick.

"As soon as we have had a cup of coffee and a biscuit," Ned replied. "Now you keep your pecker up. I've got a scheme half-hatched in my head which I think I can work out for your benefit. It will be a regular lark."

"You mean to help me to escape?" said Dick.

"Of course, there would be very little fun in your stopping here," returned Ned, "it will be a *stunner*. Ta-ta. Don't look too happy, or they will suspect something. Good-bye."

He waved his hand and vanished from the tent. A few minutes later some cocoa and biscuit was brought to Dick for his breakfast.

While partaking of it he heard a command given for the men to run the boat down to the water, and the grating of its keel on the sand and small stones followed.

Then came the measured strokes of the oars, and he knew that they had started across the narrow belt of sea.

He had good reason to fear a possible capture of his friends, for it was not easy to hide away four men even on an island of considerable extent, especially with two like Tu-tu and Tokoa Fay.

Tu-tu at all events was an incumbrance.

He could not be stowed away easily, nor move with celerity. In case of discovery and open pursuit, he would have as much chance of getting away as a porpoise on land.

"If they only find and catch him," thought Dick, "all will be known. He is sure to let out that the others are there, and then the island will be ransacked to find them."

After breakfast he was allowed an hour's exercise up and down outside with two men in close attendance upon him. He was then taken back to his tent, and remained there all day.

The entrance to it was kept open a little way, so that he could look out, and perhaps also so that the sentry might look in, for one only was on duty by day.

It was a quiet day and passed very slowly, save to those who were busy in the sailors' camp which had been formed on the other side of the stranded vessel.

Dick could hear their occasional laughter and the clinking of tools as they worked at some huts they were erecting.

For this purpose boards had been taken out of the "Cyclops."

Night came again and the boat came back as darkness fell.

It brought with it the news of another missing one.

Ned Dawson had disappeared and could not be found.

The men spent hours in searching in every direction, shouting and calling for him by name, but not any sign of the boy could be discovered.

Lieutenant Groves made his report to the captain.

" No news of Mr. Fontenoy, sir."

" Bad, Mr. Groves. Found the boat ? "

" No, sir—and another missing officer, sir. Mr. Dawson."

" How and when ? " asked the captain.

"About three hours after landing, sir," he said, " we could see traces of footsteps, and we followed them away to the north, to the wood at the base of the hill yonder. There he was lost."

" How ? "

" He disappeared, sir."

" Did any of the men see him go ? "

" No, sir."

" Confound the boy," said Captain Harrison, "as if we hadn't enough trouble without his giving us more. He won't take any harm for the night, but he must be sought for and found in the morning."

" I don't think the men will care much about the job, sir," said the lieutenant.

" Why not ? " asked the captain.

" They say the island's haunted."

" Bosh! "

" No doubt, sir, but for all that it is a strange place. We discovered some stones with curious carving on them, and the trees seemed to me as if they had been planted."

" Of course they have, by nature."

" No, sir, by man. Over yonder the design is clear enough. There are circles, and squares, and diamonds, and stars set out as well as a landscape gardener would do it at home, and there is one line of palms that is a perfect resemblance of a huge serpent."

" Mr. Groves," said Captain Harrison, sternly, " I am ashamed of you, talking about a place being haunted."

" I only tell you, sir, what the men say."

" Then tell me what you say."

" Well, sir, I don't like the place. It is pretty to the eye, but it is uncanny. It seems to me to be a giant garden, and on my word, sir, I should not be surprised to see a man forty feet high walking about it."

" Anything more to report, Mr. Groves?"

" No, sir."

" You can retire."

Captain Harrison had cut him short as if he despised the idea of a haunted island, but he felt very uneasy.

Of course, if haunted at all it would be by living and probably dangerous men.

Ghosts have only the power to scare, even if they DO exist, which a good many sensible people doubt.

But sensible people are often wrong, and Captain Harrison was not dogmatic on that subject.

The disappearance of Ned Dawson had certainly an ugly look about it.

For one to be taken out of a body in broad daylight without a struggle or a cry was indubitably mysterious.

Even if he designed to flee he would have some considerable difficulty in getting away unperceived.

The uncanny feeling was general.

Sailors, are proverbially superstitious, seeing, as they do, so many things that are wonderful and unaccountable even to scientific men.

The return party had a series of yarns to tell, and the events of the day did not lose in the course of narrative and comment thereon.

Up to a late hour they lay upon the sands talking, and then the order was given for all to go to rest.

Only the sentinels, watching over Dick, remained awake—save Dick himself, who had indefinitely learnt that something had happened, but could not quite get at what it was.

Inside the tent all was black as a cavern in the bowels of the earth.

The thick canvas shut out the faint light of the stars, and Dick lay in almost complete darkness.

He could not see anything in the tent, even his own hand when he held it up.

He was aroused from a fit of rather gloomy thought by hearing a soft sound on the left.

He turned his head in that direction and saw a faint narrow bit of light near the ground.

It was about two inches wide at the base, and rose up to a point.

As he watched it, he saw it widen out, and grow taller, and the effect at first was rather startling.

Then the truth came to him with a rush.

Some friend was at work outside, slowly and carefully ripping up the bottom of the tent.

Who was it that had come thus to his rescue?

Fearing to create an alarm by the slightest movement, he lay quite still, watching the opening widen out, until it was large enough for a man to creep in or out.

A hand appeared at the opening, and even in the faint light Dick could see that it was white and delicate.

It beckoned him to come forth, and be wary in movements.

Then it disappeared, and Dick, gliding off the couch, listened for the movement of the sentries outside.

The two men were whispering by the entrance.

For a time they had stopped their usual circular

perambulations.

It was now or never.

Dick sank upon his hands and knees, and crept towards the opening made for him by the friendly hand.

At that moment the sentries ceased to whisper, and resumed their rounds.

CHAPTER XVI.

DICK'S RESCUE—ON THE ISLAND—PLANS FOR THE FUTURE.

DICK held his breath. He expected to hear a cry of alarm and the sounds of a struggle as the sentries pounced upon his would-be rescuer, whom he rightly judged to be Hanson Seaforth.

It was the delicacy of the hand of which he had caught a glimpse that led him to that conclusion.

The sentries passed round twice without noticing anything and then halted again.

"Bill," said one, "there's something moving yonder."

"I heard it too, Tom," was the reply.

Dick heard them running away together, and his heart fairly sank within him. He felt sure that Seaforth had been discovered

But it was not so.

"Come out," softly whispered the familiar voice.

Dick, who had been all this time on his hands and knees, was through the opening in a second.

Outside it was very dark, for there was a haze over the stars, but he could just see the form of Hanson Seaforth close by.

Without a word Seaforth took his arm and together they glided away, without speaking.

There was no need for any caution in that respect to be uttered by either.

All the seamen, save those on guard over the tent, appeared to be asleep. The camp was still.

Seaforth led Dick round by the "Cyclops," bearing away from the sleeping men. Both he and Dick were light-footed, and they made no sound on the sandy soil.

Fully half-a-mile was traversed before either spoke and then Seaforth stopped and softly laughed.

"I don't think that has been badly done," he said.

"I cannot thank you, I have no words," replied Dick, "but I am sorry you risk so much for me——"

"Never mind the risk," said Seaforth, "I've done it. There really is nothing of me, and I lay as close as a root in the ground as those fellows went by. Then I gulled them with a stone tossed into the bushes. Listen!"

They both stood still, but there was no sound of alarm from the direction of the camp. Dick's escape had not been discovered.

"All right," said Seaforth, "now we can join Ned Dawson, who is with the boat."

"Ned Dawson!" exclaimed Dick.

"Yes! the young scamp, in pure love of adventure, gave his companions the slip to-day. There was a search party after us, you know, and he is with me. Tartub's on the island getting your supper ready."

"You seem to have made pretty sure of getting me away," said Dick.

"Well! we thought it was no use thinking of failure," replied Seaforth. "Here's the boat. All right, Ned, I've got him."

The boat was lying nose on the beach, and Ned Dawson sat in the bow. He gave Dick a hearty welcome, and the boat being pushed off, Seaforth bade Ned take the oars.

"Let me have one?" said Dick.

"There is no need of it," said Seaforth, "we have only to pull easily and the tide will carry us over. It is running out fast, and between the islands there is a regular race."

This was the fact, by pulling a little against tide the boat was carried across the narrow neck of water, and the other island was speedily reached.

Seaforth kept a sharp look-out for some particular place where he wished to land, but he could not quite make it out in the gloom. However, when the boat grounded he said it was near enough, and they stepped out.

Having drawn the boat up a little way they left it for the time.

Seaforth was the guide, and after a walk back of about a furlong he faced inland, and in a few minutes came to what looked like a high wall.

In the gloom the summit was hidden from Dick's view.

It was, however, not a wall, but a side of the hill which Tartub and Seaforth had scaled on the day Dick was taken prisoner.

At the base of the cliff, as it may be called, there was a fringe of bushes—one of which Seaforth held aside, showing a wide fissure in the rock.

"Enter," he said, "and behold the house of the gnome king."

There was a faint light within, sufficient to show Dick the irregularities of the ground he had to walk over.

Having passed through the opening he found himself in a low cave, about thirty feet deep. On the right was another opening, from whence the light proceeded.

The three friends, as they may now be called, had to walk with care, for the floor of the cave was covered with broken masses of stone, all rough, and some that were pointed, dangerous to fall upon.

On reaching the opening they found themselves on smooth ground, and ahead was a larger cave.

The extent of it Dick could not see, for in the centre of it a wood fire was flaring.

Over the fire, suspended from a tripod of tall sticks, was an animal that looked like a lamb, undergoing the process of roasting.

Jimmy Tartub was keeping it going, and just behind him Tu-tu and Tokoa Fay lay stretched at their ease.

"What cheer, Tartub?" sung out Ned Dawson.

"Hello! there, sir!" replied Jimmy, "you've come back a little early. I gave you another half hour. How are you, Mister Stornaway?"

Dick shook hands with him, and nodded to the

blacks, who had risen and saluted him.

"You seem to take *it* quite as a matter of course,' Dick said.

"Well, I've got confidence in Mister Seaforth," said Tartub. "He's cool, you see. Never in a hurry and there's no flurry. Now, sir, the kid's cooked, and we shall have to eat it in the rough, I'm afraid, till we gets time to make wooden plates, but better be without the plates than the food, says I."

Seaforth explained to Dick that they had come upon quite a colony of goats on the north side of the islands, and had captured one of the kids that morning.

Up to now Dick had not asked anything about the boat that had brought him over.

With his mind occupied in escaping, he had taken it quite as a matter of course. Now, as he sat partaking of the rough but welcome meat he began to wonder how his friends became possessed of it.

Of course it was the boat in which Gorton Fontenoy and Muzzle had landed, and that much Seaforth laughingly told him when he made an enquiry on the subject.

"And what has become of Muzzle and Fontenoy?" asked Dick.

"Tartub has charge of them," said Seaforth.

"I've got 'em right enough, sir," said Tartub to Dick "Nobody's hurt. They gave in without any fight, didn't they Mr. Seaforth?"

"They came ashore here," said Seaforth to Dick, "presumably to explore the island, but as soon as they were out of sight of the ship they squatted down for a confab. Unhappily, they squatted down close to where we happened to be."

"And Mister Seaforth," said Tartub, taking up the thread of the story, "he goes up to 'em in his cool way, and says, 'You had better not show fight. The odds are against you,' and he takes Mr. Fontenoy's sword and asks Muzzle for his cutlass, which Mr. White Liver gives up without a word."

"So you have them prisoners?" said Dick

"On parole, sir," said Jimmy Tartub, "all to-day, as I may still call it, for I allus reckon it isn't another day until you've gone to bed and had a sleep. All to-day they've been lying in here with us while the "Cyclops" men were looking round for what they didn't find. To-night they've got their parole to sleep where they they like, and orders to turn up early in the morning."

"Now, Dick," said Seaforth, "you know pretty well all there is to tell. You are tired and want sleep. The floor of this cavern is dry, and I dare say you can make shift with it for a bed for once. To-morrow we will try to find you better lodgings."

"Do you sleep here?" said Dick.

"By-and-bye," said Seaforth, "but we have a little work to do—outside."

"Can't I help you?" asked Dick. "Really, I am stronger than I look——"

"Really, you will do as you are told," said Seaforth. "Go to sleep."

Dick demurred no longer.

Tu-tu and Tokoa Fay—the former near his precious umbrella in a corner—were already snoring, so Dick stretched himself on the hard ground, and two minutes after his friends had retired he was sound asleep.

When he awoke there was faint daylight in the cave and Jimmy Tartub was putting some wood on the ashes of the fire, and close by Seaforth and Ned Dawson were squatting on the ground, talking in whispers.

Tu-tu and Tokoa Fay were gone, but in their places were Gordon Fontenoy and Muzzle.

They were standing not far from Tartub looking down sulkily at the ground.

As Dick rose up Fontenoy raised his eyes.

He evidently expected to be spoken to by Dick, probably reviled and insulted, but Dick took no notice whatever of him.

"Good morning," said Seaforth, "I hope you slept well?"

"Not so much as a dream has troubled me," replied Dick. "I feel fifty per cent. better"

"COME OUT OF IT, YOU TWO MAJE... ...G ALLOWED HERE!" SAID TARTUB.

"There is nothing like a hard bed for real health," said Tartub.

"I want to know," said Fontenoy, breaking into the conversation, "how long I am to be kept here?"

"Until you are released from your parole," replied Tartub.

"Seaforth," said Fontenoy, "you know how wrong all this is and the risks you are running?"

"Oh! yes," replied Seaforth carelessly.

"Dawson, I don't so much blame," said Fontenoy; he's only a boy——"

"Oh! don't talk rubbish," said Ned; "boy or not, I know what I am doing."

"Well! for both of you it may prove to be a serious matter."

"It is serious," said Seaforth; "life is serious."

"At the very least you will be dismissed the service," said Fontenoy. "Let the authorities look on it in the lightest possible way, and they must view it as a mad prank that cannot be overlooked."

"I know that," said Seaforth.

"What will your father think of it——?"

"My good Fontenoy," interposed Seaforth, "what my father may think of it is no concern of yours. Do not be so anxious about him. Probably you may have to think of your own paternal parent ere this business is finished."

"Then again," said Fontenoy, "you do not suppose that Captain Harrison has given up the search, for me——"

"He must give it up," Seaforth replied; "at least for the present. We took the liberty, last night, of crossing over and burning the other boat."

"It will be a temporary inconvenience," said Ned Dawson.

Fontenoy clasped his hands together, and for a moment seemed as if he would break into a fit of fury, but he controlled himself, and said:

"You have been cunning, but it only adds to your responsibility."

"Never mind, so long as it is not yours."

Dick, who had been silently listening to what passed, was troubled to find how deeply his friends had involved themselves on his account.

He was grateful, of course, and vowed in his heart that he would one day repay them.

"Mister Fontenoy," said Tartub.

Fontenoy turned upon him haughtily.

"You are an officer and a gentleman," said Tartub, "and will be treated as such while here, but Muzzle is before the mast, and he's got to work. Go out, you lazy skunk, and look up a few bits o' dry firewood."

Muzzle did not immediately obey, so Tartub took him by the collar and, twisting him round, bestowed upon him a hearty kick.

"Now then," he said, "sharp's the word. No skulking here."

Dick now noticed a heap of things in the cave he had not observed the night before.

Following his glance Seaforth explained what they were. "Mast and sail for boat," he said, "also a cask or two for water. We sail to-day, you know."

"What?" exclaimed Dick.

"Yes, old fellow, we put to sea in an open boat—and risk it. Fact is, it won't do to stop here. We've shut off all intrusion for a little time, but how long? About half a day—not more."

"How are they to get at us?"

"A raft will bring them," said Seaforth, "and you may trust them to get it together and float it somehow."

Dick had not thought of that, but he saw that Seaforth had taken a sensible view of the situation.

There was present safety, but on the whole it was precarious.

Tokoa Fay now came in. He had been outside watching the opposite shore.

"See now—boat gone," he said, "much run about—Heaveho!—big fun."

"Ned," said Seaforth, "go out and report."

While Ned was gone, Tartub got the fire up, and Muzzle, who had been stimulated by the kicking.

showed considerable activity in bringing fresh supplies of fuel.

The cave being lofty no inconvenience was felt from the smoke, and it seemed to have some means of gradually dispersing itself.

Water to drink—kid's flesh and fruit to eat was the breakfast, and when Ned Dawson came back they partook of it.

Fontenoy was invited to join them, but he sullenly refused, and sat apart.

Muzzle was, to his great wrath, told off to mess with the two sable monarchs.

"It's an honour you won't get every day," said Tartub, with a grin.

Ned's report was to the effect that Dick's escape had been discovered ; and, judging by the movements of the "Cyclops's" men, he was inclined to think that they believed Dick had got out of the tent and appropriated the remaining boat without any outside assistance.

At present they were doing nothing towards the construction of a raft.

After breakfast the whole party went outside. Muzzle and Fontenoy bringing up the rear.

Then Dick, for the first time, got a clear view of the spot.

It was just at a bend in the island, out of sight of the "Cyclops."

The great hill, mountain it might be called, sloped almost down to the sea, and there was a horseshoe corner in the land forming a miniature bay.

On the shore lay the two boats, everything movable in them being taken out and hidden away. Even the bottom boards had been removed.

"For even gentlemen on parole can't allers be trusted," said Tartub.

One of the boats was small, but the other was larger, and would carry half-a-dozen people, giving them room to move about. In the fore part it had been constructed to carry a mast.

"That's our craft," said Tartub. "and as soon as

we have watered and provisioned her we set sail."

They had brought there barrels from the "Cyclops," which they had found "kicking about the shore," as Ned said. The whole would hold about thirty-six gallons of water.

There were half-a-dozen springs in the cliff, to supply them with the needful fluid, and Tartub set Muzzle to this work, rolling them down to the boat.

Food was the chief thing they were anxious about.

Kid's flesh was very nice, but it would not keep in that climate, and the only thing really eatable was fruit.

Some of the melon species which had been discovered were very solid and good eating, and possibly a week on fruit would not be very disastrous.

Tartub's residence among the blacks had been of serivce to him, and in addition to what might be called soft fruit, he proposed to take cocoanuts.

Tu-tu had been dispatched to get a supply ready, on the spot near where they had been wrecked.

"We have to sail round there," said Seaforth, calmly, "and can anchor to pick them up."

They had no anchor ready, but a sailor's ready wit had sufficed for them to design something that would answer their purpose.

A big stone at the end of a rope will keep a boat stationary in quiet weather.

It is needless to enter into all the details of the morning's work.

Tokoa Fay and Ned Dawson sought out the fruit, and brought it in. Dick, Seaforth, and Tartub stowed them away, and prepared the boat.

The casks of water were so disposed and secured as to act as ballast.

The regular mast of the boat the night marauders had not been able to obtain, but they had secured a couple of light spars, and one of them Jimmy turned into a mast and rigged up a very good sail.

The oars and other things, which had been hidden under some bushes, were brought out and replaced.

About ten o'clock Tu-tu came waddling back.

He had got together a supply of cocoa-nuts, and placed them handy, "Just whar medicine men brought canoe in," which was his way of speaking of that decided wreck.

He had also left his umbrella with the cocoa-nuts as a sort of fetish guardian over them.

While this work was going on Gorton Fontenoy sat upon a rock, looking on and saying nothing.

In his mind he was revolving certain probabilities as to his own fate.

Did they intend to take him with them?

If not, what would they do with him?

In his heart he was half afraid they meant to kill him after all.

It was what he would do if their respective places had been changed.

It would be so easy to say that they killed him and hid away his body in the cave, what chance was there of his friends ever knowing anything of his fate?

These fears were natural to one of his really cowardly disposition.

He would exhibit a certain amount of bravery as an officer, but the true grit was not there.

He might rush up with others into action, but alone he would never walk coolly into the teeth of peril as many heroes have done.

There was nothing of the hero in him.

At last the boat was ready and the voyagers were ready to depart.

The boat lay a few yards off shore held by her improvised anchor. To get to her would ensure a wetting up to the knees, but that was not worth a thought.

"Take your seats," said Seaforth, "I, as captain, self-elected but without opposition, will be the last on board." I have a few words to say to Fontenoy before we go."

Tu-tu and Tokoa Fay were sent into the bow of the boat, Dick and Ned settled in the stern, the former taking the tiller. Jimmy Tartub announced himself as sailing-master.

CHAPTER XVII.

THE STRANGE SIDE OF THE ISLAND—A VESSEL AT
ANCHOR—LIMITED TREASURE TROVE.

"THIS 'ere bit of a rig up will want working by the man as made it, or a calamity may happen," said Jimmy Tartub.

"It looks all right," said Ned.

"We'll say more on that point," said Tartub, "when we've tried it."

Seaforth did not immediately follow his friends.

He remained with his eyes on Muzzle and Gorton Fontenoy, who stood side by side with a look of relief on their faces.

They were not to be killed or taken away, nor any violence done them.

"Fontenoy," said Seaforth, "send that fellow away. I want to speak to you."

He pointed to Muzzle, who did not stir. Fontenoy motioned for him to go.

"There's nothing to be said here that I don't know about," he said. "Why should I go?"

"Remain then," said Seaforth. "I have no wish to part such *close friends*." Fontenoy winced. "I only wished to say that after the EXHIBITION I HAVE MADE OF YOU HERE never speak to any one of cowardice. As for myself and Dawson, no doubt, in one sense, we are ruined by what we have done."

"I am glad you admit that," interposed Fontenoy, sarcastically.

"I only name it casually," said Seaforth. "I think the future will be all right enough. I hope so anyway. I wish to warn you, Fontenoy, not TO LIE when you make your report to Captain Harrison. You have not been ill-treated, but simply detained to show what a pair of arrant cowardly rascals you are."

"Seaforth," cried Fontenoy.

"Why should I mince words with you?" asked Seaforth, calmly. "I know as you know what most on

board the ' Cyclops' think of you.   Rash as my conduct has been, I do not fear individual condemnation
from them.   At the same time I know that I shall be
condemned—unless I can prove that my conduct is
justifiable."

"You may be able to wriggle out of it," sneered
Fontenoy.

"Well," said Seaforth, "I hope you will be able to
wriggle out, too.   We shall see.   There is the second
boat, the one you came in, to return by.   Half-an-hour
after we are gone you will have a favourable tide to
take you over.   One oar will be left for you.   That
will suffice.   I need not tell you how to use it.   Good
day."

Seaforth then waded up to the boat and climbed in.

Jimmy Tartub had got his sail spread and hauled
the anchor up.

A very light breeze carried the boat out of the miniature bay.

Not one of the party looked back on the two men
they had left ashore, with their hearts full of bitterness.

What story had they to go back with ?

There was nothing heroic in it, only that which was
humiliating and ludicrous.

There was the boat left for them with its one oar, a
part of the absurdity of the situation.

"Muzzle," said Fontenoy, "I CAN'T go back.   We
had better stop here and take our chance."

"Chance o' what ?" asked Muzzle.

"Anything," said Fontenoy, desperately,   what
story have we to tell ?   We shall be the laughing stock
of the whole ship.

"That's better than starving on this 'ere island," said
Muzzle.

"You may think so," replied Fontenoy.   "Go back
if you like, I remain here."

As the little craft moved before the wind the panorama of the opposite island opened out before the adventurers.

Away down south lay the stranded " Cyclops," with

men swarming about her, all evidently in a disturbed state, owing to the loss of their only remaining boat.

Dick and his friends at first intended to sail boldly down the narrow strip of water between the islands, but the wind was shifting and they steered northwards, having also the race of the sea in their favour.

It was now apparent that they were espied for half-a-dozen men came running along the beach to get a nearer view of them.

But the tide and wind were too swift, and they speedily gave up the chase.

Dick's destination, the place he aimed to reach, was Melbourne, and the hope of himself and friends was that they would come across some trading vessel bound for the Antipodean port.

"I shall try my luck in the bush," said Hanson Seaforth, grimly, "that is, if they cashier me."

"So shall I," said Ned Dawson, "I've long been beastly tired of being cooped up in a ship."

"You are safe, anyway, from cashiering," said Seaforth, "they can't charge you with DESERTING A WRECK."

"By George!" exclaimed Ned, brightening up, "I never thought of that. I don't see how they can."

They kept a look out for the boat they had left with Fontenoy and Muzzle, but it did not leave the island while they were in view of the spot which they had left.

The breeze freshened for a time and carried their craft round a headland out of sight of the "Cyclops," and brought the northern end of the island in view.

None of them had visited it before, and had only caught glimpses of it from the hill.

From there it seemed to be all monotonous wood, but sailing round the coast showed that it was the richest and most beautiful part of the island.

Along the shore there was a line of fantastic cliffs and rocks, the latter being very peculiar.

They looked as if they had been softened by heat, and then twisted into all sorts of forms by some giant moulder.

It was so curious that the desire to go ashore took

possession of all save Tu-tu and Tokoa Fay, who were
not impressed with any form of natural beauty.

The picturesque and the charming were quite thrown
away upon them.

Outside this island there was the open sea, and
Jimmy Tartub had no doubt it was not far out of the
track of vessels.

"Given a strong sou'-wester," he said, "and I don't
think that we could be here many days without sight-
ing a sail."

The wind played into their hands and helped them
to gratify their longing to go ashore.   With startling
suddenness it died away and they found themselves in
a dead calm.

So they pulled in near the shore and dropped their
humble anchor in about a fathom of water.

Now, indeed, they had a full view of the freaks nature
had played with the island.

It was a pinnacle of rude stone fancy work, inter-
spersed with luxurious foliage and flowers, growing
within a hundred feet of the sea.

Along the shore ran a narrow belt of sand that was
as yellow and almost as bright as gold.

At first they thought it was gold, but a closer in-
spection showed it was merely a matter of colour.

Surely it was one of the strangest and most weirdly
beautiful spots ever visited by man.

There was no regularity in the form of the beach. It
ran in and out among the fantastic rock with all the
windings of a country brook.

A hundred little caves and bays indented the shore.
and a short way inland there were deep pools almost
entirely enclosed with curiously shaped stonework that
might be the result of a convulsion of nature, or the
results of gigantic manual labour in its crudest form.

Feeling secure from intrusion or surprise they
wandered here and there without, however, going far
away from the boat.

Ned, boy-like, went off farther than the rest, and on
him fell the honour of a great discovery.

Being tempted by a grove of fruit trees to visit it, he

sauntered up, and found it was but a narrow belt of a wood. Beyond was a small inland lake, supplied by a narrow rivulet from the sea.

At anchor in that lake was the hull of a ship.

The sight of it fairly took Ned's breath away, and he had a good long stare at it before he could believe his eyes.

Then, convinced that it was a reality and not a dream, he hastened back to the others, who were now resting on the beach, watching the slowly heaving sea in lugubrious silence.

As Ned came up Jimmy Tartub opened his mouth and said slowly:

"A calm like this lasts sometimes for days. It's just possible that we may have to be here a week."

"That's a good look out," said Seaforth.

"Here, you fellows, I've got a find," cried Ned.

"What is it?" asked Dick.

"A vessel in dock," said Ned. "Come and look at it."

"Don't sell us, Ned?" yawned Seaforth.

"It's no sell," replied Ned.

Leaving Tu-tu and Tokoa Fay basking like a pair of turtles on the sands, they accompanied Ned back to the inland pool. There they had a silent stare of a few seconds' duration.

"I think this is about the rummiest go I ever met with," said Tartub.

"We had better bring the boat round and go on board," suggested Dick.

As the hull of the vessel was a hundred feet away, and it was just possible a shark or two might be sleeping in the port, they adopted Dick's suggestion in a body, although the swim was nothing in other respects, and several bits of rope hung temptingly over the side.

They trudged back and as they were getting into the boat Tokoa Fay suddenly sat up.

"Here, you not go without Tokoa," he said.

He plunged into the sea and made for the boat, which was, however, already under weigh, Tartub and Dick pulling.

"Get back," cried Jimmy, "we don't want you beggars as dead weight."

But Tokoa Fay had succeeded in getting hold of the boat and he was hanging on with his eyes half out of his head.

"Don't leab me," he gasped, "blessmereyes, oh! you good Tartub."

"Here, come on," said Jimmy, laying hold of his top knot of hair, "I wish you wern't half so fond of me, I do."

At this moment Tu-tu opened his eyes and slowly sat up. As soon as he saw the boat pulling away with the now happy Tokoa Fay in the bows, he set up such a yell that, as Seaforth said, it was odds on their hearing him at the other end of the world.

They motioned to him, signifying that they were not going away for good, and would soon return, but he either could not or would not comprehend.

With an agility that was perfectly astounding when his fat is taken into consideration, he bounded along the shore in pursuit, and kept up with them until they came to the inlet which led to the pool.

They left him there, wedged in between two rocks where he had fallen.

Tokoa Fay laughed derisively, and Tu-tu heard him. Hatred boiled and bubbled in Tu-tu's heart.

The ship was reached, and having secured the boat to the vessel's bow, they climbed on board.

Before they had gone far they found there was little left as treasure trove.

Everything movable had been taken away.

The captain's cabin was quite empty save for a few strips of torn paper, and the only things left to reward their search were two pair of trousers, one spotted and the other checked, evidently once used for some entertainment on board.

"Most likely part of the get-up when they had the usual fun crossing the line," said Seaforth.

There was absolutely nothing to guide them to the secret of the vessel being there.

Its very name had been obliterated from the stern.

Every record, or anything that would have answered as a record, had been destroyed or taken away.

"What is the meaning of it?" said Dick. "If it had been pirates they could easily have sunk the vessel, or fired her, and yet it is clear she has been plundered."

"And not so long ago," said Seaforth. "She hasn't been lying a year."

"But why take the masts down?" asked Ned. "They have been sawn clean off."

' That was done to hide her from view," said Dick. "Come, Tartub, you have had some experience of the sea. Can you explain this?"

"I'm darned if I can," Tartub replied. "I'm disappointed all round. One usually expects to find a bit o' something in a craft shut in or cast away like this. Now I wonder if——"

He paused, and thoughtfully scraped his chin with his forefinger.

"If what?" asked Seaforth.

"The parties as were last aboard here *are still on the island*," said Tartub.

This was a startling idea, and a short silence followed as each and all cogitated on it.

"I should say they are," said Dick.

"And I think so, too," replied Seaforth, "or their odies are."

"Well! I said it was the rummest place I ever saw," said Tartub, "and I stick to it. Anyway, we'll make use o' these 'ere coloured breeches. The spotted pair is big enough for Tu-tu, and my old friend Tokoa will be proud to get into t'others. Anyway, it'll make 'em more decent."

They left the ship so strangely placed, and so curiously deserted, and moved back to where they left Tu-tu.

He was still wedged in where they left him, and not being particularly incommoded, had fallen asleep.

Having awoke him with a hearty smack, Tartub gave him a helping hand out of his difficulty, and showed him the joyous garment designed for him to wear.

Tu-tu was quite overcome.

Of all the gorgeous raiment he had dreamt and hoped for, he had never conceived anything half so beautiful.

He did not think much of Tokoa Fay's checks, of which that sapient monarch was equally proud, and Tokoa openly derided his spots.

"You call dem breechers, sir. I say dem rags, dam muck," said Tu-tu.

"What yourn, sar?" asked Tokoa Fay. "Jess rags. I not low one ob my wives to wear dem."

While they were wrangling on the merits of their respective garments the others were holding anxious consultation.

There was, as they all admitted, something very peculiar about the island, and the sooner they got away from it the better they would like.

They had a pair of oars in the boat, but rowing was exhausting work, and they could not hope to make much headway in the heat of the day.

"Heaven send us the wind again," sighed Dick.

"It's the deadest calm as ever I knowed," said Jimmy Tartub.

He wetted his forefinger with his tongue, and held it steadily up for a few minutes. It is an old sailor's trick, and if there's a breath of air going it is sure to be felt.

"Not a whiff," he said, "and look at the sea. Sinking down as flat as a mess table."

"Well!" said Seaforth, "there is nothing like taking things easy, and I vote we have a smoke. I have half a dozen cigars in my pocket, the last of the race. There's two a piece. Ned, you don't want to smoke; you are better without it."

But not even this soothing weed helped matters.

The influence of that strange, uncanny island tended towards depression.

"Hanged if I stop here," said Seaforth, breaking a long silence.

"I think, sir," said Jimmy Tartub, "that we had better stop here. This calm means another storm brewing. I've been watching the sky and I don't like the look o' things."

"Well! we are safe here," said Seaforth.

"We must not forget the boat," said Dick; "if that is wrecked how shall we get off here?

"Better row her round to the pool and draw her ashore. She'll have strange company in that ere deserted vessel, but it's better than none.

"Anyway," continued Dick, "the ship shows that it is good anchorage ground. The last storm did not harm her."

"All right, sir. I can take her round."

He was about to start, when a sort of caterwauling among the bushes startled him and the two young men. Ned had wandered off again and was rummaging among the rocks picking up and examining all sorts of curious stones.

"Save us," cried Tartub; "what's going on?"

"I think I recognise the tones of Tu-tu," said Dick quietly.

The caterwauling increased in volume, and Jimmy, picking up a stick from the ground, said:

"Cats I never could stand, and a row like that is simply poison to me. I must take the fight out of them ere two monarchs."

He hurried in the direction of the sound and Dick and Seaforth followed him.

It was the two monarchs engaged in deadly combat, clawing and spitting at each other, like the feline creature who makes night hideous at home.

"Come out of it, you two majesties," said Tartub. "No fightin' allowed—not unless you can do it on reglar principles. Let go of each other's hair, will you? You ain't women."

He showed no respect to their majesties, dealing them a hearty whack or two apiece that had the effect of taking all the fight out of them.

They let go of each other, and retreated to a short distance, rubbing the assaulted parts of their anatomy with a vigour that betrayed the fact that he had not smitten them in vain.

"What dat for ?" asked Tokoa Fay.

"You hit king—what nex ?" gasped Tu-tu.

"I'll settle the hash of both on you," said Tartub, "if you go a clawin' each other.   What's the matter ?"

"He say my breeches cuss tings," said Tu-tu.

"And you say mine worse dan dat," said Tokoa Fay.

"You two listen to me," said Tartub.   "At home you were very great pussonages, I've no doubt, but here you don't count for more than an ornary duke or summat o' that sort, and don't you fight again unless it is the wishes of your 'art for to get a larruping."

Tu-tu and Tokoa Fay did not answer him.

They continued to rub themselves and glare at each other until he left them.

Then each put out about five feet of red tongue at the other and parted company.

The boat was brought round to the pool again, and Tartub was about to moor it when a thought came into his head.

"Why not go aboard that ere craft for a bit," he said. "A storm's bound to come.   See yonder, them bits o' smoke like clouds, and I fancy it will be a warm 'un."

"It's a good notion," said Seaforth.   "We can moor our craft alongside."

"And then, you see," continued Tartub, "in a big wind ashore here, all sorts o' things are flying about and it's clear that ship can stand agin 'em.   She rode out the last cyclone."

It really seemed to be the best thing to do.   So Ned and the two rival monarchs were hailed, and they returned in a body to the strangely deserted ship.

It was about two hours since they left it, and having made the boat secure they took out everything destructible.   The water barrels alone were left in the boat.

Tartub saw to the fastening of the boat, and he secured it with a double painter or rope, drawing it close up under the bow of the vessel.

Then he cast an eye aloft and touched Dick on the arm.

"In half-an-hour, Mister Stornaway,' he said, "it'll

be on us. Lor, sir, I've seen so many of 'em. They're as common as blackberries about here, and this will be a stiff 'un. When it comes it will be jest as well to go below."

Here an exclamation was heard from Ned Dawson.

The boy was standing at the head of the companion staring down below.

Seaforth, who had been looking about him, in his calm, indifferent fashion, asked what was the matter.

"Somebody's been here since we left the ship," Ned replied, "look there. That thing was not here when we were last on board."

They were all by his side now, and following his pointed finger they saw lying on the stairs, an old, well worn leather glove.

CHAPTER XVIII.

ON BOARD THE STRANGE SHIP—TU-TU IN A GALE—
MOVED FROM HER MOORINGS—THE STRANGE
FIGURE ON THE SHORE.

A GLOVE.

It was the strangest thing ever discovered under similar circumstances. Stranger even than the one foot-print Robinson Crusoe discovered, and never properly accounted for, centuries ago; for a man cannot get about very well without his feet, but on lonely islands who would walk about wearing gloves?

They passed it from one to the other, examining it.

"It's a good glove," said Seaforth, "and has been taken great care of. See how carefully it has been mended."

"But not by a woman," said Dick; "the stitches are tolerably neat, but not neat enough."

"The question is," said Ned, "was that glove here two hours ago?"

"It warn't," replied Jimmy Tartub emphatically; "I'll oath that."

"It was not here," confirmed Dick, "for I looked about carefully for signs of those who had once been aboard the ship."

It was an amazing mystery, although not of the class to excite their apprehensions.

A thought occurred to Seaforth.

"Was it in the pockets of those old clothes we've given to Tokoa Fay and Tu-tu?" he asked.

"It wasn't," replied Tartub. "I rummaged 'em over before I brought 'em up this way."

"It's no use speculating," said Dick. "Perhaps we shall know what it means before long. Here comes the storm."

A gust of wind swept over the ship, making it rock a little, and they heard it go moaning away across the seaThen came a lull below.

But above the clouds were flying along before a mighty current of air, and Jimmy, having cast his weather eye aloft, said it would be a "buster."

He bade the others go below while he kept on the companion to watch the progress of the storm.

Tu-tu's umbrella was in the boat, and its owner, getting anxious about it, asked if he might bring it on deck.

"In course," said Jimmy, "but it will stand a good chance of being blowed away."

"Me take him b'low," said Tu-tu.

Jimmy did not object, and the others having gone below Tu-tu waddled across the deck, and lowered himself into the boat with a sudden flop that tried the solidity of its bottom.

Another gust of wind swept by.

"Hurry up there," cried Jimmy, whose head just peeped out of the companion way; "it's a comin'."

"Me berry much smack," gasped Tu-tu; "get hard knock. Me sit down too quick."

Another whirl of the wind set the ship rocking.

Tu-tu's umbrella was seen to rise a little above the ship's side and then subside again.

"Come along with that 'ere thing," said Jimmy Tartub.

"Me comin'," replied Tu-tu, "but no get up."

Whirr!

Tartub ducked his head before the rush of wind, afraid, as he said afterwards, of having his hair shaved off.

It was a fierce blast, short and sharp, like the wind of a passing cannon ball.

When he raised his head again he saw a wondrous thing.

The wind had not entirely subsided as it did at first, but was blowing pretty hard after one moment's rest, and borne before it was Tu-tu.

He had hold of his umbrella, which was fully distended and acted as a sail and bore him swiftly across the pool.

About half his body was submerged and he was carried along at an angle of forty-five or so.

Tartub had a view of his face and never before had he seen a pair of eyes so far out of a man's head.

But notwithstanding his terror Tu-tu held on.

No mortal man could help him, so Tartub made no effort to do so. Nor did he call out anything to alarm the rest. Higher rose the wind.

Tu-tu was carried safely ashore, where somehow he got upon his feet and still holding on to that precious umbrella he started off.

He had to do one of two things.

Run or abandon the precious evidence of his kingly dignity.

The latter he would not do without a big fight with the elements.

Jimmy Tartub saw him bounding away like a school-boy running a race, occasionally leaping several feet into the air, assisted in the rising by the umbrella.

And so he bounded away and was lost to sight.

"Well! I've been darned many times in my life," he said, "but never so much as now. If the wind rises any more old Tu-tu will be taken aloft."

Settling down lower in the companion he listened to the rising wind and through the opening above watched the clouds that were racing by.

Suddenly the rain began to fall in big drops that fiercely beat upon the deck.

"Hallo!" thought Jimmy, "that's a bit heavy."

Heavily it fell and little streamlets trickled down the

stairs. Jimmy was still under the lee of the companion way.

Then, as the storm increased, he saw that he would soon be drenched. So he went below, and found his friends in the empty cabin.

This was open to the companion way, for the door was gone, having been carefully taken off the hinges.

As they could not shut themselves in, the buzz and roar of the storm almost precluded conversation.

That the discovered glove was a continued source of wonderment was evident, for Seaforth was still examining it, but he got no further information about the wearer.

Tartub had to tell the story of Tu-tu's fate, and, by dint of talking his loudest he made himself understood.

"He'll be blown right off the island," said Tartub, in conclusion, "and if he can only hold on long enough, will go right away to Europe."

It was evident by their faces that Tu-tu's disaster was not looked upon in a very serious light.

Tokoa Fay lay down in a corner, and gave way to laughter, which was the more noticeable because he could not be heard, and made horrible faces while indulging in merriment.

And now the cyclone was upon them.

They judged it was far more violent than the one they had experienced, when reckoned by the rocking of the ship at her moorings.

The rattle of the rain as it fell upon the deck was deafening.

And ere long in began to stream down the companion and flow into the cabin, so that they were speculating upon being drowned like rats in a hole.

Dick went up the companion to have a look out, and speedily came back again.

"The air is alive with leaves and branches," he said.

They could not hear him, but they judged by the signs he made that the storm was indeed phenomenal.

The window of the cabin was so encumbered with

outside dirt that they could not see out, but suddenly they could feel that the vessel had been torn from her moorings.

"To the deck," signalled Tartub.

They went quickly up—Seaforth foremost, and as soon as he put his head out he had to hold his cap on with both hands.

When he stepped out he seemed to be whisked away by the wind like a straw.

But no great harm had come to him.

When Dick emerged, he saw Seaforth up against the poop. He had gone as far as the wind could carry him, and was so far safe.

But the hull of the ship—what of that?

It had been torn away from its anchorage, and was being driven towards the narrow neck of water that led to the sea.

For a moment it seemed possible to Dick that they might be carried right out to sea, but that was hardly to be expected even by the most fortuitous concurrence of circumstances.

The ship was driven in that direction, but at the mouth of the narrow way she struck heavily on the rocky shore and heeled over so that she lay on her beam ends.

Sailors never ought to be taken by surprise, but our friends were, and they went tumbling in a heap down to the side.

Tokoa Fay went clean over the bulwarks and fell upon his head with a force that would have severed in two a cranium of ordinary density.

But he got up and commenced rubbing his hip, which had been grazed as he went over, ignoring his head.

So all question as to its substantiality was set at rest.

On rising our friends had a look about them, and then they got an idea of the tremendous force of the gale.

It still raged, but the worst was over, and they could just keep their hats on by holding tight.

The small lake in which the vessel had been recently moored was seething and boiling like a witches' cauldron.

The water was thick with leaves, branches, and rubbish blown into it.

Two thirds of the trees in sight had been blown down and lay in heaps, tossed in some cases one upon another.

The rain had almost ceased, and the clouds in the sky were dividing.

In a few minutes the short, sharp, and terrible storm would be at an end.

What had become of their boat they could not see, but that it was wrecked there could be no doubt in the minds of any of them.

This was a dismal look-out, but it was useless to repine, so they awaited the subsiding of the storm, which in half an hour was a thing of the past.

CHAPTER XIX.

AFTER THE STORM—TU-TU AND HIS UMBRELLA—DICK HAS THE STRANGEST EXPERIENCE THAT EVER FELL TO THE LOT OF MAN.

" THIS is a go," said Tartub. "Cracked like a nut under a steam hammer."

He alluded to the boat, which they had discovered was under the hull of the ship—smashed to match-wood.

The old ship, too, had not stood the shock so well as she might have done, and here and there she gave out signs of having had her timbers started.

Half an hour's heavy sea would have broken her up.

But there was no sea there worth speaking of, and if no more storms assailed her she would hold together for years.

" I'm beginning to think that this island is haunted," said Tartub. "There seems to be no getting away from it."

Matters were, indeed, in a queer way.

They had now no means of quitting the island, and even if not discovered by the men of the "Cyclops," the prospect of being boxed up there was not inviting.

" But *nil desperandum*," said Dick. " Night is

near ; we must knock up some sort of shelter."

"We will do that," said Seaforth, "but what of Tu-tu?"

"Tartub and I will go and look for him," Dick said.

The search was not a very prolonged one. He was not above a mile away.

They found him shut up in his umbrella, with his legs peeping out. Inside he was mumbling some prayer to his fetish.

Tartub laid hold of his heels and drew him out, while he yelled and kicked until he saw who it was.

A wonderful change had come over his majesty even in that short time.

He seemed to have lost a lot of his fat, and had a shrunken, baggy look about him.

The run before the storm had brought about the results of very violent training. It had trotted many pounds of fat off him.

"Blarm you," said Tartub, "what d'ye mean by shutting yourself up in that way ?"

"Me no do it," replied Tu-tu, tearfully, "umbella shut on me, so held tight."

"You are a darned image," said Tartub, "bring it along."

Tu-tu was very glad to find himself with his old friends, and cheerfully accompanied them back.

The others had been busy constructing a shelter for the night.

Tokoa Fay had brought his native teaching into play, and had carried in some trees that had fallen, and were crudely laced together, with their tops about fifteen feet from the ground.

A rough, open hut was thus formed, big enough to allow them all to sleep in comfort, or with as much comfort as the state of the ground permitted.

Food, of a farinaceous order, was in abundance, and so far they were all right for one night, at least, and in even spirits, if not high ones, they lay down to rest.

After the storm they talked little about that glove.

But it was in the minds of all.

Stretched on the ground. near what may be termed

the door of their hut, Dick lay thinking of it long
after the others had succumbed to fatigue and were
asleep.   Dick was thoroughly wide awake, and felt
there was no sleep for him, at least for hours.

After a time he did what most men would have done
under the circumstances, he arose with the intention
of going softly out, and walking up and down until
fatigue induced repose.

As he was going out he glanced back upon his companions, dimly seen in the faintly permeating starlight.   How still and quiet they look.

But for their regular breathing he would have felt
like one among the dead.

" A strange band," he mused, " brought together by
my misfortune, involved in the fate of one whom they
do not know by name."

He sighed, and for a moment there came over
him a feeling that it would be better for him to be at
rest.

But he cast it off and stepped lightly into the open air.

No storm now, but a dead calmness.   The stillness
of complete repose was upon all things.

To the left of him lay the hull of the ship like some
monster washed upon the shore.   Before him lay the
ruined woods of the island.

Near the spot a very chaos was to be seen, and there
was something weird and impressive in the grouping of
the uptorn trees.

They presented the appearance of having been put
together by giants, as some children will play with a
bundle of sticks.

Some were laced together, others simply rested on
each other, many were crossed, as we see them in
timber yards to let the air get at them, and many
were broken in the middle, exhibiting curious jagged
ends that stood up like fantastic chimneys of some old
mansion.

" Sometimes," said Dick, " I feel that it is all a
dream, so marvellous, so strange is it all—how will it
all end ? "

He sighed again, as he asked himself this question.

and to his amazement, and it may be said momentary terror, his sigh was echoed behind him.

He was standing between the rough sleeping place and the stranded vessel, close to a heap of torn-up trees.

To that he charged the echo, and to test it he softly clapped his hands together. But he did not look back.

He felt that something living was not far away.

The noise he made was not echoed, but in its place he heard a distinct movement among the trees.

He turned then to face whatever form of foe he might have to encounter.

No arms were in his possession for defence. If a dangerous enemy was indeed near he would have to trust to his hands.

And what he saw, for a moment, chilled his very blood.

Rising up behind a heap of sticks and trees he saw a white face, with two eyes that seemed to him to gleam like those of a wild animal.

"Who is there?" he asked in a hushed voice.

He was not naturally susperstitious, but he could not believe it was mortal he looked upon.

"Are you a spirit?" asked a tremulous voice.

There was a curious restraint in the voice, as if the speaker were endeavouring to master a new tongue.

For all that there was no foreign accent in his voice.

"No," replied Dick, and then, led away by a sense of grim humour, he asked, "Are you?"

"I think not," replied the other, "but I hardly know."

"Come out," said Dick "and let me see what you are like."

"You will not harm me?"

"No."

The stranger then slowly and carefully emerged from behind the wreckage, disclosing the form of a small man, neatly dressed in a suit of tweed and a tall hat.

In his right hand he had a cane, and Dick noticed that he carried *one glove.*

As far as Dick could make out in the fai

saw before him a sort of dandy one sees in the afternoon lounging in the park or in the thoroughfare of the west end of the metropolis.

But over all was a faded air, a worn-out appearance that was apparent even in the starlight.

Whatever form of earthly wonder Dick might have encountered in that strange island he could not have been more staggered than he was by this man.

For a minute or more he could do nothing but stare, while the stranger pulled down his shirt cuffs, yes, he wore cuffs—and took up an attitude of graceful repose.

"I suppose I am awake," thought Dick, "but hang it all—excuse me, sir, but are you a native here?"

"I am," was the reply, "if residing here alone makes me one."

"How long have you been here?" asked Dick.

"Really," replied the other, after some reflection, "I don't know. I have tried two or three times to keep a record of the days, but I could not do it. I am, therefore, convinced that Robinson Crusoe and his notches on the post are nothing but fiction."

"Well," said Dick, "I believe that is the general idea."

"You think so?" returned the other, wearily, "I did not look on the story in that light. I wish I had. May I ask whom I am addressing?"

"My name for the present is Dick Stornaway."

"For the present. Ha! Then mine for the present is Banks the Dandy. It was a name they gave me at school, and it stuck to me in after years. You observe something odd in my speech?"

"It is a little odd."

"So would yours be, Mr. Stornaway, if you had had nobody but yourself to talk to for an indefinite period of time."

"Can't you give me any idea how long you have been here?" said Dick.

"Judging by my feelings, about forty years," was the answer, "but I don't think I've been here more than two. You are a stranger, I presume."

It was just the way some native of a town would

have addressed a new-comer, and Dick involuntarily laughed.

But the stranger kept up his gravity and his genteel attitude.

"You are disposed to be merry, sir," he said. "May I ask where the jest comes in?"

"I ask your pardon," said Dick, "but really our meeting is so very odd."

"It's an odd world," sighed Banks the Dandy. "You are alone, I suppose?"

"No, I have five companions with me."

"Indeed, sir, and is it your purpose to settle here? We shall form quite a colony."

"I assure you," said Dick, "that I intend to get away as quickly as possible, and if you desire it you may go with us, if fortune favours us."

"I shall not regret it," was the answer, "for as I am a gentleman, a lonely life on an island is a fraud—a contemptible fraud."

Dick was going to laugh again, but he restrained himself.

His newly-found companion went on :

"Are your friends ad—ad—what's the word?—adjacent?" he said.

"They are all sleeping yonder," replied Dick. "I could get no rest, and came out to tire myself."

"I have passed many sleepless nights," said Banks the Dandy, "and can sym—sym—oh, sympathise with you. But I do not care to risk too much of the night air. A loss brought me out to-night. Not a very great one perhaps. A glove. I believe I lost it on board the 'Thunderbolt.'"

"That is the name of that ship?"

"Yes, but pardon me, the dew is heavy and the air chilly. May I ask you to visit my humble abode? We can converse more freely there."

"With pleasure," said Dick, whose curiosity was quite equal to his amazement. "Is it far?"

"Not any great distance About the length of Bond Street. Permit me to show you the way."

He started off at the strolling pace of a fashionable

lounger. swinging his cane, and Dick walked by his side.

"I can ease your mind about the glove," he said. "We found it this afternoon."

"Indeed. I am in—in—oh, indebted to you. How difficult it is to remember words one has not spoken for a time."

He led the way round the now quiet pool to the upper end to a pile of broken ground which Dick had observed some hours before.

As they drew near to it our hero saw an opening which he rightly judged was the entrance to a cave.

Banks the Dandy bade him wait a moment while he went in and lit "the lamp."

"I do not wish you to hurt yourself by falling over the furniture," he said.

"What on earth is coming next?" Dick asked himself.

But he said nothing, and waited patiently for a few minutes, giving himself an occasional pinch to make sure he was awake.

At length a light was discernible in the cave, and Banks re-appeared at the mouth of the cave.

"Welcome to my humble home," he said. "Enter."

Dick obeyed and passed into the cave, where he saw a sight that gave him additional astonishment.

It was not a spacious place as caves go, but it was very large for a single apartment.

It was furnished with all sorts of things, tables and chairs, evidently taken from the ship. There were sleeping bunks, books, and a score other things. From the roof swung a ship's lamp.

It was not burning very brightly, and Banks the Dandy apologised for its defectiveness in that respect.

"My stock of oil is running low," he said, "and I have to econ—econy—economise."

Dick now observed that just within the cave there was evidence of an effort having been made to fix up a door, but without the success that would have attended the labours of a good carpenter.

The frame was there and the door was there, but

both were lop sided.

"I tried to make it a comfortable home-like place," said the Dandy, " but I am not a builder. I am a muff at that sort of work, so you see I abandoned the thing."

" I am sure the place looks very comfortable," said Dick.

He hardly knew what to say. Everything was so very odd.

"It *looks* comfortable," said Banks the Dandy, " and Robinson Crusoe might have gone into ecstasies over it, but he was an ass. I say it advisedly, he was an ass, and he was moreover untruthful. Life in a cave is as poor as life can be. He was never honest enough to talk about the bats and insects. I have suffered much from them, having a horror of such things. As for his goats and his parrots and all that, my blood boils when I think of the humbugging way he wrote about them. Sit down, please."

Dick sat down, and his strange companion did some rummaging in a locker, finally bringing out a bottle and a glass.

"Port wine," he said, " the only bottle left, I kept it in case of guests—or sickness."

He poured out a glassful and handed it to Dick, who took it, because he felt he wanted something to enable him to stand up against the dreamlike experience of the night.

He had a good look at his companion now, and saw that he was still young, not more than five or six and twenty, but looking very weary and worn.

His clothes were old and had been mended in every conceivable place, and the hat he carefully put upon the table had a suspicious limpness about the crown.

"Yes," he said, with a sigh, "I look on Crusoe as a man who ought to be kicked. Will you have another glass of wine ? "

"No, thanks," replied Dick.

" You are sure ? "

" No, indeed."

" Then I will take a little myself. Excuse my drinking out of your glass. It is all that is left to me. I had another, but it was broken by a goat I tried to tame. I saw the wretch prowling about here, watched him in and endeavoured to keep him. His behaviour was most violent, and he butted me in a vicious way I have not forgotten."

He drank a little wine, and sensibly brightened under its influence.

"Truly, sir," he said, "I am rejoi—rejoiced to see you. I wait the departure of solitude with ju—ju—ju —jubilation."

"No doubt you do," said Dick, "and I trust that our stay here will not be long, but excuse me, how did you get to and from the ship?"

"I have one small boat which I hide away," was the reply, "it was left me by the nefarious villains who abandoned the vessel and me to this fate. It is true I desired to be left behind, because I hate low company, and I— I—had faith in Robinson Crusoe. Enough; you shall hear my story by-and-bye."

"It will interest us all," said Dick. "If you will excuse me now, I will go back to my friends. We shall be glad to see you early in the morning."

"Can I not offer you——a bed?" said the Dandy.

"Thanks—no," replied Dick, "they might be alarmed when missing me in the morning."

"True—I forgot that," said the Dandy; "it was thoughtless of me. Pray give them my compliments and say I shall be glad to see them at breakfast. Humble fare, but a hearty welcome. Say about an hour after sunrise—will that suit you?"

"Admirably," replied Dick, falling into the humour of the strange situation. "Good night and thank you."

"Good night," said the Dandy, extending his hand, "I shall sleep more peacefully than I have done for a long time. Man is a gre—gre—gregarious animal— he must have society or he will suffer. Robinson Crusoe knew that when he wrote his book, but he was a humbug and a fraud. Good night."

Dick shook hands with him, and left the cave wondering if when the morning came he would not find that his strange experience had been nothing but dream.

CHAPTER XX.

DANDY BANKS ASTONISHES MORE THAN ONE PER-
SON—ANOTHER WRECK—DICK'S DARING TRIP—
THE DOOMED SHIP.

NED DAWSON was one of the first to awake, which
was like a boy, but, like some boys, though aroused he
was not disposed to get up.

So he lay with his head on his two clasped
hands surveying his companions in the growing morning light with a leisurely criticism on their sleeping
attitude.

Both of the savage marauders slept with their
noses and knees nearly together, an attitude often assumed by young white people when the nights are
cold and the clean white sheets strike chilly.

Jimmy Tartub was snoring, having quite a gift in that
direction, each sound he gave out being expressive of
immediate choking or pending apoplexy.

Not that either of these evils was, at the time, in
store for him. It was only his way of showing that
he slept soundly.

By the light Ned judged that it was about six
o'clock, and, after a series of yawns, he was about to
try to get to sleep again when Dick Stornaway opened
his eyes.

He looked at Ned, and gave him good morning.
Then the memory of the previous night's adventure
flashed upon him.

Again he thought it might be a dream.

But, rising quickly, he looked in the direction of the
cave, and saw a column of white smoke rising slowly
in the air.

Banks the Dandy was preparing breakfast, and it
was all true.

"Wake up, all of you," said Dick, "I have a story
to tell you that will astonish you a bit."

They were awakened by the sound of his voice, and
as soon as they had got the sleep out of their heads he
told them the story of meeting with the Dandy.

THEY FOUND TU-TU SHUT UP IN [...] WITH HIS LEGS PEEPING OUT.

It is needless to say that they were astounded, and even Seaforth had to lay aside his ordinary phlegmatic bearing.

"How long has the fellow been here?" he asked.

"That," replied Dick, "I have yet to learn. Also, how he came here at all."

"I don't ask the question in a snobbish way," said Ned; "but is he a gentleman?"

"He acts like one," replied Dick.

"Well, that's enough," said Seaforth. "Not that I would quarrel with any man's manners unless he were vulgar or rude. So we are to breakfast with him?"

"That is his desire," said Dick, "and see, he is preparing the festive board."

"What can the fellow have got for us?" mused Ned. "I'm hungry enough to eat grilled shoe leather."

They all had a wash at an adjacent spring, and made as good a toilet as circumstances permitted.

Then they sallied forth to keep their appointment, Dick and Seaforth leading, and the two monarchs bringing up the rear.

"You will please to remember," said Jimmy Tartub to them, at starting, "that quarrelling and fighting when you are out visiting ain't good manners. On the fust sign of a rumpus between you two off go both your heads. I've been a weavin' a spell to bring that ere cat—as—trophe about. D'ye hear?"

They heard and believed for was not the white man's power a potent thing? Silent and restrained they brought up the rear. Banks the Dandy received his company courteously, but without effusion.

On a clear white sail spread upon the ground he had spread breakfast, which consisted of fish, and something which looked like putty, but which afterwards proved to be passable bread made by the host, and fruit and coffee.

For the latter there were cups, saucers, and spoons. There was, likewise, a small quantity of sugar.

"I thought you would prefer the open air to the cave," said Banks. "Caves are either very damp or close. In either case not desirable places to entertain

our friends in. Romances have a great deal to answer for."

"You believed once in a life in a cave?" said Seaforth.

"I did," replied Banks the Dandy, with a sigh, "but it won't do if you can get another abode."

"There was the ship," hinted Dick.

"Not there," answered Banks, shuddering. "No, not after what I witnessed there. Enough, it is not a story for the breakfast table."

In the daylight Dick could see how poor was the apparel of the dandy.

It was literally worn thread-bare, but everything he had on was scrupulously neat and clean.

He could be compared to nothing better than a faded flower.

There was also in his countenance the curious pinched eager look one sees in the faces of those who struggle against poverty to keep up appearances.

But he was composed and hospitable, pressing his guests to eat and partaking of little himself until he was sure they were satisfied.

Tokoa Fay and Tu-tu sat a little apart by choice.

Their manners were not of the class that stamps the family of the Vere de Veres and they were fully conscious of it.

"White man eat one way," said Tokoa Fay, " black man eat no way."

Notwithstanding the novelty of the surroundings everybody talked and laughed as if it had been an ordinary picnic.

Banks the Dandy did not laugh, it is true, but he smiled in the gentle deprecating way of a man who is naturally grave but tolerates mirth for the sake of others.

"I have enjoyed my breakfast anyway," said Ned Dawson; "the coffee was prime. I hope you have a good stock of it, Mr. Banks."

"I regret to say," replied the Dandy, "that I used the last this morning. I reserved it for my birthday."

" When is that ?

" Really I have lost all count of, dates.   It was my ntention to guess at it."

This naïve confession set them laughing, but the Dandy did not even smile.   Rising he begun to clear away the fragments of the feast.

Jimmy Tartub assisted, and Tokoa Fay and Tu-tu lent a hand, but the rest had the good sense to see that the Dandy looked upon them as honoured guests, and expected them to behave as such.

Therefore they did nothing.

" Mr. Stornaway," said the Dandy, " I promised you last night to show you my boat. It is a crude specimen of the art of boat-making, but it has served my turn."

" It is not one of the ship's boats then," said Dick.

" No," replied Banks, shaking his head mournfully, " it is only fit for me.   The nefarious villains I have before referred to knocked it together for my use inland.   It is not seaworthy."

And truly, when he had drawn it out of its bed of rushes, it was indeed a rugged affair, with as little real make and shape about it as there is in an egg chest.

It was made of straight planking, and there was no keel to speak of.   The rowlocks were merely four wooden pins fixed in the sides.

Dick was terribly disappointed.

He had been indulging in hopes of the Dandy having a boat that would replace the one they had lost.

Now they were as much as ever prisoners on the island.

However, there was a fair size party of them, and they need not despair. With so many heads and strong hands to match it would be odd if they did not hit upon some means of getting away.

Their host put everything away after breakfast in a neat and orderly manner, carefully stowing the earthenware in a locker in the cave, and shaking out and folding the sail as if it had been a fine linen table cover.

" I had two linen cloths when I first started here," he

said, "but to confess the truth—I was driven to converting them——into shirts."

This confession sent Ned into a fit of laughter, which the author of it took good-humouredly.

He produced a cake of cavendish, which he offered them to cut and smoke, but all except Tartub refused.

As the day was advancing by this time the power of the sun began to be felt, and they withdrew to the shade of some of the trees the storm had left standing.

Tokoa Fay and Tu-tu, however, preferred basking in the sun.

"It's enough to bake their brains," said Ned Dawson.

"If they had any," replied Jimmy Tartub, "but don't you fret, sir, on that account. Niggers like them have only got cocoa-nut milk in their heads."

Not being prepared to discuss this physiological aspect of the nigger Ned let the assertion go as a fact.

Banks the Dandy was now asked if he objected to give an account of how he came there. In response he gave a ready negative.

"There is nothing particularly wonderful in my story, I suppose," he said, "but you will be the judge of that. As the facts are in my head so I will endeavour to relate them.

"It was about two years ago—a month more or less —when the good ship 'Barbaria,' sailed from Sydney to London with a general cargo, and about twenty thousand pounds worth of gold dust.

"She carried no passengers but one young man who had been out to the colony to test the romance of the life of a digger, and found it like living in a cave—a bit of a fraud.

"Of course I don't say it would be a fraud to every one," said the Dandy, "but to young men like this one, who was like myself, gentlemen, endowed with a wonderful imagination—the reality is miles behind the fancy.

"Disappointed, if not absolutely disheartened, I was going home, and owing to the pecuniary inducement was travelling cheap. I was acting as cook's mate, in fact, and personally I do not see anything degrading in it.

"I had to work my passage over or to stay where I was, and I preferred the work.

"The crew was a rough one, the roughest I had ever seen on board a ship, and to a gentleman, which I humbly hope I am, their language was shocking.

"I ventured to remonstrate with them more than once, but all I got was what the vulgar call 'chaff' for my pains.

"One morning these men rose up and mutinied.

"Bad as they were considered to be, we never expected that, and all except those who had a share in the plot were taken by surprise.

"So sudden was it that the majority, including the captain and the officers, were killed and tossed overboard ere they had recovered from their astonishment.

"The cook and myself were spared.

"We were both useful and harmless, so we did not suffer with the rest.

"But we had a hard time of it, which I need not enter into beyond stating that they treated us like dogs when they were sober and acted like ungrateful brutes when drunk.

"Some of the crew had no share in the mutiny, but in point of numbers they were not strong enough to stop it.

"So they yielded to circumstances and became passive mutineers.

"The price of their neutrality was death.

"One night, I remember it well, the others suddenly fell upon them, and hiding in the crosstrees into which I had sprung was the unhappy witness of as hellish a piece of butchery as ever disgraced mankind.

"This time they killed the cook and I alone was left.

"Why they spared me I don't exactly know, unless it was for the same reason as before, because I was useful.

"Well, gentlemen, their purpose was plunder. They

originally intended to sink the ship, but they happened to light on this spot and they brought her in here. The masts they cut down and left the wreck of the rigging hanging in confusion about the sides.

"The ship had good stores and they made merry for a week or so on shore. Some times they quarrelled and one man was killed, but on the whole they got on very well considering what blackguards they were.

"At last they decided to divide the gold, and with their chests put to sea in the boats.

"They said it was their intention of getting into the track of vessels so that they might be picked up. They could swear the vessel was wrecked in a gale.

"Then came the question of what was to be done with me," said the Dandy, "and some were for putting an end to me, while others said it was no use killing a puppy dog, which was personal and untrue, for if I am a gentleman, careful of my dress and manner, it does not follow that I am a puppy.

"Before they went, two of them, kinder than the rest, knocked up that boat for me.

"You will want it," they said, "to go to and fro to get a few things from the ship."

"It was kind of them, and if ever I meet with those men under distressed circumstances I shall certainly endeavour to repay them.

"Left alone, you may guess my life," said the Dandy, in conclusion. "I cleared away the wreck of the rigging, and by degrees got out the stores which I brought ashore, and lived in yonder cave an imitator of the life of Robinson Crusoe. In my boyhood I often wished for the chance of doing so, as a man I have found out that it was a foolish wish.

"A solitary life is unbearable, horrible. No beauty of scenery, no amount of romantic comfort can make it endurable. It is not good for man to live alone. He was not designed for it, and he who is without his fellow to talk to and look up to, is a most pitiable object.

"The long days, and the still longer nights, have set their mark upon me. I am not the man I was, nor do

I think I can ever be again. Occupation has saved me from going stark, staring mad. I have never permitted myself to have an idle hour and that is the secret of my being alive, clothed and in my right mind, to tell you this day my strange, if not wonderful story."

He ceased, and for a few moments there was silence. It was broken by Seaforth.

"Dandy," he said, "you are a good fellow and a brave one. You are also a brick. Let us shake hands all round with you as a simple but explicit expression of our feelings."

And this was done to the satisfaction of all concerned.

"And now," said Tartub, "our next move is to scheme some way of getting off this island. I say, Mister Dandy."

"Mr. Tartub," said Dandy.

"You have kept a look out for vessels, I suppose?"

"Oh, yes, but I have never seen a sail but twice, and that was far away at sea. I do not think we shall be rescued that way."

"We must make a raft," said Dick. "Build it in the lake so that there will be none of the troubles of launching."

"Another good idea," said Seaforth. "Dick, as usual, to the fore. Let us go down and inspect the old ship. She will supply us with materials."

Now all this time there had been a secret spy on them. In the long grass behind the trees Gorton Fontenoy lay listening to every word.

He had been drawn to the spot by the smoke of the breakfast fire.

Already he had found out the weariness of a lone existence, and was longing to return to his friends.

He had only to return to the old spot and signal them for the boat to be sent to him.

Then he could tell the grand news.

Dick, Seaforth, and Ned were all deserters, and to recover them with one haul would be a great thing.

So he rose up and stole away to bring the men of

the "Cyclops" upon those he hated, while they, unaware of impending disaster, talked cheerily and laid their plans to escape from the island.

CHAPTER XXI.

FONTENOY'S SUFFERINGS—PREPARING TO CAPTURE THE DESERTERS—ANOTHER WRECK.

THERE was no delay about the building of the raft. Under the guidance of Jimmy Tartub, who had once been wrecked, and helped to make one that floated for a week on the sea, they all went to work.

Dandy Banks had a good store of axes and other implements, which the mutineers had kindly left him, because they were of no great value, and would be a dead weight in the boat.

He had also a good collection of nails and screws, and had been especially careful in taking care of all ropes and cables.

They began their task with hopeful hearts, while Gorton Fontenoy, already tired of solitude, made his way back to that point where he hoped to be seen by his old friends.

The cyclone had shaken all the pride out of him. He would rather go back, and face the charge of cowardice or anything else, rather than live on that island for a week.

The feeling which prompted him to send off Muzzle alone was decidedly ephemeral.

He was too late to signal to his friends that day, for it was growing dark when he arrived in sight of the headland opposite where the "Cyclops" lay.

With a weary heart he threw himself down under the lea of a rock and slept.

He had had nothing more than fruit to eat that day, and water only to drink. He was in a low, depressed condition, and was troubled with horrible dreams.

In the morning he awoke weary and unrefreshed.

After a breakfast of wild melon and a drink of water, he set forward for the headland, and about ten o'clock arrived there footsore and tired as a lost dog which has been seeking its old home for days.

The "Cyclops" was still there, but the camp, so far as the huts erected were concerned, had been swept away. A considerable portion of the wood beyond was also down.

He could see the men busy cutting up timber and preparing another camp, and on the shore not far from the "Cyclops" was the boat by which Muzzle had returned.

Putting himself into a prominent position Fontenoy took off his cap and waved it.

They neither saw nor heeded him.

We need not elaborate upon the day of torture he endured.

At intervals, as often as his waning strength permitted, he waved his cap, and waved it in vain.

Sometimes he shouted, but his voice could not travel so far.

He prayed, he wept, and cursed alternately without any result until night was at hand, and then somebody on the other side saw him.

Immediately, or as soon as the men could get into it, the boat was pushed off and came speedily across the narrow neck of water.

The revulsion of feeling, from dark despair to joy was too great for Fontenoy, and he fainted away.

They found him lying senseless on the sand, and lifting him into the boat took him back again.

There was no demonstration of joy when he was on the other side, and not even when he had been restored to consciousness, was he congratulated on his recovery.

The first person he saw on opening his eyes was Captain Harrison, who was in one of his sternest moods.

"I must congratulate you, Mr. Fontenoy," he said sarcastically, "on your timely repentance."

"I hope you do not misunderstand me, sir," Fontenoy replied with his head down.

"Oh, no," replied Captain Harrison, "you simply deserted like the others, only you lacked the courage to stand by your friends, or perhaps they declined the honour of your company."

" I never sought it, sir."

" Then Muzzle has lied. He told us that you had made friends with the deserters and had gone away with them."

Fontenoy was bitterly angry with Muzzle, but he dare not give the feeling vent.

" You shall judge, sir, how far I have made friends with them," he said.

And then he told Captain Harrison all he had heard and seen, and offered to lead a body of men to the spot and capture Dick and his friends.

It was too late to do it that night.

Already the sun was down, and darkness rolling up like a cloud.

Captain Harrison dryly said that he would see what could be done in the morning.

We must now return to our friends, who worked until it was dark and then went to rest.

As soon as there was a ray of light in the morning, they were up and resumed their task.

Dick had not absolutely recovered from the terrible mauling he received when wrecked on the island, and his friends insisted that he should knock off early in the morning, and take upon himself a lighter duty.

Dandy Banks told him of a spot on the coast where he could find clams, and suggested that he should take the boat and paddle down to the mouth of the rivulet, which was near the place he indicated.

Dick accepted the task, which, ordinarily, would have fallen to the lot of Tokoa Fay or Tu-tu, who were, however, useful as labourers.

The tide was running out, so Dick had an easy task.

He had only to lie in the stern of the box-like boat and steer with an oar. A very short time brought him within view of the sea.

Casting his eyes over the wide expanse of water, he saw steadily bearing towards the land—a ship.

The wind which had blown off the land during the cyclone was now set in from the sea, and at first Dick thought the vessel was on the shore tack, and would soon veer round.

There was no time to go back and apprise his friends of its arrival. All he could do was to endeavour to attract the attention of those on board.

As he hastily drew his boat ashore and sprang upon a rock something peculiar in the vessel attracted his attention.

There was a strange disorderly appearance in the rigging, and she was coming towards the shore BROADSIDE on.

The wind was very soft and her progress slow, especially as she had the tide against her.

There was indeed the prospect of a calm, and then she would be born away on the retreating sea.

Dick had had some experience of the sea, and had learnt a lot from listening to the older salts on board the " Cyclops," and he could tell by theory at least that the vessel would not reach the island. Then the idea of going out to the ship occurred to him.

It is true that the boat was frail, but the sea was fairly smooth, and it was worth the risk.

Possibly the ship had been deserted as going down, as many a vessel had been, and had not fulfilled the fears of its crew.

Certainly it was very odd that she should be, as it were, blundering about the sea in that fashion.

Dick put the boat off again, and now taking both oars pulled steadily and carefully out to sea.

He now found that he was indeed in a crank craft that might turn turtle any moment, but his curiosity was so great that he was induced to go on.

With great skill and care he carried the tub over the waves, pulling easily and steering her with the tide until he was close upon the ship,

Then all doubts as to her being without living men on board were soon dispelled.

The rigging was in a state of wreck, stays torn away, and the sails for the most part split and flapping loosely against the masts.

Only two or three of the sails were fast and by these she was being blown towards the shore.

Her progress was so slow that Dick had no difficulty in getting to the windward side and fastening his boat to a rope that was dangling overboard.

Having secured it he climbed the same rope and threw a leg over the side.

Then he paused half dazed with the scene of horror that was before his eyes.

The deck was strewn with dead men.

In every attitude expressive of a sudden and awful end they lay.

There were no weapons strewn about.

No sign of a desperate fight for life.

On these men the Sword of Destruction had fallen suddenly, even as in the Assyrian of old.

Has not the poet written—

" The Angel of Death spreads his wings on the blast,
And breathed on the face of the foe as he passed ;
The eyes of the sleepers waxed deadly and chill,
Their breasts but once heaved and for ever were
　　still."

—Even thus did it seem to have been with these men on whom Dick looked with a heart almost as cold as theirs.

CHAPTER XXII.

THE SHIP AND ITS DEAD—ARMS FOR ALL—THE RAFT FINISHED—THE MEN OF THE " CYCLOPS "—JUST TOO LATE.

ONLY for a few moments did Dick hesitate, and then he dropped quietly to the deck to get a nearer view of the dead men.

Their faces were wan and sickly, because the hue of death rested on them, but there were no signs of the terrible wasting of a lengthened illness.

Nor were there any signs such as he had been taught to believe would follow death by any virulent disease.

They lay about the deck as if they had all fallen down and died without a groan.

He counted the dead bodies on deck.

Seventeen was the number.

That would be a small crew for such a vessel, and there was only one officer among them, so he concluded that there were more below.

Should he go down and inspect the cabins?

It was a test of his courage and nerve, and he naturally hesitated.

There were three big boats, any one of which would do away with the necessity of using the raft which his friends were engaged upon, but when he tried to loosen one, he found the ropes were jammed into the davits, and would have to be cut away.

If for no other purpose than to get an axe, he must go below, for he could not see one on deck.

The companion was open and he descended.

On the bottom of the stair sat a man, with his head bowed forward, apparently asleep.

This was a startling discovery, and Dick was about to speak to him, but he saw in a moment that it would be useless.

The man was dead.

It was one of the officers, and passing him by with a shudder, Dick entered the cabin, which he judged was the captain's own.

He was right.

And the captain was there, seated in a chair, with the log book open before him.

He too was dead.

And on the floor, where he had fallen, was another officer, stretched out in death.

In one moment must death have come upon the whole ship's company.

What had been the cause of it?

Dick had heard of travellers perishing on the Andes under the withering breath of the *Blast of Death*.

High, on some of the tops of the mountains which form the great chain running from north to south of Southern America, they tell us there are poison winds which kill as they sweep by.

Was it possible that some such blast had swept over this ship and taken the lives of all on board?

It was not only possible but reasonable to believe in.

Nor could these poor men have long been dead.

In that climate an exposed body soon becomes unbearable.

Only a few hours could have elapsed since they died. This was a terrible idea.

Might not the same destroying influence sweep down on the islands, and if it did, what then?

All would die.

Friends and foes would perish alike and no man survive to tell the story.

Sick at heart Dick took up the log book and put it under his arm. Then he quickly searched the cabin for weapons, of which he and his companions were in need of.

In a long chest he found several rifles and revolvers, and in a cupboard there was ammunition for both.

His next task was to lower one of the boats and put the stores into her.

He found the carpenter's room, where there were tools galore, and having selected an axe he cut the boat clear of all obstruction and lowered her.

The ship was now stationary.

The wind had almost ceased, and he must be quick, as the tide would soon be carrying him to sea again.

The arms, ammunition, a few tools, a sextant and a compass he placed in the boat and then pushed off just as the tide was beginning to exert its influence over the wind. It was a heavy task he had before him.

The boat ought to have had at least four men to pull her with ease.

And he had the tide against him.

But Dick saw in that boat a means of saving them all, and he set manfully to work.

Inch by inch, as it were, he battled against the retreating waters, and drew nearer to the shore.

The death ship was born slowly away over the calm sea.

Dick pulled with might and main.

And he would have pulled yet harder if he had known that twenty men of the " Cyclops," headed by their captain, were coming across the island to arrest the " deserters " from the ship.

Gorton Fontenoy was their guide, and he had announced the walk as a matter of four hours or so.

At starting he was sure he knew the way.

Had he not gone to and fro only the day before, and was not there landmarks to go by.

And yet it was these landmarks which put him out just a bit.

Some of the fantastically-shaped rocks that stood upon the plains seemed to have changed their places during the night.

One that he thought was to the right of the way was now plainly on the left. Some were not to be found, and others he had not noticed were there before his eyes.

The four hours walking had not brought him within sight of the pool with the wrecked ship.

But ahead of them lay the sea, and far away on the right they could see a vessel apparently at anchor, and a small speck between it and the shore.

The latter was Dick in the boat, and the former was the strange ship he had visited.

Happily, the captain of the " Cyclops " had not brought a telescope with him.

So he made a guess at the nature of the vessel, and put it down as a trader, which had dropped anchor and sent ashore for water.

"We must communicate with her," he said, "perhaps they can take some of us on board."

"And the deserters, sir ?" said Fontenoy.

" Oh, hang the deserters," replied the captain, testily, " my first duty is to think of saving my crew."

" He hasn't much heart in this job," thought Fontenoy, bitterly.

Captain Harrison led his men to the beach, as the shortest route to reach the boat.

But he soon found he had made a mistake.

Ere long they came to a clump of rocks, inaccessible on account of their quaint shape, and these had to be skirted, which took him at least a mile out of the way.

over one of the roughest ways ever trodden by man.

When they reached the beach again, several of the seamen were limping, and the rest were tired.

So a short halt was called.

The ship and the black speck of a boat were again in sight, the latter a little nearer ashore, and the other further off.

Captain Harrison shaded his eyes with his hands, and took a long and steady look at her.

"She seems to be standing out to sea," he said, "but she's got a slovenly lot on board."

The men were growing weary of their task.

The idea of it being an enchanted island had taken deep root in their breasts and they were half disposed to rebel against being taken any further.

But discipline and common sense prevailed.

Rations had been brought and after a little food and a drink they started on again.

At every half mile there was one of these barriers, a clump of quaintly shaped rocks that could only be climbed with the greatest difficulty or not climbed at all.

"It is confounded travelling," said Captain Harrison. "Fontenoy, I am afraid you have led us all wrong."

"I don't think so, sir," Fontenoy replied,

"Have you ever been here before?"

"No, sir."

"Then you must have come wrong."

"I think we are going in the right direction, sir."

To this the captain offered no reply.

As a matter of fact Gorton Fontenoy was on the right track.

The only thing wrong in the matter was that the track was difficult to traverse.

It was now a question of time.

Between the party from the "Cyclops" and Dick an unconscious race was going on.

Each was straining every nerve to reach a certain goal.

The question was—Who would be first there?

F

CHAPTER XXIII.

MAKING THE RAFT—WHERE IS DICK?—WHERE THE ENEMY?—A HURRIED FLIGHT ON A HALF-BUILT RAFT.

"I CALL it hard work building a raft," said Jimmy Tartub, "blessed if I don't. Look here, at this rate we shall not have it ready to-day."

They had only as yet succeeded in getting about a dozen timbers together and the afternoon was half gone.

This, however, was the main portion of the work so far as strength was concerned.

It was the very centre of the structure.

Other planks and timbers were to be lashed around it, but in the centre part was to be fixed a top mast on which Jimmy proposed to rig up a sail.

This was a job he set about at once.

Tokoa Fay and Tu-tu were sent for the materials, while Ned, Seaforth, and Dandy Banks went on with fixing the outside parts of the raft.

The Dandy was not of much use except to hand up the ropes to bind with, and steady the planks during the process.

But he worked as well as he could, and with a will. No man can do more.

When Jimmy had fixed the mast he proceeded to fix round it sundry boxes, containing the remnant of the Dandy's stores, and articles that might be useful.

These served to keep the mast firm, steady the raft, and were useful as seats.

"Get a raft solid in the middle," Jimmy said, "and she will bear a bit o' rough work at sea."

Suddenly Ned Dawson said: "Dick's a long time gone."

Then everybody thought the same, and a reference to Seaforth's watch showed that Dick had been five hours away.

"Time goes when a man is busy," he said.

"I hope nothin' aint happened to him," said Jimmy uneasily. '

"What could have happened to him?"

"Well, we can't tell."

"Ned," said Seaforth, "just get up one of the trees on that knoll there, and have a look about you. You haven't forgotten how to climb I suppose?"

"Not that I'm aware of," Ned replied.

He chose a tree of the fir tribe, tall, straight, and with little foliage save at the crown.

Ned was up there as nimbly as a cat, and on getting up a sufficient height, took a survey of the land towards the sea.

What he saw brought him down with a run.

"I say, you fellows," he cried, as he dashed towards them. "Here's a go!"

"What is it?" asked Seaforth.

"Harrison and at least a score of the 'Cyclops'' men coming this way."

"Whew!"

"How far are they off?" asked Jimmy Tartub.

"They will be here in a quarter of an hour."

Blank despair for a moment settled on them all.

"The raft ain't finished," said Tartub, breaking a dismal silence, "we can't go."

"We must go," said Seaforth. "A quarter of an hour? There's not a moment to be lost. The tide is still running out and we can work her down to the sea."

"We've no water on board," said Tartub.

"Can't help it," returned Seaforth. "Here, where are the poles we cut to steer her? Get aboard. Push off, my lads. There's not a moment to stay for luxuries. Water, indeed. We must do without it for a day or two." .

He spoke lightly and cheerily, but all knew that there was cause for serious apprehension.

The retreating tide was still slowly sucking the water out of the port, but there was not much of a current to assist the craft towards the sea.

As for the poles to be used for steering, they were simply the trunks of young straight trees, which had been blown down.

Tokoa Fay and Tu-tu had trimmed them but an hour before.

They were destined, however, to be of great service.

The incomplete raft was not more than sixteen feet square, and could hardly be called a sea-going thing, but under the circumstances it was better than nothing.

"We shall be sure to pick up Dick by the sea," Seaforth said. "Did you see anything of him, Ned?"

"I hadn't time to look," Ned answered. "As soon as I saw the 'Cyclops'' men I came down smart."

The raft slowly moved through the water.

Seaforth and Tartub each took a pole and used it as they do with punts in shallow water.

Then the heavy craft began to lumber along.

Barely had they got clear of the pool and into the narrow belt of water when Captain Harrison and his men came in sight of the spot.

They approached by the fallen trees, and were so engaged in picking their way that they did not see the raft.

The afternoon was now far spent and night at hand.

Given another twenty minutes grace and darkness would be falling.

The hull of the old ship soon caught the attention of the search party.

There was no exclamation of surprise, for Gorton Fontenoy had spoken of its existence.

But they felt elated that they had reached their destination at last.

"Steady, men," said Captain Harrison. "Be wary, or they may elude us."

The men halted, and their leader had a good look round in the hope of seeing the party they were in search of.

But as he looked in every direction but the right one of course he saw nobody.

"Perhaps they are in the cave, or on board the ship," suggested Fontenoy.

Captain Harrison divided his men into two parties.

One, under the command of Fontenoy, went off towards the cave.

The other he headed himself, and led the way to the ship. Steadily the raft pursued its way towards the sea.

Slowly the night approached.

The sun was going down and a few minutes more of grace would suffice.

The captain quickly posted his men about the hull, and then alone clambered on board.

Crawling across the sloping deck he got to the companion, down which he peered.

" Seaforth !—Dawson !—Stornaway ! " he said, " I call on you to surrender yourselves."

Naturally there was no reply.

The sun dipped down and the light faded from the earth.

Five minutes more of grace and our friends would be safe.

Slowly the raft went on its course in sight of the pursuers and yet unseen.

The light went out of the sky and a tropical night was there.

At that moment Captain Harrison raised his head and looked towards the raft.

In one moment he saw it dimly, and then it was shrouded in darkness.

" Was it really there, or did I fancy it ? " the captain hurriedly asked himself.

Then, like a smart man, he resolved to waste no time in speculating, but go and see if it were a vision or not.

Leaping down, he called on his men to follow him, and hurried along by the margin of the water.

But the darkness deepened fast, and his eyes, as yet unused to the sudden change, could but imperfectly see his way.

He soon began to stumble about, and the sailors tumbled here and there, confounding the rough ground.

" What are we running arter ? " said one.

Captain Harrison halted.

He had heard what the man said, and felt very much like pursuing a will-o'·the-wisp.

"I thought I saw a raft moving down the estuary," he said, "but I may have been mistaken. It is useless to attempt to follow it to-night."

"Or at any other time," muttered one of the sailors. "I'll bet it warn't anything but the ghost of one."

Then, for a time, things worked for the benefit of our friends: but, apart from being pursued, they had another source of anxiety.

"Where was Dick?"

They were near the sea, and could see no sign of the rough boat in which he had departed.

A few moments more, and objects a few yards away would hardly be discernible.

"It is safe to cry out now," said Seaforth, as they drew out into the deep water.

Putting his hands to his mouth he called out "Dick!"

Back from the sea came a faint reply, "Here!"

Then out of the gloom emerged the boat, with Dick, almost utterly exhausted, just holding the oars.

"Catch hold," he said faintly, "I'm nearly done."

"Why, what is this?" asked Seaforth, "a ship's boat, where did you get her from?"

"Tell you by-and-bye," said Dick, faintly. "Why did you start with the raft?"

"Because the 'Cyclops' men were upon us," replied Seaforth, "I say, old man, you are quite done, and we have nothing to give you."

"Pardon me," said Dandy Banks, "I have a little wine here, in a flask, which I saved for an emergency such as this. May I beg of Mr. Stornaway to accept it?"

"Banks," said Seaforth, "you are more than a brick, you are a chief corner stone."

＊ ＊ ＊ ＊ ＊ ＊ ＊

It was morning on the sea, and the raft and boat were still in company.

All through the night the calm had lasted, and to make progress at all the boat had been attached to the raft.

Each in turn had taken his place in the boat to row, save Dick, who slept at the bottom of the boat overcome with fatigue.

Pulling the big boat against the tide had been a task almost beyond his efforts.

All's well that ends well, but all, however, was not ended yet.

The morning found them so far away that the islands were only as patches of cloud in the distance.

The tide had in due time turned, and running out bore them away from the scene of their recent adventures.

And now they began to feel the want of water.

Before the sun was up an hour the majority of them were thirsty.

They had a few melons with them, and one being cut up, a slice was given to each. This warded off the longing for water, but they knew it would not long suffice to quench their thirst.

The hot still air was oppressive, and with dread they looked forward to the advancing day, with its burning heat and copper coloured sea.

But nobody uttered a word of apprehension or complaint.

Whatever they felt they kept to themselves.

Time was wiled away with casual talk and by-and-bye came the heat they dreaded.

The sun passed nearly directly over their heads and its rays fell upon them like fiery rain.

That they could have borne if they had but possessed water to drink.

Ned being the youngest suffered most, but he had no more complaints to make than the rest.

It was his first great experience of the suffering induced by thirst, and the like of it he had never dreamt of.

If this was the experience of the first day, what would the second be like and the third?

Could they bear it?

Every now and then a piece of melon was handed to

each by Jimmy Tartub, who acted as caterer. By this means extreme pangs were held at bay.

In the evening a cool breeze sprang up, blowing in th eright direction for them, and Tartub hoisted his little sail.

Slowly the raft moved on.

"To-morrow," said Tartub, "if the wind keeps in our favour we shall get into the track of vessels and be bound to be picked up."

"Perhaps," thought Dick.

It will not do to shout before we are out of the wood, and so it proved with our adventurers.

The wind shifted in the night, bearing them away west in a parallel line with the track of vessels they were hoping to get into.

Parallel lines do not meet, and the change of wind was a great misfortune in their eyes.

It was useless to attempt to sail the raft in any direction, except right before the wind, so they kept on through the dark night, wondering what the morning would bring forth.

It brought them a most welcome sight.

Right ahead of them was land, either a very large island or the continent of Africa.

That it was the latter Tartub was almost convinced, but Seaforth took their bearings, and discovered that they were many miles from any known land.

But whatever it was it was welcome. There they would find the much needed water, and fill an empty cask they had brought with them.

When they neared the land, the sail was lowered on the raft, and Seaforth and Dick went ashore in the boat to reconnoitre.

There was a prospect of the land being inhabited by savage and dangerous foes.

They took no visible arms with them, but each had one of the revolvers which Dick had discovered on board the ship with its dead crew.

Ned Dawson accompanied to keep the boat from grounding. It was very heavy, and might not, if left by the tide, be got off without considerable exertion.

There was nothing fantastic or weird on this island.

The shore was rather rugged, the rocks having been broken up by the action of the sea.

The tide was going out again, and between the boulders were a number of small fish resting on the bottom, or darting about in search of some means of escape to the wide sea.

The two friends walked warily on, seeking some evidence of the presence of man, but at first could find nothing. At last as they reached a retired corner among the rocks they came upon something of import.

It was a man's hand and arm sticking straight up out of the sand.

Dick was a little in advance of Seaforth, and they both stopped short.

There they stood for a few moments staring at the strange object thus brought before their eyes.

It was the hand and arm of a black man.

The fingers were extended as if life was still there, but they did not move.

"Dick," said Seaforth, breathlessly, "what do you make of that?"

"Nothing," replied Dick.

"Let us go and see," said Seaforth, "what is—what is—*attached to that hand and arm*."

CHAPTER XXIV.

STRANGE AND STRANGER STILL—CIVILISATION IN A LONE LAND—DICK FALLS IN WITH ROUGH ACQUAINTANCES.

As the two friends advanced nearly to the mysterious arm the expression of their faces gradually changed, and finally, instead of horror, they expressed simply astonishment and surprise.

"It isn't flesh and blood," said Seaforth, "but STONE."

And so it was.

The arm was only a portion of a statue which had been overthrown and left upon the sea shore, when the tide had partially buried it in the sand.

They ascertained, by scraping around it, that the

statue was still entire. At all events the greater part of it must have been there, for they failed to move it.

The figure was of most beautiful workmanship, and was, undoubtedly, that of a man with arms extended.

"About the oddest thing I ever met with," said Seaforth.

But ere long they found it was not a lone figure.

A little further inland, lying among sea weeds and rubbish, they found half-a-dozen splendid specimens of Indian statuary, and further on portions of a temple that had been razed to the ground.

At this point the land was out of the reach of the tide.

But the greater surprise was yet to come.

Urged on by curiosity they penetrated further inland, and arrived at a large hollow, which had recently been excavated by man.

Here were hammers and picks, and all sorts of tools used for the purpose of unearthing the secrets of the soil, all of them in a condition to prove that the use of them had been quite recent.

Probably only a few days had elapsed since the digging had been actively going on.

The discovery was so amazing that they could for a time but stare at it in speechless surprise.

"Now, Dick," said Seaforth, "help me to clear my head over this business. What do you make of it?"

"We have come to some civilized land. That's my idea," replied Dick.

"It is not on the maps. Here, what is this?"

Seaforth ran forward a few paces and picked up a piece of board, on which was burnt the following inscription :—

"Do not be alarmed, we shall be back soon."

"Well, I'm hanged, or bothered, or what you like," said Seaforth, "look at it. I should say that it hasn't been burnt in more than a few hours."

"And there are the ashes of the wood fire," said Dick, pointing towards a white heap.

They hurried towards it, and found the ashes still

warm. Whoever had been there could not have left the place more than a few hours.

Mystery on mystery.

"There is only one thing we can do," said Seaforth.

"What is that?" asked Dick.

"Wait here until to-morrow; meanwhile, of course, we had better go back to our friends and open their eyes."

"And suppose, said Dick, "that our unknown friends should come and go again? One of us had better stop here."

"I'll stop, your idea is a good one, it is quite clear from that board somebody is hourly expected. Whoever it is they can't be very dangerous; thieves and bandits don't excavate as a rule."

They were now about two miles from the shore, and in an hour or so Seaforth could get back again.

So he went, and Dick was left alone.

About the digging, on the upper side, there was a lot of wood, and Dick's eye soon discovered a track from the diggings into the trees. Having nothing better to do, he followed it, to find fresh surprises in store.

At a short distance in among the trees, he came upon a number of huts arranged in a row. There were perhaps a dozen in all.

They were not built simply of wood, but many of them had walls of stone, portions of some buildings which had been overthrown near the spot.

Some good carpentering work was exhibited here and there, and in two of the huts was a glazed window.

Dick went up to one of them and knocked at the door.

Getting no answer he gave it a push, and it swung back readily on its hinges.

The inside was equally astonishing.

It was as rough as it need be, but great efforts had been made to give it a civilized appearance.

A table, seat, and jug stood by the window, and in the window itself, on a deal shelf, were two flower-pots.

Overhead hung an old bird-cage without an occupant.

On examining the flower-pots, Dick found they were roughly made—manufactured there, probably by some lover of flowers.

Who was he? What was he?

Dick took off his hat and sat down on the seat to think.

The whole thing was so astounding that he was justified in the idea that it might possibly be a hallucination.

"I have gone through with a great deal lately," he said; "perhaps it has been more than I can bear."

It made him quite weary to think of it, and he rested his head upon his arms as he tried to work it out in his mind.

The day was hot, almost to oppressiveness, and the air acting on him as anodyne he fell asleep.

A quarter of an hour afterwards, footsteps resounded outside, and three rough men entered the hut.

At the sight of Dick each whipped out a weapon and stared at him in surprise.

The next moment their manner changed.

"He's only one, and sleeping," said the foremost "but who in the name of Jehoshaphat is he?"

"Don't know," replied another. "Some friend of the Professor's, I suppose. Dropped down from a balloon."

They all laughed at this, and despite their rough appearance, did not appear to be a bad sort of fellows.

Coming softly up to Dick they carefully looked him over.

"Seems a right sort of chap," said one.

"But HOW came he here?" asked another.

"Dunno—let's wake him up and see."

A gentle shake of the shoulder sufficed to awaken Dick, who sprang to his feet.

"All right, guvenor," said the man nearest to him; "friends here—right away."

"Pardon me," said Dick, "but I was not aware——'

"Of course you wasn't," interposed the other; "more were we. It's a case of mutual stagger."

Then explanations ensued, with which we need not trouble the reader *in extenso*.

Dick learnt that the names of his new acquaintances were respectively Staines, Timbs and Burles.

They were part of an excavating party sent out by the English Government under the guidance of a certain Professor Ruddle, to search and excavate on Bayley's island, as the long stretch of land was called.

A report made by the captain of a cruiser who put in there for water had led to the expedition.

Some great discoveries had been looked for and some had been made.

The Professor was satisfied on certain mooted points of African history and he expected to make a great name on his return by writing a book thereon.

He was absent for the day, as recorded on the burnt board, "shooting around, as they had," the men said.

The Professor always told them not to be alarmed if he were absent, although, as the men said, they were never alarmed and could take care of themselves.

Best news of all was that two ships were hourly expected—one to take the Professor and sundry relics of his expedition back to England, the other to convey home a number of experienced diggers who had been engaged for the service.

And these men came from—Australia.

Staines, Timbs and Burles were among them, and when Dick told them that of all places in the world he most longed to get at was Australia, they reckoned they would be right down glad to take him with them, and his friends too.

"Speaking of friends," said Dick, "reminds me that mine by this time will be looking for me. Will you come with me and be introduced to them?"

Having signified their readiness to accompany him, Dick led the way back to the excavated ground, and there they found Seaforth awaiting them.

CHAPTER XXV.

THE PROFESSOR—ARRIVAL OF THE SHIP—A
FRIENDLY ACT—AWAY TO MELBOURNE.

THE number of men under the care of the professor
turned out to be twenty-one. They were all rough,
strong fellows, accustomed to digger's work, and
formed a noisy, as well as amusing assembly when
all had gathered round the camp-fire that evening.

The professor was a little man, a wiry enthusiast,
who lived in the past, and could talk of little else but
ancient things.

He was kind and courteous to our adventurers, but
he did not take much interest in any but Tokoa Fay
and Tu-tu, who, as African monarchs, were a bit of a
study.

He saw nothing ludicrous in them, not even in their
nether garments, but talked seriously to them about
their ancestors, who, he said, were a portion of the lost
tribes of Israel.

Tokoa Fay and Tu-tu were much gratified to hear
this, as they would have been if he had told
them they were first cousins to the man in the moon.

The meeting with the professor was most fortuitous, but as the short stay our friends made with
him was uneventful we need not linger upon it.

Eight days after the meeting a ship hove in sight,
and she proved to be an English steamer of fifteen
hundred tons burden.

She had brought with her men and machinery for
getting on board such relics as Professor Ruddle
deemed necessary.

This was a work that would occupy a week, and while
it was in progress the ship arrived to take the diggers
and a few of the smaller specimens of ancient statuary
to Melbourne.

Their services not being wanted for the loading
they embarked at once, and our friends went with
them.

A jolly evening was spent before parting, and all sorts of good wishes accompanied the toasts that were drunk.

Before leaving, Dick and Seaforth had an interview with the captain of the English steamer, and told him the story of the "Cyclops," giving him all the necessary instructions about finding the wrecked men.

He promised to look them up, and take as many on board as he could accommodate.

The rest he would see were provided for until assistance could be sent to them.

"It is only our duty," said Seaforth; "but, of course, Harrison, when he gets home, will do his best to get me cashiered."

"And me too," said Ned Dawson, "but it won't matter: I'm going to turn bushranger."

So the ships parted company, and the "White Wing" headed for Australia.

Dick was in the highest spirits.

He saw, in the unexpected meeting with the Professor, an omen of the success of his mission.

What that mission was, we now record, as he told it to Seaforth.

It was a starry night, and they had been about a week at sea. The two friends stood by the side, watching the rippling waves.

They had been silent for awhile, thinking.

"Dick," said Seaforth, suddenly.

"Yes, Hanson."

"You have promised to tell me your story, why not do it now?"

"It is strange, but I was just then thinking of doing so," said Dick.

"I am not moved by vulgar curiosity, Dick, on my word, I'm not."

"No, I am aware of that, Hanson, nor have I any mighty secret to tell you. The only reason for my being reserved has been the fear that what I HOPE might not be fulfilled."

"Well, go on, old fellow."

"Hanson," said Dick, "you are a man of family

AT THE SIGHT OF DICK STORNAWAY EACH HELD OUT A WEAPON AND STARED AT HIM IN SURPRISE.

_____"

" Oh, hang all that."

" Yes, I know, but really you must listen to me: you are a man of family, to whom honour is dearer than life."

" As it is assuredly to thousands of others."

" As it is to me," said Dick, with a slight stiffening of his neck. " But there is one thing dearer to me than my own honour, and that is my mother's good name."

Dick paused a moment, and Seaforth turned his dreamy eyes wonderingly upon him, but he was silent.

" My mother's good name," said Dick.

" Is your father dead?" asked Seaforth.

" He died fifteen years ago—he was murdered in the bush in Australia," Dick answered.

" I remember him, although I was very young when I lost him for ever ," said Dick. " He and I, and my dear mother lived on a small farm far up the country outside Melbourne. I should say it was quite a hundred and fifty miles away—might be more. Our life was a lonely one, but as a child I thought nothing of that.

" He was a fine, handsome man, with a rich, flowing beard. We did not get many visitors at the house, and what there were had very little in common with him. He was not proud in a snobbish way, but he had a high bearing."

" Which he could not help," suggested Seaforth.

" It was inherited and cultivated in his earlier life," said Dick; " the bushmen always called him ' Duke,' and as I have learnt from my mother since, in mockery at first, but in earnest afterwards. Who he was or what he was he never told them, nor was my mother sure then, but she knew he was high born, and, as he assured her, had married her honestly, in the family name, which was Feverton.

" He did not deny that he had a right to a title, but always vowed that he would never assume it. ' When I am dead and gone,' he would say, ' let my boy go home and claim his own.' "

" Did he never give any reason for his exile ? " asked

Seaforth.

"Nothing, beyond its having something to do with a quarrel with a younger brother, who had deeply injured him. Well, one day he was missing from home, and we never saw him alive again.

"It was his custom to ride out in the morning, and look after his stock, generally returning a little before or after sunset. That night he did not return, and on the morrow he was found dead in an adjoining wood, shot in the back.

"It was not known exactly who did it, but there was talk of one Morgan having done it, and afterwards boasting that he was well paid for the job, but in that wild part there was no legal machinery to bring the crime home to him."

CHAPTER XXVI.

DICK'S STORY FINISHED—PROSPECTS OF A LIFE IN MELBOURNE.

DICK was silent for awhile, dwelling on the sad death of his father. Hanson Seaforth did not interrupt his meditations by uttering a word.

"I can only tell you what took place afterwards from what my mother told me," said Dick. "I dimly remember the journey across the sea to England, and our travelling by rail to the heart of the country, where we went to a big house which I now know to be Feverton Court, the home of the Earl of Staunton.

"We saw there a white-haired old man, the Earl, who listened to my mother's story, and asked for proofs.

"Her story was that she had married my father, who was the Earl's eldest son, in a church in Melbourne, the name of which she could not call to mind.

"My mother is the daughter of an English settler in the bush, and my father made her acquaintance accidentally while wandering there. He had left England after a quarrel with his family, but the nature of it he never mentioned, and I do not know it now.

"What the old Earl said to my mother was this: 'Get me the certificate of your marriage, and I will believe your story. I will also own your son as heir to the earldom.'

"Beyond that he would not go.   He would not help her with money or instruct anyone to make inquiries. She was poor and could do nothing.

"To live she had to work, and like an honest woman she laboured for her bread.

"At first she used to speak of her hardships—but people laughed at her.   They put their interpretation upon her story, and what it was I leave you to guess.

"To me she would never have breathed it, but one day, two years ago, it accidentally came to my ears, and then I knew that I had a task before me which it would be criminal for me to neglect.

"We were still poor—very poor—but I had been educated.   The old earl had paid for that, and had, indeed, offered to assist my mother to live.

" She refused the offer made to herself, but allowed me to receive the education, which would be needful if ever, as she said, 'I got my own.'

" Seaforth," said Dick in conclusion, " the old earl is dead—and the father of Gorton Fontenoy is the Earl of Staunton.   Neither Gorton nor myself saw anything of each other until we met on board the " Cyclops." For some reason or other he has never been spoken of by the family name of Feverton, but simply as Gorton Fontenoy, and it was only by chance that I knew who he was.

"I was Dick Stornaway, bearing my mother's maiden name, and he did not know me.   Nevertheless, we are rivals for the coronet of an earl.   Of that I do not think so much as my mother's good name, and to find out where she was married, and by whom, is the object I have in going to Melbourne."

"If it is to be found, old fellow, we will find it," said Seaforth.   " You have a clear field—for Fontenoy is either boxed up on the island yonder, or, if rescued, will in all probability be taken to the old country."

" I never quite understood him," said Dick thoughtfully, "but from the first he hated me.   Perhaps he knew more than I suspected"

"His father has been at the bottom of it all—depend on that," said Seaforth. "He was the cause of your father going abroad, and through him your mother was treated so scurvily. What sort of character does he bear?"

"Bad," said Dick; "he is a tyrant, and is much disliked."

"Like father—like son," said Seaforth. "Do you know what my idea is?"

"No."

"It is this: 'An eye has been kept on you and your mother, and your every movement watched. Gorton Fontenoy knows who you are.'"

"But he could not know my object, for not a word of it has escaped me except to you; even the dear mother I have left behind knows nothing of it. She thinks I am going to Australia to make a home for her, as she longs to return thither."

"Well, we shall see," said Seaforth; "time will tell everything, old fellow; I wish you good luck. How ever things go I'm your friend. If you can do nothing better than settle down in the bush I am with you."

And they shook hands over it.

"What's the congratulatory hand-shaking for?" asked a voice near.

It was Ned Dawson, who came lounging up with his cap on the back of his head, the image of sea-going ease and carelessness.

"We think of settling in the bush," said Seaforth, "and are shaking hands over it."

"Take me in," said Ned.

"What will your people say?" asked Seaforth.

"Oh, there's a big family at home," replied Ned, "and I'm the pickle of the lot. They wont be sorry to get rid of me, especially if I should be able to write home and say that I am getting along swimmingly."

"We will take you in—provisionally," said Seaforth.

Before another day had elapsed Dandy Banks and

Jimmy Tartub had also been elected as members of the band of probable settlers, and Staines, Timbs, and Burles promised to give them the benefit of their experience.

Anyway, they would all have to work somewhere, and life in a town would be distasteful to all.

What Dick wanted was a house from where he could run into Melbourne occasionally, and pursue his search for the certificate of his mother's marriage.

Melbourne is now a big place, and wisely he did not hope to be successful in a day.

It might be a work of days—months—or years.

And as he thought of the latter prospect, he sighed.

CHAPTER XXVII.

AT THE WATERSIDE SALOON—MORGAN AND CHUNKS —A PROSPECTIVE CRIME WITH TEN THOUSAND POUNDS REWARD.

SIX months have elapsed, and it is summer in Melbourne. Christmas Day, the antipodean midsummer-is at hand, and Melbourne lies sweltering under the burning sun.

In one of the narrowest streets, and streets in Melbourne are not as a rule narrow, not far from the banks of the Yarra-Yarra River, several men were drinking in the bar of one of the lower class saloons.

There were a rough lot, such as a nervous man would shrink from in a lonely place, and were indeed members of the ruffianly class with which Melbourne, like other big towns, is afflicted.

They were discussing certain matters of interest to themselves, but not to the reader, when a heavy footstep was heard, and a powerfully built man, with grizzly hair and beard, entered from the street.

" Hallo, Morgan," said one of them, " where did you spring from ? "

" Give me a drink, Chunks," replied Morgan, " I'm stone broke."

" So bad as that ? "

" Cleaned out last night at Griffins, and never was

bad luck so bad as now."

"Bad luck is always bad," said Chunks, philosophically.

"You don't grip," returned Morgan. "I want a few sovs. now bad. Who's got any?"

The majority there looked as if they had been "stone broke," too, and had no need to say anything on the subject. Others said they were short.

Chunks was silent.

"Come," said Morgan, "you can help a man. I can pay you back a dozen times over in a month or two."

"Luck's been against you for years," said Chunks, "but it ain't that—there's your drink. About this money now. Suppose I lend it, away it goes at Griffins' table."

"No, it won't. I want to send a wire to the old country."

Chunks stared.

"Send a wire?" he said.

"Yes, a telegram, if you like it better, to an old friend. OUR old friend, Chunks."

"No, the Hon——"

"No names," said Morgan, hurriedly, "and he's an earl now. I say, can't we get into a quiet corner and have a chat?"

"Come up to my room," said Chunks. "I'm hanging out here just now."

He led the way down to the back of the saloon, and up a short staircase to a small room commanding a view of the river dotted with boats and small shipping.

The larger vessels, say those drawing twenty odd feet of water, cannot go farther than Port Phillip, from whence the winding river takes eight miles to reach Melbourne.

Straight across the land the railway reached it in two.

The two men sat down by the window, and after a peep out to see that nobody was listening outside, Chunks said:

"In the name o' tarnation what's up now?"

"I'm going to ask him for money," replied Morgan.

"You won't get it."

"Why not?"

"He washed his hands of us twelve years ago. Told us to go and do our worst, which we dursn't do."

"That was on the old job," said Morgan, "but the thing has broken out in a fresh direction."

"How can that be? You settled him.'

"The father, yes; but the son is living, AND HE'S HERE."

Morgan leant forward and whispered these words with a hissing sound. Chunks, who was a small-eyed evil-looking ruffian, stared at him, breathing hard.

"I allus guessed the game," said Morgan, "t'other stood in the way of the one in the old country, and although he was pretty keen in hiding who he was, I've found it out at last."

"How?"

"You hear me, Chunks. The party who employed me is now Earl of Staunton, and t'other was his brother. I got at that only yesterday."

"But I don't see——"

Morgan made an impartial movement, and Chunks stopped short.

"For some months past," said Morgan, "there's been a party o' settlers in an open forest, Gipp's Land way. They're a mixed lot, gentlemen, a sailor, and a couple o' niggers, and they git along somehow, working hard at their farm and gradually collecting cattle, one on 'em being continually coming down Melbourne way—and I spotted him on the chance that he might be worth sticking up. But he kept out of the saloons, and never did anything as I could see, but go *to church.*"

"Go WHERE?" asked Chunks, as if a most horrible specimen of human depravity had suddenly been opened out before his eyes.

"To church," repeated Morgan. "Not at reg'ler times like them other varmints, but when nothin's been going on, and he's been a scanning the registers for summat which I've got at through enquiring. He wants to know where Feverton was married."

"What for?" asked Chunks.

"I think you get more dunderheaded every day," said Morgan, "why, he's Feverton's son, and Feverton would ha' been Earl o' Staunton if he'd lived, and this young chap is the real earl. Oh, I've worked it all out in my mind, and I tell you there's *money in it*."

Chunks now fairly gasped.

He could see a big thing hovering in the distance, and the loan of a few pounds to Morgan might be a most lucrative investment.

"It don't matter to me or you," said Morgan, "who's earl—but we've got to make a bit o' something for ourselves, Chunks, as I'm a livin' man, I mean to have ten thousand pounds out o' this job."

"Ten thousand pounds!" said Chunks, and then there arose before his eyes the cheerful prospect of weeks and months of debauchery.

"What's to be my share of it?" he asked.

"HALEVS," replied Morgan, "if you work with me right through. Will you do it?"

"WILL I?" exclaimed Chunks. "Here's my paw on it."

Then their coarse-grained hands met, and clasped in a fervent grasp.

"Don't try to do it alone," said Morgan, "because you can't."

"I never said I could," replied Chunks.

"No," said Morgan, "but I saw it in your eye. I KNOW WHERE FEVERTON MARRIED STORNAWAY'S GAL, AND YOU DON'T."

"You do!" exclaimed Chunks.

"Yes," said Morgan, "I've got the earl here—under this," pressing his thumb upon the window-sill, "and what's more, I don't think the young feller will find it without me, so it work's all round."

"Morgan," said Chunks, "you are a genius."

"That's why I'm allus so poor," returned Morgan, drily. "Now, then, out with your tin, and I'll send on a wire that will galvanise his lordship."

Chunks took out a leathern purse, from which he extracted five sovereigns, and Morgan, bidding him wait there, went out to wire to the Earl of Staunton.

He was absent for an hour, and then came back to wait for a reply.

He and his companion spent the day drinking and smoking, and it was late at night when the answer came.

"Call on Mr. Jecks, Waterside Street."

"Same party as I saw before," said Morgan. "Fancy the old scamp being still alive. Why, he was an old 'un when I took on the first job."

"Were you well paid for it ?" asked Chunks.

"Five hundred," replied Morgan, "but I didn't know the worth of it or I'd a had five thousand. Anyway, we'll make up for it now."

CHAPTER XXVIII.

THE HOUSE IN THE OPEN WOOD—DICK'S RIDE WITH MORGAN—LEFT TO DIE.

AMONG the other beauties of Victoria are the open forests, which are vast plains dotted over with trees so wide apart that herbage grows between, and cattle get good grazing.

Some open spots are large enough to be farmed, and on one of these our friends had made their home.

They had built themselves three log huts, one for living and sleeping of the whites, a smaller one for Tu-tu and Tokoa Fay, and the other for domestic work.

The two African monarchs were the servants.

Trained by Jimmy Tartub they soon learned to cook and wash and live like civilized beings, and like their less savage brethren they did not always get on so well as they might.

But it was only in the absence of Jimmy Tartub that they dare quarrel, for he carried with him a stoutish stick which he called his Peace Provider, and he never hesitated to use it with sufficient freedom to make their majesties jump and skip and howl.

The white men farmed, and with a little stock.

mostly strayed cattle without an owner, they did very
well in a humble way

Dandy Banks blossomed into quite an agricultural
character.

One of their neighbours, or what was a neighbour
there, living three miles away, rode over and gave them
a little instruction, lent them an old plough, and
promised them a mount on horseback whenever they
wanted one.

His name was Garland, and he was the son of
an English farmer, who, finding times hard, sent him
abroad.

Before long he exchanged three horses for some
cattle, and although he made believe that he had got
the better of the bargain, they knew that it was a
friendly act and a sacrifice on his side.

They all rode occasionally, and it was a treat to see
Jimmy Tartub on horseback.

He was, as he said, all over the ship, but kept
aboard, which meant that he was sometimes on the
neck of his steed, and sometimes behind, but always
held on.

However, we will not dwell too long on the details
of this life in the open forest.

It was pleasant, but uneventful.

Dick used to ride into Melbourne once a fortnight,
taking three days—one day riding there, a day of rest
for his horse and of research for himself, and then a
day's ride home.

They used to watch for his return, looking to see some
signs of success in his countenance.

But he came back each time more gloomy, and for
a whole day afterwards would be silent.

Then he would recover himself, and become as cheery
and hopeful as they could desire.

They all knew his story now, and longed for success to
crown his efforts.

Every mail he sent a letter home to his mother,
telling her that he was happy, and giving sundry details of his friends and the farm, as if he had no other
ambition.

One day, they had been eight months on their farm, and it was about seven weeks after Morgan and Chunks held their consultation, the former of the precious pair rode up to the settler's house and asked for a drink of water.

Evidently the liquid was very strange to him, for he sipped it very carefully, and after some hesitation asked if he might stay there for the night.

They did not like the look of him, but in that country no stranger was ever sent away if he asked for a rest, and he was allowed to come in.

He did not give a name, and he was not asked for one, but he said he was in the cattle trade, and had just made arrangements for a thousand head to be driven into Melbourne.

He was going on to-morrow to make arrangements for their slaughter and disposal of the hides.

Dick's time to go to Melbourne was again due, and although he would rather in general have ridden alone, he settled to go with Morgan.

He was led to do so by the ruffian's talk of Melbourne and its surroundings.

He knew every place, and ninetenths of the settlers around, then and for many years past.

Scores of stories which could not fail to be interesting he told them in the evening, and finally came to the narrative of the murder of Dick's father.

It was a bold thing to do, but Morgan was a bold man.

"I knew both the man and the fellow who was said to have killed him," he said, "ah, it was a bad business."

Dick did not say anything about his own interest in the story, but he asked him a few questions indirectly bearing on his mother's life.

"She was old Ben Stornaway's gal," said Morgan, "a splendid wench, and could have married any man hereabouts if she had liked—but the English swell carried her off. All gals here or elsewhere go for swells."

For a moment Dick hesitated and then with a slight huskiness in his throat he said:

" They were married hereabouts, I suppose ? "

" No," replied Morgan, laughing. " To marry you want a parson, and maybe a church, and there's neither for many miles round. No—they went to Melbourne. It wasn't much of a place then, and I remember the church was a wooden one."

" You were there ? " said Dick.

" I was," replied Morgan, " so were lots of others. All that could go went. It was a regular kick-up, it was."

He told this bare-faced lie without moving a muscle to betray him, and Dick thought he saw light at last.

He could not confide in this man, but he could ride with him into Melbourne, and indirectly lead him on to show where that church now was, and then——

It was all a trap, and he fell into it.

Morgan stayed the night, and early on the morrow rode away with Dick.

The face of our hero was illumined with hope. His friends thought they had never seen him look so handsome. But they felt as if they were parting with him for a long while.

" I don't like the look of that fellow," said Seaforth. " If Dick had any money about I should not have let them go together, but I took care to speak of the limited means he possesses."

" One of us might ha' gone with him," said Jimmy Tartub.

And then, in a very dissatisfied frame of mind he went away to give Tokoa Fay and Tu-tu a "twisting."

He found the two sable monarchs engaged on the weekly wash, both at one tub, owing to a scarcity of that article.

They were, at that moment, in a state of high tension.

If they had done their washing facing each other there would have been ample room for both, but they must needs get side by side, which somewhat cramped them.

As Tartub drew quietly up to the door with his Peace Provider in his hand they were elbowing each other, and nagging in a suppressed way.   Having their backs to Tartub they did not see him.

"Who you crowding on?" asked Tu-tu.

"Get you carcase higher up," growled Tokoa Fay.

"Move 'long, you nigger."

"Git furder away, black man."

Then as they pushed and struggled the tub rocked and was in imminent danger of being upset when Tartub stepped in and brought about Peace.

It was a very simple process.

No words, but simply two cuts with his Peace Provider.

In a moment they divided, and each went to his own end, using a hand covered with soapsuds to rub the assaulted part of their anatomies.

"You let me catch you at that game again," said Tartub, "and I'll flay the pair of you. If you can't agree go out, like cats in the night, and fight it out in the bush."

Leaving them rolling their eyes and spasmodically rubbing the linen and the smarting part of the frame in turn, Tartub went back to his friend.

Dandy Banks and Ned Dawson, with hoes on their shoulders, were about to set out to weed a bit of the land.

Seaforth, with his arms folded, leant against the side of the house looking in the direction Dick and Morgan had taken.

"Tartub," he said, "I don't like Dick's going with that fellow. I think we ought to ride after them and go too."

"Well, I should be more comfortable, sir," replied Tartub.

"I suppose we can leave you for a few days," said Seaforth to Dandy Banks and Ned.

"I believe," replied Dandy, "that I am now sufficiently proficient in agricultural pursuits to get on for a short period without instruction."

He carried his hoe as a master of ceremonies does his wand and bore himself generally in the old way.

A change of pursuit brought him no change of

style.

Ned rather liked the idea of being "boss" for a time, and eagerly said that he could rub along.

So Tartub handed over the Peace Provider, and in a quarter of an hour they were riding in pursuit of Dick and his companion.

Seaforth did not hurry his horse because he knew that if he tired it at starting, he would have difficulty in completing his journey.

Tartub was not sorry, as riding for him meant much rolling about, and considerable peril to his neck.

They rode all day, save for two needed halts at farm-houses for refreshment for themselves and horses.

At each place they heard of Dick and Morgan having been there an hour before and ridden on.

So far, well.

If mischief were intended it would probably be attempted ere Melbourne was reached, although there was no certainty about that.

Many men had been decoyed from the country into gambling dens, and there killed in a brawl got up for the purpose.

Then, of course, nobody was to blame.

Melbourne was reached as the afternoon was waning, and they road to the place where Dick usually put up his horse.

It was an Inn with stabling attached, with quite an old country air about it.

The horse was there, but Dick had gone away with his companion, who intended to put his horse up at another place.

The ostler at the inn heard them say something about taking the train to Port Phillip.

"What on earth can they want there?" said Seaforth.

He and Tartub hastened across the town to the railway station, where they learnt that two men, who answered the description of Dick and Morgan, had been there and just missed the train.

All officials told them that they had set out to walk

the two miles, and the younger man rolled as if he had been drinking.

Seaforth now began to be really alarmed.

Dick never drank except in the most moderate way, and as for being rolling drunk he knew that, ordinarily, that was impossible.

"I'm sure there is something wrong about the fellow," Seaforth said, "although I cannot tell what it is."

Dick and Morgan had been gone about half an hour, and in the usual way ought to have reached Port Phillip.

There was not another train for two hours.

"We will walk, Tartub," said Seaforth.

The hill was mostly an open one across the land, and was indeed the straightest road.

They started off, walking at a brisk pace so as to reach the Port ere night set.

Nearly a mile had been traversed when Tartub, looking on ahead, saw some dark object lying between the rails.

A moment later, and Seaforth saw it too.

Not a word escaped either, but the fear of one was the fear of the other.

And that fear was verified when they came up to the dark object, and saw that it was Dick lying still as if in death.

CHAPTER XXIX.

WHILE THERE IS LIFE THERE IS HOPE—NEWS OF THE "CYCLOPS"—THE HUNT FOR MORGAN.

SEAFORTH was the first to recover from the shock, and stooping down he raised Dick's head.

On his face there were no signs of injury, nor on the breast, but under him was a pool of blood.

He had been shot in the back.

The wound was still bleeding, which was evidence of the injury having been quite recently inflicted.

Hanson Seaforth cut open Dick's shirt, and to stop the flow of blood plugged the wound with a piece he tore from his handkerchief.

"It is better than nothing," he said, "and now Tar-

tub, you must go and get some help. Run back to the
station. Ask them if they will send a doctor, on a
trolly. Dick could be taken back on it."

"He is still alive, sir," said Tartub dubiously.

"Yes," replied Seaforth, who maintained a wonderful calmness, although he felt in reality deeply
agitated, "he'll be all right if we get the doctor in
time."

Tartub helped Seaforth to lay Dick on the bank and
then sped away.

He could run at a pinch, and now he put a spurt
on, for it was a matter of life and death to a dear
friend.

Seaforth sat with Dick's head on his knee, watching
for some sign of returning consciousness, and presently
it came.

The bleeding of the wound having been stopped the
faintness passed off and slowly he opened his eyes.

"That's right, Dick," said Seaforth, "don't move,
don't even talk, but keep quiet a bit. You got a
hurt."

Dick's eyes suddenly brightened with anger, and
he looked quickly about him in search of his assailant.

"Where is that ruffian?" he asked.

"Never mind him at present," returned Seaforth,
" we will hunt him up by and bye."

"What have I done that he should attempt to take
my life?"

"That we will see anon too. Now be quiet, there's a
good fellow."

"But how came you here?" asked Dick.

"Oh! we came to Melbourne——"

"Who are we?"

"Tartub and I. We came——"

"I see," said Dick, "you had grave suspicions and
followed that scoundrel and myself. It is a great
thing to have such friends."

He lay back and looked as if he were about to go off
again, but, rallying, he looked around him, and saw the
railway line.

"I was crossing that when he stepped behind me and

shot me down; I fell on the line. Hanson, did you find me there?"

"Yes."

"Then it was the ruffian's purpose to leave me there to be cut to pieces. Who is this man? and what have I done to him that he should want my life?"

Seaforth did not answer him.

He was unable to solve the problem, and he could see that Dick was excited by talking, so he held his peace, and Dick, closing his eyes again, lay back.

Tartub must have hurried along, for in less than half an hour the whirr of the approaching trolly was heard.

It was the sort of thing the platelayers use when they have a distance to travel to work, and in it were three men—Tartub, the doctor, and one of the company's labourers.

They brought with them some cushions and rugs, and a rough bed was already arranged for Dick.

The brake was put on and the trolly stopped.

Leaping off, the doctor, a young energetic looking fellow, hastened to Dick's side. With a nod to Seaforth he proceeded at once to examine his patient.

He was looking very grave as he proceeded, and finally he said, "We must get to Melbourne without delay."

"Is it a serious wound?" said Seaforth enquiringly.

"I can say more about that after a closer examination than I can give it here. The bullet has gone very close to the spine."

"It has not broken it?"

"Oh, no. In that case he would have to remain here, but a bruise alone is a serious thing.

With great care they lifted Dick on to the trolly.

He groaned like one in a troubled sleep, but did not open his eyes.

"My house is very near the station," the doctor said; "he had better be taken there."

As the trolly, under the guidance of the labourer, glided back the doctor sat by Dick, watching every movement he made.

He was very restless, and two or three times half-opened his eyes, but without recognising anybody.

The station was reached in a few minutes, and the news of an attempted murder having got about, a number of people had gathered on the platform awaiting the return of the trolly.

The police were also in attendance, and did good service in clearing the way and helping to carry Dick to the doctor's house.

On a plate fixed to the door Seaforth saw that the name of the doctor was Headlam. A quiet, pretty woman, who proved to be his wife, met them at the door, and at once made herself unobtrusively useful.

Dick was laid on a couch in a room on the ground floor, and all but the doctor, his wife, and an assistant went into another apartment during the examination.

It was the patients' waiting-room, with the usual books and papers for the use of those who had to sit there for a time.

One of the police officers accompanied Tartub and Seaforth.

He wanted to get as much information as he could, and they gave him a description of Morgan, which he at once recognised.

"That's Morgan," he said, "one of the most hardened villains in the colony. Had your friend any money?"

"Only a few shillings," Seaforth replied.

"Did Morgan know of it?"

"He was perfectly aware of it."

"That's odd. Morgan never wastes powder and shot unless there is something to be got by it. Was there any ill-feeling between them?"

"They never met until yesterday, and all the harm we did the ruffian was to give him a supper and a night's lodging."

The officer reflected for a few moments, but nothing satisfactory came to his mind to help him.

"There is something behind the scenes," he said,

" there must be."

Then he wanted to go into Dick's history, but Seaforth declined to go far back into matters which Dick might, possibly, wish to be held in reserve.

Seaforth, however, did not deny that Dick had a history, but preferred that he should tell it himself.

"If he lives," said the officer.

"Yes," replied Seaforth, "and if he dies—which Heaven forbid—I will tell it."

The officer went away, and Seaforth and Tartub being left to themselves the former took up a paper from the table.

It was an English one, and by its date he could see that it was two months old. Notwithstanding its age the contents could not fail to be interesting.

During their life in the open forest the settlers had heard little or nothing of the old country. They had all written to their friends, but, as yet, received no reply.

Seaforth's letter to his father, the baronet, was characteristic, and we may as well take this opportunity to give a copy of it :—

" Dear Sir Harold,—I have left the Navy, and taken to a settler's life. You may have me called a deserter, but I am not one in the true sense of the word. I won't disgrace the family name whatever I do. Hope soon to send you a good account of our flocks and herds. I have some good fellows for companions.—Yours, very affectionately, HANSON."

No reply, as we have said, had been received to that letter, and Seaforth was not so sure that he would get one unless it was a " stinger."

Whatever was coming he waited for it with his usual philosophical patience. Tartub did not read much.

He was like most sailors—nothing of a bookworm—so he sat staring at the pictures on the walls until an exclamation burst from Seaforth's lips.

" The ' Cyclops ' people are home," Seaforth said.

" That's good news anyway, sir," replied Tartub.

" Not a soul lost," said Seaforth, " as far as I can see. All the officers are here, bar those in the bush, and the list of men is complete, I think. Muzzle is here."

"He's a bad lot," said Tartub. "I judge by what I've heard of him."

"He is."

"If ever he and I meet, I mean to see who is the better man."

"He's done nothing to you," said Seaforth, with a quiet twinkle in his eye.

"I'm not going to wait for *that*," replied Tartub, "there's a score for us to settle.

The entrance of the doctor cut short their conversation. Seaforth rose up from his seat with an anxious face.

"Your friend," said Dr. Headlam, "is in some danger, but with care he will, I hope, recover. It is a most interesting case, and I think you had better leave him here."

"We could do nothing for him up at the farm," said Seaforth sadly.

"Of course you could not," replied the doctor. "I don't think we need take his depositions to-night, but if he gets any worse it must be done."

"Can I see him?" asked Seaforth.

"No, it will be better for you to leave him with us,' was the reply, "Of course you will take steps to have his assailant arrested?"

"Yes! he is well known. His name is Morgan."

"THAT villain," exclaimed the doctor, "why he hasn't been hanged years ago I don't know! But he is like a will-o'-the-wisp, the police never seem to know when to have him."

Seaforth and Tartub left the doctor's house sad enough, but they talked as hopefully as they could, and it was settled that Tartub should go back to the farm with the news of the attempted murder.

Seaforth would stay in Melbourne until Dick was better, or——well! they did not like to think of that contingency. So Tartub mounted his horse and rode away, and Seaforth remained behind to watch the issue and to assist the police.

A hue and cry was raised at once. Bills were printed

and all good citizens called upon to lend their aid towards the capture of the well-known outlaw, Morgan, whose name had long been a terror to peaceably disposed people.

But with so many means of escape the prospect of his being captured was not, in the eyes of those who knew, a very brilliant one.

CHAPTER XXX.

DICK'S RECOVERY—THE RETURN TO THE FARM—MORGAN AGAIN—A MIDNIGHT VISITOR—A SURE SHOT.

For a whole week Dick lay between life and death.

It was, as the doctor said, an interesting case, not only from the surgeon's point of view, but on account of its romantic surroundings.

The doctor's wife was extremely anxious that such a handsome fellow as Dick should not die.

"Think what a loss it will be to some nice girl who ought to marry him," she said.

"Just the way you women look at such cases," her husband said. "If he had been old and ugly how different would have been your view of the case."

At the end of the week he began to mend.

The crisis passed, and youth and strength came out the conqueror.

"For all that," the doctor said, "he must be taken good care of for months. All he wants is an easy life."

Nothing had been heard of Morgan.

The police visited certain houses where he might possibly be, and, naturally, failed to find him.

"Gone back to the bush," the police said, "and it's about as useless to hunt him there as it would be to try and find a particular rat."

A fortnight later Dick was taken to the farm.

They rigged him up a sort of lounging saddle, which could be strapped right along the back of a steady old horse lent them by the doctor.

As for fees, the good fellow would not hear of them.

"Pay me one day when you grow rich," he said

laughingly, it has been a most interesting case, I assure you."

"When I grow rich," thought Dick, sadly, "shall I ever be so?"

Only fools profess to despise wealth, and Dick naturally would welcome a good income, especially if it brought with it a good name.

Seaforth and Tartub formed the escort, and now, for the first time in the colony, they carried revolvers in case of attack.

The journey occupied two days as they had to go at a walking pace, and a right royal welcome awaited Dick.

Ned Dawson and Dandy Banks had been very busy.

The log huts were decorated with wild flowers and ferns, and Tokoa Fay and Tu-tu, to their great delight, made veritable Jack-in-the-Greens of.

When Dick appeared in sight a salute of two guns was fired, and on his arrival at the hut he was received heartily by Ned and with courtly grace by Dandy Banks.

Dick, in the eyes of Tokoa Fay and Tu-tu was the chief of "White Medicine Men," and they wanted to grovel in the dust before him.

Tartub had, however, taught them to pull their fore-locks and scrape their legs back in sailor fashion, and on second thoughts that was the salute they gave him.

A right royal meal of wild pigeon, rabbits, fruit, corn-cakes, and other bush luxuries was laid out on the table, and with hearty appetites they fell to.

They were all very jolly, but there was one grave face among them, and that was the property of Dandy Banks.

He looked every now and then at Dick with an anxious expression which Hanson Seaforth presently observed. Then he too became a little grave.

After supper—for so they called the meal, although it was partaken of at five in the afternoon—Seaforth lit a cigar, strolled out leaving Dick resting.

Dandy soon followed, as if by appointment, and

they drew a little apart from the house.

"Now, Banks," said Seaforth, " what's up?"

"I had a little adventure this morning," Banks replied. , "I had been down to the creek to get some water, and was returning through the grove when I came upon a man sleeping."

"Not anything unusual."

"No, but it was not an ordinary man. He was lying on his face or I should have known him at once. I aroused him as I passed, and he looked up. It was that man Morgan."

"What did you do?" asked Seaforth.

"What could I do?" replied Dandy Banks. "Had I been possessed of a weapon of a better nature I would have slain him, but having nothing but a stick I gave a polite good-day, as if I did not know him, and passed on."

"To that I say—well done, Dandy," returned Seaforth. "Did you see any more of him?"

"Oh, yes; I continued to observe him as he strode away. He went west, and walked in a hurry for awhile, but afterwards he slackened his pace, and from what I judged he did not intend to leave the neighbourhood.

"Have you said anything to Dawson about this?"

"No, I thought I would not mar a happy day."

"It was a kind thought, Banks. Now in future you must be armed. If you get another chance at Morgan shoot him down. I have bought revolvers for all, save the niggers, and for the present one of us must always be with Dick.

Eventually Seaforth decided that Tartub and Ned ought to know of Morgan having been in the neighbourhood, and Dick to be kept in ignorance of it.

"Not that he would be troubled with fears," Seaforth said, "he would want to be up and after him. I know Dick feels very bitterly against the man, not only for having attempted his life, but because he inspired him with a false hope.

Dick in short was determined to settle accounts with Morgan whenever and wherever he met him

Night came and the settlers retired.

In such places as the bush and open forest, the pioneers of civilisation have few of the luxuries of life.

Bedchambers and feather beds are not in vogue with them. They sleep hard and are none the worse for it.

A piece of matting was placed next the ground, and on it was placed a mattress, then a blanket, and a sheet and another blanket for a covering. That was all.

Their beds were taken up by day, and made just before going to bed.

Seaforth that night contrived to have his bed near the door, and Dick's the furthermost from it.

"Out of the draught, you know, old fellow," he said.

"Really, I am neither sugar nor salt," replied Dick "I am ready for work to-morrow."

They were soon asleep, Seaforth sleeping very lightly as was his wont.

Dandy Banks having had a hard day directing the place slept soundly, so did the others.

Seaforth had been asleep about an hour when he suddenly awoke.

He was not conscious of having heard any sound, nor had anybody touched him.

Neither was there any sound outside to be heard, now that he was awake.

For several minutes he lay quite still.

Not a sound was heard.

There was not a breath of wind to rustle the leaves of the trees, and the movements of cattle outside.

What need was there for his having awoke so suddenly?

And now that he was awoke he found he could not sleep again.

He was as wide awake as if he had slept the usually allotted hours of rest.

Tartub was sleeping on his right about three feet away, and between them overhead was the opening which served as a window to their house.

It was unglazed and closed with a sliding shutter working inside in a double groove, one at the top and the other at the bottom.

This was usually left an inch or two open to let in the fresh air, and this night was no exception.

Seaforth could just see the narrow slip with the starlight behind it.

The night was clear and the stars were very bright, Sirius was visible to his eyes.

He shifted a little to get a better view of it, and watch it glide by the narrow opening as he knew it would in obedience to the motion of the earth.

But Sirius did not disappear.

On the contrary, the star got a wide margin around it, and Seaforth began to puzzle his brain to account for the phenomenon.

Then in a moment he got at the truth.

The shutter was being slowly pushed back in the grooves.

It was necessary for him, lying almost immediately under it, to get out a little to see by what agency this was being effected, and as every little sound is often distinct at night, he had to do it with the utmost caution.

Inch by inch he worked his way off his bed, and then slowly turned round and looked up.

Now he could see *four fingers* grasping the shutter.

Half of it had been slowly forced back, and when the other half was down the window would be big enough for an active man to get through.

Seaforth had taken the precaution, as indeed all " in the know " had, to lay his revolver ready for use.

Quietly he took possession of it and waited to see a face at the window.

" Would it be a cowardly thing to shoot him dead ? " Seaforth asked himself.

He did not like the idea, although he would have shot the fellow readily, whoever he might be, if he had been outside.

In a moment his resolution was taken.

He would meet that man.

His clothes lay by his bedside, and in a few moments he had put on his trousers and was in one sense dressed.

He had only now to open the door and step out to find himself face to face with a midnight visitor.

The fastenings of their forest home were very simple, a latch for use by day and a wooden bar at night.

The latter he soon drew out and placed carefully on the ground. Then, revolver in hand, he raised the latch and stepped out.

Before him stood a burly figure, just in the act of peering into the now fully opened window.

The slight noise made by Seaforth on emerging caused the fellow to look round.

A savage oath burst from his lips and his hand went to his hip.

Seaforth gave him no time to draw his weapon and use it, but rushed at him, and struck him between the eyes.

He fell to the ground, and Seaforth threw himself upon him.

"Move," he said, "and you are a dead man."

"All right," replied the other, "I give in. Nobody's dead. I only wanted a little grub and a drink."

"That's a good tale," said Seaforth, as he extracted the other's weapon from a pocket in the back part of the belt of his trousers. "That's all right. Lie there, and don't move unless you want to quit all earthly business."

"I give in," was the answer, "that's enough; what more can a man do?"

Then Seaforth arose, and at that moment Dick came out of the hut, and stared wonderingly at him.

CHAPTER XXXI.

THE CAPTIVE TURNS OUT NOT TO BE MORGAN—
HE PLAYS THE GAME OF FOX, BUT IT DOES
NOT PAY.

"WHAT'S the matter, Mister Seaforth?"

It was Jimmy Tartub, who put his head out of the door in a way that denoted he had no more clothes upon him than he slept in.

"I think we've got him," replied Seaforth.

"Never, sir?"

"Fact; on with your clothes and come out here to help me."

Tartub wore no superfluous attire and he was soon ready.

The captive, meanwhile, lay very quiet.

"Get up," said Seaforth, with more ire than he usually exhibited.

Chunks got up and stood with his hands folded before him, the image of humility.

But for all that Seaforth did not quite believe his story.

"We will take care of you," he said, "until the mounted police come along, and see if you are known."

This was not at all to the taste of Chunks, and the change in his face was very marked.

"Get a rope, Tartub," said Seaforth, who still kept a sharp eye on his captive.

Tartub soon had one, and between them they served Chunks in a manner that left him little chance of doing the rope trick.

Then they put him in with the two African monarchs, and, having wakened both, gave them instructions to keep guard, and watch over him during the night.

"But I say," said Chunks, "don't put me with derned niggers."

"Don't be so mighty particular for one night," replied Seaforth, "now, you understand, you Tu-tu and Tokoa Fay, don't lose sight of him, and if he makes one movement to escape, call out murder."

"If you lose him," said Tartub, "mysterious spell will be wove so that all the hair will drop over your face, and your heads become as bald as an egg. You will also get your feet turned round and have to walk backwards for the rest of your days."

He and Seaforth then returned to their beds, and and the others unconscious of what had taken place.

They lay down as they were, in case of an alarm, and were soon asleep again.

Chunks left to himself reflected somewhat in this fashion :

" Well, I'm derned. It just comes o' trying to work alone, but Jecks said whoever did it was to have the money, and as Morgan had bungled the job I thought I'd try my hand. It's the derndest mess of a job I ever made. I've got to play low down to git out of it."

Tu-tu and Tokoa Fay were true to their trust. The fear of that terrible spell not only kept them awake one at a time, but absolutely prevented both from sleeping at all.

With the lantern ready on hand, so that its light was thrown upon Chunks, they squatted facing him with their eyes fixed on him with dreadful persistence.

It soon got monotonous to him, and at last terribly irritating.

" Can't you take your eyes off me one minute, hang you ? " he asked.

" When Massa Seaforth come back in de morning," replied Tokoa Fay.

"Take 'em off my eyes then," argued Chunks, "look at my nose, my chin, anywhere but in that blessed straightway."

He was trying in a quiet way, as he talked, and he felt that with time he might be able to get out of his bonds. But the quick eyes of Tokoa Fay soon saw what he was doing.

" Jess you sit still," he said, " or me call Massa Seaforth."

Chunks inwardly groaned, and after a protest to the effect that he would rather die than try to get away, he wished he might die if he wouldn't, he gave up the job.

In the morning, when his capture became known to all, he was visited by all the friends in turn, but none of them recognised him.

"I don't see how you should," he whined, "when I ain't been three months in the country. I landed with a hundred pounds, intending to buy a little farm, and I lost it all one night gambling."

It was difficult to believe him, but there was a likelihood about his story which led them to think it might be the truth.

If it was true, they were decidedly in the wrong to keep him bound like a felon.

He vowed by all that was good and true that all he wanted to find was where the food was kept, and when they gave him his breakfast he ate it like a ravenous wolf.

Half the day was gone, and no mounted police having rode by, Seaforth said he would release him if he would give his parole not to go away without permission.

Of course Chunks gave it as he would have given anything else, and he was set free.

All but Dick then apparently went away to work in the field.

Chunks remained in the nigger's hut for half-an-hour, and then came out yawning and had a look about him.

Half a mile away he could see three or four figures moving about among the trees, and Dick sat by the door reading.

Chunks sauntered up to him and touched his hat.

"All alone, sir?" he said.

Dick raised his eyebrows a little and smiled.

"Anything in that?" he asked.

"Oh, no," replied Chunks, "but some people might think I was not a chap to be trusted."

"I have not thought about it," Dick said.

The eyes of Chunks began to glint in an evil way.

He saw that Dick was weak, and if he once got a grip on him he could not only silence him for the moment but for ever.

And then the reward would be his.

He could hide away in the bush until the hue and cry blew over, and then make tracks for America by one of the San Francisco vessels.

' Of course I felt it hard to be treated as I was," he said, "coming just promiscuous like in the place, but I don't bear any malice, bless you."

"I don't see why you should," returned Dick.

"No malice," said Chunks, coming a little nearer. 'I say—what's that behind you?"

Dick turned to see what he meant, and in a moment Chunks was upon him. His strong hands closed upon Dick's throat, and in a minute it would have been all over.

But Seaforth calmly stepped out of the hut and deliberately shot the murderous villain down.

With a bullet in his breast he staggered back—threw up his arms—and fell.

"It's all over with me," he said.

"You have earned your fate," said Seaforth, sternly. "Much as I dislike shedding blood I think I have only done my duty here. I only pretended to trust you, but if you had been worthy of it you would have found friends in us. Dick, old fellow, this is no sight for you—go in."

"Can't we do something for him?" Dick asked. "Seaforth, I cannot sufficiently thank you, but I know you are generosity itself——"

"It's no use," said Chunks, faintly, "a man knows when he is dying, and I'm done for. I can tell the truth now—I came here to murder you——"

"What have I done to you?" asked Dick.

"Nothing—but there is ten thousand pounds to be had for your life—oh! I am going—trace Morgan—Jecks—Waterside Street—Lord Staunton—I—I——"

He made one frantic effort to rise to complete his story and then fell back—dead.

The report of the revolver was heard by the others working, and in a few minutes they came running in to learn the story of Chunks's fate.

It was now clear to all that desperate efforts were being made to take Dick's life, but who was the originator of the nefarious efforts they had yet to find out.

It so happened that two of the mounted police came by that evening, and the story of Chunk's arrival and

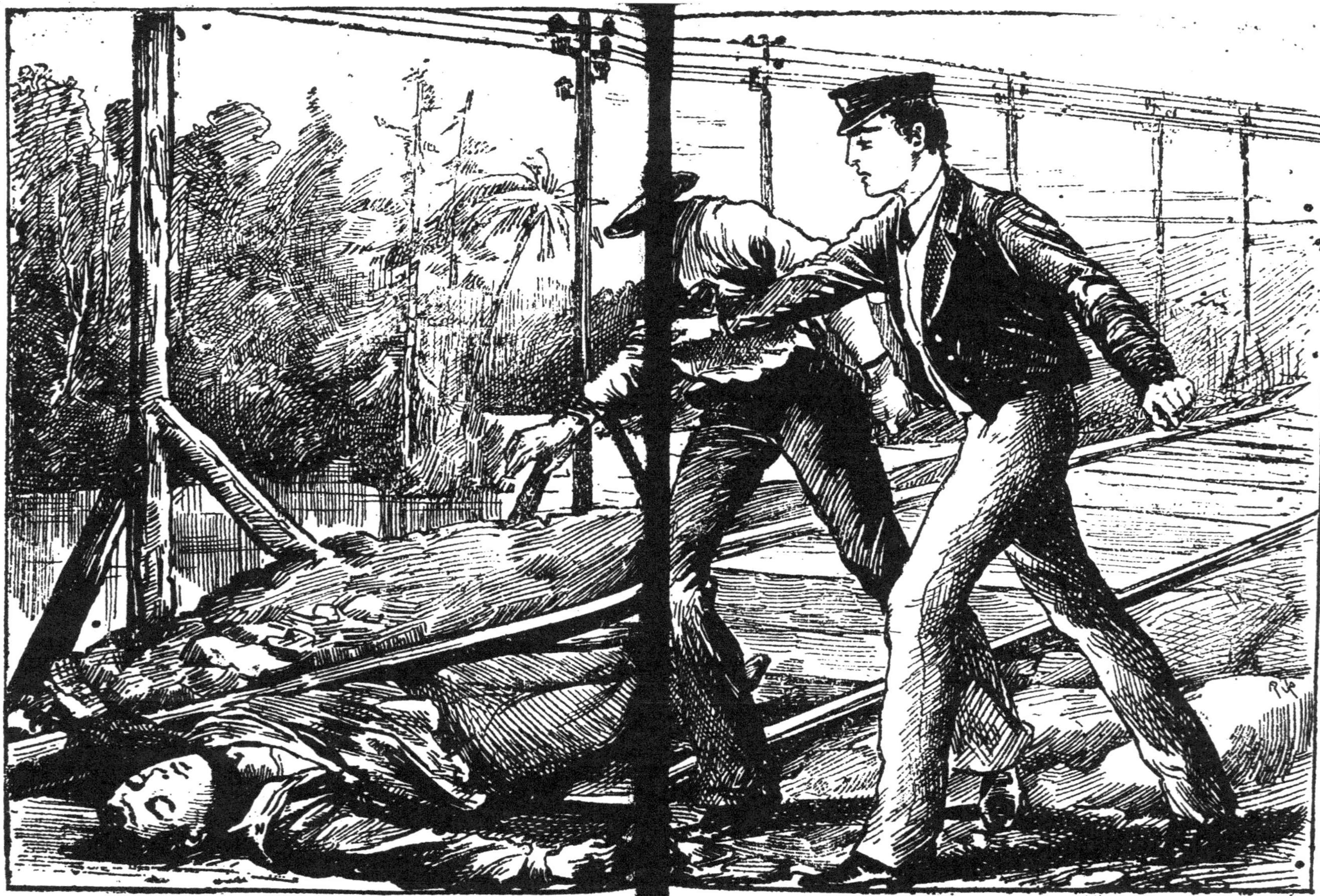

THEY CAME UP TO THE DARK OBJECT ... IT WAS DICK LYIN S'ILL AS IF IN DEATH.

all that followed was made known to them.

One of the men knew Chunks as a desperate character, and assured our friends that they need not be at all disturbed about him.

"Bury him in some convenient spot," he said, "and we will report the matter to headquarters."

Whether that was done or not our friends never knew, but certain it is that no further notice was taken of the fate of the ruffian.

"Jecks—Waterside," said Seaforth after the police had gone on. "I wish I had thought of asking them if they knew anything of the name."

But he had forgotten it, so he arranged to ride into Melbourne on the morrow, to make inquiries.

"This matter has got to be sifted to the bottom, Dick," he said.

"I suppose so," Dick replied, "but you had better leave it to me. Why should you bother at all about it?" To which questions Seaforth only smiled by way of reply.

Dick was not yet fit to go, so Seaforth, after leaving injunctions for the rest to remain with Dick, and do no field labour for a day or two, rode away in the morning, and, keeping on, reached Melbourne in the afternoon.

There he put up his horse, and asked for Waterside Street.

He was directed thither, and on reaching it, found that it was eminently respectable, in appearance, at least.

For the most part the houses were occupied by business men, and the name of Mr. Jecks, on a brass plate, soon caught his eyes.

There was no statement as to what his calling was, simply "Mr. Jecks," and although the plate had been a very good one once upon a time, it was now in a very dirty, battered condition.

By the look of it, one would have guessed that passers-by took delight in battering the said brass plate. Seaforth thought so, and he was standing in the doorway, wondering what sort of person this Mr. Jecks was, when the door opened and somebody ran against him.

"Fontenoy!"

"Seaforth!"

The meeting was such a surprise to both, that after the first exclamation, they could only stand and stare at each other.

At last Fontenoy managed to stammer out:

"Who would have expected to see you here. What are you doing?"

Seaforth had now recovered his wits, and with some coolness, replied:

"That is a question I might put to you."

"Oh, I can tell you," said Fontenoy, "we have some property over here, and, as I have left the navy, I thought I might as well run over and see after it."

"May I ask what property?" asked Seaforth.

"You may ask, of course," replied Fontenoy, coolly, "but I don't feel called upon to tell you."

"Fontenoy," said Seaforth, "you know me pretty well, I never lie, and I don't beat about the bush; you do both."

"Sir!"

"Oh, don't give me any airs, in the first place you have no property here."

The face of Fontenoy began to change colour.

"Lie the first," said Seaforth, "and in the second place, if you had any you would not be here to look after it. Who is this man Jecks?"

"Jecks," said Fontenoy, "I don't know such a man."

"There's his plate," said Seaforth.

"Yes, and there are others," returned Fontenoy, "I need not call on Mr. Jecks."

"*But you have done so,*" returned Seaforth, "here, come back with me and see the man."

"I won't," returned Fontenoy, violently.

"You shall, or I will call the police and give you in charge for conspiring to murder."

"Give ME in charge?"

"Yes, Fontenoy; one of your *agents* was shot up at our farm last night. He made certain confessions before he died, shall I tell you what they are?"

The face of Fontenoy was terrible now to look upon, so deathlike was its hue, and his hands trembled."

" Now," said Seaforth, "you have your choice, come back with me, or I will call the police, and risk giving you in custody."

" I tell you I don't know the man," said Fontenoy.

" Come back and see him."

" Very well," said Fontenoy, " if I must I must, not that I have had cause for fear, but you were always a dogged fool, and I don't want any disturbance."

Then they turned back, and went upstairs together.

CHAPTER XXXII.

SEAFORTH V. FONTENOY AND JECKS—A GENTLE
HINT—FONTENOY PLAYS AN ARTFUL CARD.

THE room occupied by Mr. Jecks was on the first floor. It was a dingy little den, with little in it but a chair or two, a table, a newspaper, and an odour of mingled rum and tobacco.

Jecks, in person, was not very inviting.

He was old—very old—although it would have been difficult to say what his age was.

He might have been anything between sixty-five and ninety.

In figure he was small and spare, and a withered look about him generally.   He was like a man HALF mummified.

Seaforth opened the door of the office without any ceremony, and walked in. Fontenoy perforce followed.

Jecks must have been surprised, but he did not show it.

He was seated at the table poring over some papers, and on hearing footsteps he looked up and closely scanned Seaforth.

Then he glanced at Fontenoy, but exhibited no signs of recognition.

" Mr. Jecks, I believe," Seaforth said.

" That's my name," replied the old man in a hard, dry voice.

" I am here on peculiar business," continued Seaforth. "Your friend, Fontenoy——"

"Pardon me," interposed the old man. "My friend, did you say?"

"Yes."

"That must be a mistake. I do not know Mr.—Mr.—the gentleman you referred to."

"He is here."

"Oh, that is Mr.——I beg your pardon—what name?"

"Fontenoy."

"Oh, yes—Fontenoy," said Jecks. "But how is it that you assume him to be MY friend? As a matter of fact, I have no friends. Don't believe in them. All the good they do you is to borrow your money and revile you afterwards."

"They do not borrow much from you, I reckon," said Seaforth.

Fontenoy stood just within the door, looking about him with sullen indifference. He made no attempt to join in the conversation.

Seaforth put himself into a position to intercept any glance that might be exchanged by the other two, and went on :

"You play your part well, both of you. But for all that I am positive you are known to each other, and that you are engaged in a nefarious plot to rob a man of his birthright and his life."

"It is early for you to have had so much drink," said Jecks, drily.

"I have had none," replied Seaforth, "and your taunt is thrown away. Now, understand me. I am not to be trifled with. If either of you come within two miles of our place you will be shot, and in any case you will be closely watched. Dick Stornaway is heir to the Staunton title and estates, and we mean to prove it. Mr. Jecks, if you are wise you will come over to our side."

"Don't know anything about it," said Jecks, shaking his head. "If you don't mind, I would rather you went away and left me to my work. This is my busy day."

"I have said all I have to say," said Seaforth "and you must do as you please. But, remember this, we are not the people to be humbugged or trifled with. Good day."

Seaforth spoke very quietly, as was his wont, but he was revolving a little scheme in his mind, which he now carried out.

Having taken a brusque leave of Jecks, he brushed by Fontenoy and went out, closing the door behind him.

"Well," said Jecks.

"Curse him!" said Fontenoy.

"How did he know?"

"He says that somebody's been shot up their way."

"That's Chunks," said Jecks, "I was a fool to employ him, but he pressed so hard to be put on the job. So I engaged him as an auxiliary."

The door at this moment opened sharply, and Seaforth stood before them with a quiet sarcastic look on his face.

"You do not know each other, of course," he said.

The masks had fallen. They were completely taken by surprise, and found out when too late that, cunning as they were, others could double on them.

"I am satisfied *now*," said Seaforth, "we understand each other perfectly. Once more—good-day,"

And then he really went, as Fontenoy discovered when a few minutes later, he opened the door and looked downstairs.

Returning to the room he, by Jecks's desire, locked the door, so they could talk without fear of interruption.

"Jecks," said Fontenoy, "you seem to be bungling this business."

"If you think so take it in hand yourself," was the cool reply.

"But are you not?"

"No. It is impossible to foresee everything. I don't know the particulars of Chunks's failure. Do you?"

"No," said Fontenoy.

'Then why do you have the audacity to blame ME?"

hissed Jecks.

"The audacity?" exclaimed Fontenoy, haughtily.

"Yes—the audacity," said Jecks, "knowing as you ought to do that I could burst up the whole business.'

"You dare not."

"To the deuce with your 'dare-nots!' I could and dare. I am independent of you and your father, and I could hang him and ruin you."

The old man was not speaking loud, but his tone of concentrated quiet passion left no doubt about his earnestness.

Fontenoy began to haul down his colours.

"I spoke hastily," he said.

"Haste be hanged!" said Jecks, "it is like you cubs—you think that you can ride roughshod over everyone you think lower than yourself. Remember this—I am your father's master. I hold proofs that he connived at and arranged the murder of his elder brother."

"Hush, for goodness sake!" said Fontenoy,

"I will not hush," but speaking louder, "you spawn of a fratricide!" said Jecks, "how dare you talk to ME?"

Fontenoy was now completely alarmed and cowed.

"I apologize for what I've said—I am sorry—indeed I am," he said.

"Well! keep down there," said Jecks, with a low growl, "and don't give me any of your airs. What's to be done now?"

"I don't know."

"Of course you don't. But I do. You've told me the story of the wreck, and can't see how it will help you now. Bah! Wire home at once to say that the two officers of the "Cyclops" who *deserted their posts* are here, Unless I am much mistaken a prompt order will come for their arrest."

"Will that help us?"

"Will that help *us?*" sneered Jecks, "it will clear the ground, won't it? I don't like that cool fellow. He must be got out of the way. We must whittle that little company down until we have only your cousin to deal with.

"He's no cousin of mine," said Fontenoy.

"He is, to *his* shame," returned Jecks, "his father married old Stornaway's daughter as I can prove."

"Where?"

"That is one of my secrets?"

"That is one of the things you were asked to find out," said Fontenoy.

"Well! I did find it out," replied Jecks, suavely.

"Then you were to let us know."

"Oh, yes; and have the register destroyed and so win the game. No; I hold that trump card until I get my share of the stakes."

"And what is that?" asked Fontenoy.

"Half the prize," returned Jecks.

"Half the Staunton estates!" exclaimed Fontenoy.

"Yes, that's my price. It is a big prize," said Jecks, "but I have waited sixteen years for it, and I won't be robbed now."

Fontenoy looked at him with a troubled face. Jecks returned his gaze with a mocking leer.

"Don't waste your time talking," continued Jecks, "but go and do as I tell you. Wire, however, that the deserters are here, but only mention the officers. If Stornaway should be arrested with them we could not *finish the game*."

Fontenoy unlocked the door and left the office in a state bordering on bewilderment.

He felt that what that old villain Jecks said was right. Half the prize would have to be handed over to him.

And what would his father the present Earl of Staunton say?

Gorton Fontenoy could pretty well guess what a white heat the bare suggestion of such a thing would put him in.

As he turned into the street he saw Muzzle coming along, evidently bound for the same rendezvous.

Muzzle had put on a rollicking air of freedom, and was disposed to be chummy.

"Pretty warm country this, ain't it?" he said.

Fontenoy stared hard at him.

"Confound you," he said, "what do you mean by speaking to me in that way?"

"And confound you," returned Muzzle, firing up, "what do you mean by speaking to me like that?"

"You miserable hound."

"Look here, Mister Fontenoy," said Muzzle, "you and me at home are different parties to what we are here. There you could put your back up, but here we are pretty level. Besides, *I know too much* for you to make a football of me. If you don't want me there, may be there are others as does."

"Stop a moment," said Fontenoy

He drew in a deep breath as if he had need of strength to make a big effort.

"Muzzle," he said, "no good can come of our quarrelling."

"Then don't you begin it," replied Muzzle, "I'm not unreasonable. All I want is fair treatment. Are you going to stand a drink. Every decent chap stands drinks here."

"Wait until I have sent a wire home," said Fontenoy.

"I'll go with you," said Muzzle, "and see what it is. I can't have no back-door games played on me."

Fontenoy could only accept his offer, and together they went away to the telegraph office.

So different in all things, age, education, tastes, instinct and position, yet bound indissolubly together by the iron chain forged by mutual crime.

CHAPTER XXXIII.

THE PURSUIT OF MORGAN — SEAFORTH'S RETURN HOME—THE RIDE AFTER DICK—TWO HORSEMEN IN THE TWILIGHT.

THE pursuit of Morgan was very keen at first, but it soon relaxed as it was apparent that he had taken to the bush.

Seaforth stayed in Melbourne four days, and was busy all the time putting various agencies to work on behalf of Dick, and at the same time keeping an eye as far as possible on Jecks.

Apparently no movement was made in that direction.

Twice he met Fontenoy in the streets, but he cut him dead, which was not at all palatable to Fontenoy, who each hour was growing more uneasy.

No reply to his telegram had been sent back, notwithstanding the fact, that in case of accident, he had repeated it.

All Seaforth's efforts to find out where Dick's father and mother had been married resulted in failure, and the conclusion he came to was that he was not married in Melbourne at all.

Before looking elsewhere, he thought he had better go back to the farm for a day or two and confer with Dick.

Accordingly he started on the morning of the fifth day, and arrived there late in the afternoon to find the place in a state of commotion.

Dick had gone out after breakfast for a short ride and had not returned.

"Was he armed?" asked Seaforth.

"He took a rifle with him," replied Jimmy Tartub, "I helped him to sling it across his back."

"He ought not to have gone alone."

"He would go, sir."

The season just then was at its dryest, and trails were difficult to strike, but Seaforth thought he would try what he could do.

There was another horse, which he exchanged for his own, and having ascertained the direction Dick had taken, he galloped off.

About an hour and a half of daylight remained for him to make use of.

He had good eyes and a little instinct in tracking anyone. With proper training he would have made an excellent scout in Indian warfare.

After riding here and there, keeping pretty well in the line indicated by those at home, he came upon some faint hoof marks in a spread of long, coarse grass.

The earth itself was too hard to receive an impression, but the crushed grass showed where a horse had passed by.

Following this trail for a quarter of a mile or so, he found indications of a *second horse*, and from thence they, apparently, went on together.

Who was this second rider?

Assuredly not one of their neighbours, for on that side the land was pretty well open and unoccupied, save by some lone herdsmen here and there.

Why should Dick, in any case, ride in that direction?

However, Seaforth hurried his horse so as to get out of the open forest to the plains. Half-an-hour's riding would bring him there, and then he would assuredly know what had become of Dick.

The sun was going down, as it seemed, fast to him. It would soon be twilight and impossible for him to see the trail from the saddle.

Then the quest would become practically hopeless.

Straining his eyes he rode on, the "open forest," getting thinner and thinner, until the end of it was in sight.

Beyond, like a wide stretch of sea, was the open plain, land that was a little lower than that on which he rode.

A race for dear life.

The sun sinking, and the first shadows of evening rolling up from east.

On, on.

The last tree was reached, and the wide plain was before him.

He reined up his horse, and from the summit of a gentle slope looked down on the broad expanse before him.

At first he saw nothing but the broad, neutral-tinted spread of grass land, but in a few moments he saw two dark objects circling round each other.

They were far away, a mile or more, but he could not mistake that they were two horsemen.

And why where they circling round each other?

Friends do not indulge in such pastime, but enemies

do when they are looking out for an opening to get a clear shot at each other.

Seaforth understood it all now.

Dick had not been riding with another horseman, but after him.

He had been in pursuit of some one who had fled before him, and the reasonable assumption was that it was Morgan.

CHAPTER XXXIV.

THE BUSHRANGER—HE HAS INFORMATION FOR DICK —THE END IN VIEW.

THE sun sank, and twilight was there.

It was impossible at that distance to distinguish which was friend or foe, and Seaforth did not linger to decide.

He urged his horse on again, and rode at a hard gallop down the slope.

He kept his eyes on the two circling figures, and could now see that they each had a rifle resting on a level with his hip.

A movement on the part of one would lead to the firing of the rifle of the other.

Suddenly one made a movement.

The other followed suit.

Both rifles were raised to the shoulder and fired.

One of the men reeled and fell from the saddle.

Seaforth's heart leaped within him and a groan escaped his lips.

"What if it is Dick!" he murmured. "If so I need ride no further, save to avenge him."

As he spoke his horse stumbled and fell.

He had been riding carelessly, almost to recklessness, with a loose rein bent only on getting on, and his horse had stepped into a rabbit burrow.

He was pitched right over the horse's head upon his own, and turning right over lay on the ground half stunned.

It was some time before he could collect his thoughts, and when he had done so he found that his frightened horse had risen and galloped back in a homeward direction.

With an effort he got upon his feet, and looked about him as well as his disordered vision would permit, but he could see nothing.

The darkness of night was at hand, and in the distance all things were misty or blotted out.

Seaforth was almost at his wit's end, but after awhile something like his old coolness came to his aid.

He stood awhile thinking over his position, and endeavouring to make certain which way to go, and like a true sailor he looked up to the stars to guide him.

Ere long he had got his " bearings," and ignoring the pain which followed the severe shaking he had received, he struck out in the direction he had put down as the correct one.

It is very difficult to keep a bee line on an even plain after dark, but Seaforth, with his eyes on the Southern Cross, scarcely deviated an inch from his course.

Presently he heard a sound that set his heart beating a little quicker.

It was that of a horse trotting towards him.

Who was the rider ?

" I'll find out that," said Seaforth ; " and if it is Morgan, I'll shoot him down. No sin in that."

Putting his hand to his mouth he sent forth a ringing cry.

It was promptly answered by a cheery shout and he recognised, to his great delight, the voice of Dick.

" This way," he fairly screamed in his joy.

In a few seconds he dimly saw the form of a horse and a rider, and sprang forward, crying out:

" Here I am, old man."

Dick reined up, and their hands met.

" Seaforth," said Dick, " I have had a strange duel, and came out of it first. It was with Morgan."

" Have you killed him ?" asked Seaforth.

" No, but he is dying, I think, and I can't bear the idea of leaving him to perish like a wolf. Have you a flask about you ?"

"Luckily I have," said Seaforth, "the one I brought from the town. Dick, you have given us a turn by being so long away."

"I am sorry," replied Dick, as he turned his horse round, "but why did you come on foot?"

They were going back now, and Seaforth explained matters, and ere they reached Morgan had heard Dick's story.

Dick, it seemed, had caught sight of a man on horseback sneaking about the neighbourhood, and made up his mind that it was Morgan.

"I thought it was my affair to capture this man," he said, "and I went out to do it. I picked up his trail, and overtook him on this plain. He showed fight and we had a sort of circular duel, buzzing round each other for a quarter of an hour, and then we fired together. He fell."

"Morgan knows something I think that might be useful to you," said Seaforth, thoughtfully, "but whether he will tell it you or not is another matter."

"He must tell it soon or never," said Dick.

The sky overhead was now brilliant with stars, and by the aid of their soft light they succeeded in finding the fallen man.

He lay stretched upon the plain, as if dead, and his horse, like Seaforth's, had bolted away.

As it was a stolen one it is to be hoped that it returned to its owner.

Morgan was not dead, and the administration of a few drops of brandy brought him back to consciousness.

In a gruff voice he asked where he was, and what "the nation was the matter with him?"

"Don't you remember?" replied Dick. "You and I have been fighting."

"Yes," said Morgan, "and you dropped me. It's right enough, all fair and square. If anything I've got the balance on my side."

He spoke with difficulty, but with the air of resignation one hears of in gamblers, who have the nerve to bear their losses like philosophers.

"You attempted to take my life," said Dick.

"Yes," replied Morgan, "and that's the balance. Look here, youngster, I'm going as sure as my name's Morgan, and as certain as I'm the biggest blackguard in the colony, so I've a mind to speak out."

"If there is anything you can tell me that will help me to find out that which I seek," said Dick, "I shall be ever grateful to you."

"Look here, young fellow," said Morgan, "I owe no grudge agin you. I took on the job to kill you at a price, and you've dropped me in fair fight. I don't complain. Now tell me what you are looking after."

"I want to find out where my father and mother were married," said Dick, "I think you know something of it."

"Why do you think so?"

"I feel it."

"Curus," said Morgan, "but—I'm mighty faint. Can you——"

Seaforth put the flask to his lips and gave him a stimulating drink."

"That's better," said Morgan. "Now I can talk a bit afore I stop clattering for good. I'm going to make a clean breast of it. Your mother was old Stornaway's daughter, as good and pretty a girl as ever lived. She married your swell father, and they were a happy couple. Heaven forgive me. My lad—I killed him."

Dick said nothing by way of reply as he had already guessed what was coming.

Seaforth stood erect, looking down upon the dying man on whose rugged countenance lay the faint weird light shed by the stars.

Dick was supporting his head as if it had been that of a dying brother.

A strange impressive picture, truly.

"Yes—I killed him, and was paid for it," continued Morgan, "and mind you—I ain't going to talk any cant about being tempted by the rich man. I was ready and willing then to do anything for money. I'm dyed red, I am, bad to the backbone."

He stopped, and Seaforth, bending down, administered a little more brandy. It gave him the strength he needed to go on.

"But this isn't all I've to say," said Morgan. "Your father and mother were married—NOT in Melbourne, lad."

"Tell me where, Morgan," said Dick, "and it will go far towards atoning for the wrong you have done me."

"They were married," said Morgan, "in a little shanty of a church north side of Geelong. It wasn't much then and it ain't much now, but it's got the name of some saint, I forget who it is, saints not being much in my line. You'll know it when you see it, for there's a small round tower at the west end for the bell, and there's some fairish trees in the churchyard. Anyway, Geelong ain't much of a place for churches, and you can't miss it. Gimme a drop more brandy, Mister. I'm going."

Seaforth hastened to do so, and this time Morgan emptied the flask, but its reviving effect seemed to have deserted it.

He lay back in Dick's arms, breathing heavily, and every now and then he muttered something neither of the listeners could catch.

In a few minutes he was silent for awhile, and when he spoke again it was more clearly, and of things far away; of home and friends long deserted, and the latter perhaps dead.

It was a strange jumble of country life, evil companions, prison, temptation, and of deeds that made the listeners shudder.

Happily it soon came to an end.

Then followed another silence, broken only by his heavy breathing, which gradually got more and more difficult as the moments passed.

Suddenly it ceased, and they thought he was gone. Dick was about to lay his head down gently on the ground, when, with a spasmodic effort, he sat up alone.

"Jecks and the Earl o' Staunton," he cried; "punish em. Don't let them go scot free. There isn't much to choose between us."

He tried to raise his two clenched hands as if to call down vengeance on their heads, but the effort was too much for him, and, with a gasp, he fell back —dead.

Dick caught him as he fell, and laid him gently on the ground. Then he and Seaforth stood awhile in the presence of death—without speaking.

"Seaforth," said Dick, "it will not do to leave him here ; the carrion birds would tear him to pieces before morning. I will watch by him while you ride back for assistance to bury him."

"No—let me remain here," urged Seaforth.

"Do as I bid you, dear friend," said Dick; "believe me—I would rather remain here, for I feel that I had better be alone to wrest from the heart all thoughts of this wretched man, save forgiveness."

"It is hard to forgive such a one," returned Seaforth, "but at least he, in his rough way, endeavoured to make some amends."

"I am not his judge," Dick said, simply.

His horse was not far away, quietly browsing, and Seaforth, having secured it, climbed into the saddle, feeling stiff and sore from his recent fall, and rode slowly back.

It was necessary that he should go carefully, for a second fall might put him entirely *hors de combat*.

So Dick was left alone with the dead.

There, on the lonely silent plain, he remained by the still form of the man who had slain his father and attempted his own life, wrestling with his thoughts.

He wanted to forgive the dead, and he tried to do so. It was as Seaforth said—hard work.

But he succeeded at last. The man had been a tool, and although he was not the less culpable on that account, he was not the chief offender.

Dick's thoughts turned to the Earl of Staunton—his uncle—who had been the chief actor in the villainous drama.

But for him what suffering would have been spared. How much agony, shame, and shedding of tears avoided !

Him Dick could not as yet forgive.

"It would be unjust to let him go," Dick murmured.

And then he thought of his own wrongs, of his life on board the "Cyclops," of the attempt to ruin him, and all that had followed, but strange to say his anger was not aroused.

His chief feeling towards Gorton Fontenoy was that of contempt.

As for Muzzle, he only thought of him, as a strong man thinks of a yelping cur who has tried to bite him and failed.

And then he thought of his return home.

What would his long-suffering and much enduring mother think of him when he returned successful in his quest.

It would come unexpectedly upon her, like a message of peace from angel land.

No longer would her name be spoken of with derision. The dark stain upon it would be removed.

And then, what a vista was opened up for himself.

He would be rich, and the bearer of one of the proudest names in England.

He, the poor despised lad, the common sailor, the wanderer, would be noble among the noblest.

But all depended on the truth of what Morgan had told him.

It was scarcely possible that a dying man would lie, but the world is full of strange and wicked men, and at Dick's heart Doubt knocked and tried to enter in.

But Dick bade it go.

Then it was possible that the little church might be removed or destroyed, its records lost.

With so much depending on it, and the truth of the story, who can marvel at Dick's growing impatience with the length of the night.

He longed for the morning's dawn, to be off and away, to ride in hot haste and test the truth of the story.

At last he threw himself down upon the ground, and lay there with his eyes on the horizon watching for the dawn.

And while he watched he fell asleep.

So mimic and real death lay almost side by side under the mighty arch of the star-spangled heavens.

The dawn had barely arrived, when he was aroused by the tramp of horses' hoofs. It was Seaforth and Tartub come back together, the latter leading a third horse for Dick.

Scarce a word was said.

Tartub had brought with him a pick and spade, strapped to the pommel of the saddle, and at once set to work digging the grave.

Seaforth tied the horses together and staked them to the ground, and then went to his aid.

In a short time the grave was ready, and Morgan was laid in his last home.

They filled in the grave level with the plain, and scattered the superfluous earth around. Then stood for a moment beside the dead, and at last, in silence, mounted and rode away.

Thus was the murderer left in his lonely grave, without a mound or stone to mark where he lay.

The first rain would wash out all record of the last office performed for him, and when that was done, no man on earth could correctly say where he slept.

Desperately he lived, miserably he died, and if his deeds were remembered, he himself was " blotted out."

CHAPTER XXXV.

THE CHURCH AT GEELONG—WHO FIRED IT ?—RETURN TO MELBOURNE—ARREST.

" THERE'S the church, Dick," said Seaforth, as he reined up his horse, and pointed to a little belfry tower, peeping over a mound about a mile away.

They had ridden all the day before, only stopping for needed refreshment, and to give their horses imperative rest, and arrived in Melbourne just as darkness set in.

There they passed the night, but Dick had scarcely slept a wink, and the morning found him feverish, with bloodshot eyes, his mind in a whirl.

There was so much at stake, and a little while would decide whether the prize he sought was within his reach, or had again eluded his grasp.

" Let us go on, Hanson," he said.

Their horses were fairly fresh after the night's rest, and in obedience to a touch of the whip, broke into a gallop.

As they advanced, the small tower rose higher and higher in view, but no roof appeared, at which Dick marvelled.

At last the rugged outline of the remains of a wall appeared in sight, and the awful truth burst upon him.

The church was in ruins.

Nay more, it had only recently been reduced to that condition by the action of fire, for from a heap of fallen matter, feeble columns of smoke were arising, and Dick had but too good reason to feel that he had to thank an enemy for the work.

The disappointment was so keen that he was not strong enough to bear it.

He reeled in the saddle, and would have fallen if the watchful Seaforth had not caught him in his arms.

" Dick, old fellow, bear up; all may not be lost yet," Hanson said.

A sob that could not be repressed burst from Dick's lips, and with an effort he recovered himself sufficiently to sit up in the saddle again.

" Hanson," he said, " I can bear what I have lost, but—my mother. I can never face her again."

" I wonder how it happened," said Seaforth, musing. " I see somebody moving about yonder. Let us go and enquire."

" What does it matter ? " returned Dick, wearily. " It HAS happened, and that is enough for me."

There was a man ahead, moving slowly round the ruins, who paused now and then to throw up his arms or indulge in some other expression of despair. Towards him they rode.

He proved to be a man of about seventy years of age, and his appearance was that of a working man.

" Good morning, friend," cried Seaforth.

The old man raised his head and stared at him in

wild-eyed manner as if abruptly roused from a dream

"You have had a fire here?" asked Seaforth.

"Ah, it is so," replied the old man, with a furious gesture, "and I want to know who did it. I've been clerk here since the place was built, and it was my pride to do my duty well. Heaven forgive the man who has been guilty of this crime."

"May it not have been an accident?" asked Seaforth.

"Accident!—no," was the reply. "Yonder is my house—just behind the trees. I was going to bed last night when, as usual, I looked out to get a peep at the church before going to sleep. I saw a light gleaming inside, and came hurrying out to find out what it was. I was just in time to see two men ride quickly away."

"Did you see their faces?" asked Seaforth.

"No," replied the old man; "all I saw was that one could sit a horse well, and the other could not."

"Fontenoy and Muzzle for a thousand," muttered Seaforth.

He turned to Dick, who was sitting in the saddle with a look of resignation on his pale, handsome face. The eyes of the old clerk turned in the same direction.

"Why should it trouble him?" he asked.

"He came here to find something of importance to himself in the register," replied Seaforth, in a low tone.

"What was it?"

"An entry concerning a marriage. Perhaps you might remember it?"

"My memory is bad," replied the old clerk, shaking his head, "but come home with me a bit, and let us talk it over. I've little hope of calling to mind any-thing——but I may be able to help you for all that."

* * * * * *

That same morning Fontenoy went up to Jeck's room with an elastic step, and knocked at the door.

"Come in, croaked the old agent.

Fontenoy entered, and dropped into a chair reserved for clients.

"Well, old man," he said, "I've come to ask you to modify your terms, and name the lowest sum you will take to have done with the business for good and all."

"I have named the lowest," Jecks said.

"Hark ye, old man," said Fontenoy, "I have found out where they were married, and have seen the register myself. Yesterday, when out riding, I dropped upon a little church, and the fancy took me to go in and make inquiries. The door was open and an old man, who said he was the clerk, was dusting the seats. At my request, backed with a fee, he searched the register."

"And found a record of the marriage," said Jecks, quietly.

"Yes."

"Well, I don't see how that helps you, Mr. Fontenoy."

"Jecks," said Fontenoy, "that register is kept in a wooden cupboard—strong enough in its way, being made of oak, and fitted with a good lock, but it was not fire-proof, and last night the church was burnt to the ground. Will you modify your demands now ?"

It was really pitiful to see the face of the old man, who had sinned and worked for a grand prize all his life, saw it within his grasp, and then lost it for ever.

"You are a fiend !" he cried at last, "but I may be even with you yet."

Fontenoy laughed.

"You will have to be even with me soon," he said, "for I sail to-morrow. There is nothing more for me to do here. The Government at home have wakened up at last, and in a few hours the deserters from the 'Cyclops' will be arrested. I need not appear here in that ; it matters little to me now ; they may take the whole gang, including Dick Stornaway."

"There is one thing you have forgotten," said Jecks, fixing his piercing eyes on Fontenoy—"your father connived at the murder of his brother — I can prove it."

"That is not my affair, you know," said Fontenoy, easily, "you can't get me into trouble for that."

"But your father."

"Well, he must look after himself. If he gets into trouble it will not affect me. If you hang him I shall only be Earl of Staunton a little earlier than I could have hoped for."

Jecks stared at him as if he had discovered some great novelty in monsters, and for a few moments neither spoke.

The old man was the first to break silence.

"I have as little heart as here and there one," he said, "but I cannot hold a candle to you, young as you are. You ask me what is my lowest price, and my answer is—nothing. What terms I have to make shall be made with your father."

"As you like," said Fontenoy, rising, "I am deputed by the governor to settle matters here. I thought I might as well square up everything before I go."

"No, that was not in your thoughts," said Jecks, "your idea was to come here to mock me. Enough, I have no more to say to you HERE."

The old man leant back in his chair, fixing a glittering eye upon Fontenoy, which he could not stand.

The effect of it was to make him feel as if two keen weapons were slowly penetrating his heart, and only half satisfied with his visit of mockery he arose and left the room.

That night when Dick and Seaforth returned to Melbourne they were arrested, one on a charge of having deserted his ship, and the other with having wilfully left it at a time of peril.

They were lodged in a house under the care of a number of men from H.M.S. "Penelope," then in harbour to await the arrival of Ned Dawson.

The prisoners were treated with every courtesy, and when Ned arrived and they were transferred to the "Penelope," they found to their surprise their old captain in command.

Ned had informed his friends that the home in the open forest had been broken up. Jimmy Tartub, Dandy Banks, and Tu-tu and Tokoa Fay intended to sail by the first ship to England, there to meet their old friends and see them through their trouble.

Captain Harrison did not say anything to the prisoners on their arrival that gave them a clue to his feelings towards them, but Seaforth was inclined to think that he was their friend.

"We shall have the thing fully developed on our return home," he said, "and then we shall know our fate. If anything happens to me in the way of being cashiered, I shall feel sorry for the governor. The family pride will receive a mortal wound.'

"In which I am responsible," replied Dick.

"I am of an age to be responsible for my actions," said Seaforth, grimly; "without being exactly buoyant I am very hopeful of the issue."

CHAPTER XXXVI.
THE EARL OF STAUNTON.

FEVERTON COURT is a noble building, in the South of England, commanding a view of the most beautiful part of Sussex.

The house of the Stauntons is of historical renown, many incidents of a stirring nature having taken place within its walls during the last three centuries.

It was built at the time of Henry VIII, and at that time was of larger dimensions than it is now.

Time has robbed it of some of its outer adornments, and two of its six massive towers have fallen, but the rest have been kept in good repair by its successive owners..

Its courtyard is still intact, so is the noble gate by which access is gained thereto, and from the latter there emerged one morning, about two months after the events recorded, a tall man, on horseback. with a young man of meaner stature beside him.

It was the usurper of the title of the Earl of Staunton, and his son, whom we have known as Gorton Fontenoy.

The face of the father was haughty, that of the son defiant. High words had passed between them that morning, and if the clouds had broken for a moment, the return of the storm might be looked for.

They rode on down the slope through an avenue of

oaks of majestic size, the pride of the family for generations, and not a word was exchanged.

At the base of the avenue was a lodge from which an old woman emerged, and, with much curtseying, opened one of the massive iron gates to let them pass through.

It creaked as it swung slowly back and the Earl turned his head towards the old woman, saying:

"I told you to look to that gate yesterday—why don't you do it?"

"My lord," she said, "me and my good man have been looking to it—a greasing and a working of it—and it made no noise an hour ago."

"Don't let me hear it when I return. I hate a creaking gate."

"And well ye may," muttered the old woman, as father and son rode on, "being a Staunton, and a bad 'un—for what's the old saying of your home:

'When the main tower rocks,
And there's creaking in the gates and locks,
Which man or woman cannot cure,
There's a change of Stauntons you be sure.'

And a good change it will be whoever comes," added the old woman, as she hobbled back to the lodge.

The earl and his son rode on slowly down the road for a quarter of a mile, and had not got beyond the fencing of Feverton Park.

"Gorton," said the Earl, suddenly, "you will have to give up this prosecution, or at least your share of it. Don't go to the Court Martial."

"But I am one of the principal witnesses," replied Gorton, "and I hate the fellow. I want to crush him."

"You are a fool," said the earl curtly, "and don't know how to let well alone."

"You have to thank me for all being well," returned Gorton, sullenly.

"I am not so sure that all is well," replied the earl. "Our friends or our enemies, as they may be called, are too quiet."

"They are out of it, now." said Gorton, emphatically.

"you have nothing to fear."

"Here comes the mother of—— your cousin," said the earl, drily, "does she look like a woman who is utterly broken down?"

"She always stood up well against things, you know," returned Gorton.

They were referring to no less a person than Dick's mother, to whom the reader has not yet been introduced.

Her age might be forty, but notwithstanding all her troubles she looked younger.

Attired in plain neat fashion, she came towards them, with an elastic tread that had been gained in her life in the bush, and never entirely deserted her.

The daughter of the old settler had a fearless bearing, without exhibiting anything that could possibly be called ill manners in the presence of one so high as the Earl of Staunton.

As soon as they met, she stopped, and it was clear that her being in the neighbourhood was to gain an interview with the earl.

Mechanically he reined up, and Gorton did the same, taking up a position a little behind his father.

CHAPTER XXXVII.

THE EARL DEFIED—MUZZLE'S REVENGE—CLOSING IN.

HAVE come some distance to speak to you," the old woman said; "and you must forgive me for stopping you here. My son has returned, and is, as you are aware, a prisoner on a charge of having assaulted an officer and deserted his ship."

"Such, I believe, is the case," replied the earl, suavely.

"His *superior* officer," said Dick's mother—"your son. May I ask if it is your intention to prosecute him?"

"It is a matter I leave to his own discretion," answered the earl.

"And what does he say?" she asked, turning her dark

eyes upon Gorton.

"That I will smash the whelp that has dared to strike me."

"He is your cousin."

"Oh! no; you may say so, the world thinks differently."

The face of the woman flushed, and it was some minutes ere she could speak. When she did so it was in a lower tone.

"In blood you are akin," she said; "and for all that you have said I was the lawful wife of your uncle. Gorton Fontenoy, you are young, and if ruin should be staring you in the face, what would you do but ask for those with the power to crush you to show some signs of mercy?"

"And they would laugh at me," he answered.

"That some might," Dick's mother said, "but not all. Should Dick ever hold a power over you—"

"Ha—ha!" laughed Gorton; "that is good."

"If he should," she went on, "and fail to show a better spirit than you have exhibited towards me I will disown him."

"It is a pity you did not disown him years ago," said Gorton; "he is no credit to you."

"I am proud of him," said the mother, with flashing eyes; "for it is by his desire that I came here to-day to see if there was one spark of compassion in the hearts of those who usurp his place. But I see there is none. I will never beg of you again, and if ever you beg of me my ears at least shall be deaf to your appeal."

She stood aside to let them pass, but ere going on the earl turned his dark, lowering face upon his son in mute appeal.

"Better let it all go," he said.

"If it cost me my life," replied Gorton, in a passionate undertone, "I will go on to the end; I will degrade him to the level of the common felon."

"You talk like a fool," muttered the earl, and, facing round again, he urged his horse on.

Gorton Fontenoy followed, raising his hat in mockery to the handsome woman, whose glance of scorn pierced the armour of his brutality, and made him wince.

The earl was now galloping ahead, and ere Gorton could overtake him a wide stretch of common was reached.

Then the father gave his horse the rein, and let it fly on at will, as if he intended it to bear him away from the thoughts that troubled him.

Gorton kept within easy distance of him until he slackened the speed of his horse, and then joined him.

"You are a fool, I say!" angrily cried the earl, as if their conversation had been but momentarily interrupted. "I do not like the look of things, I say. Did that woman look like one crushed, defeated, and bowed down by shame?"

"Did she ever look like it?" asked Gorton. "Had she not ever the impudence—"

"No, Gorton, not impudence. She has the true instincts in her."

"Instincts be hanged!" said Gorton, angrily.

The earl turned his eyes upon him, and, in a quiet, incisive way, said—

"You forget yourself. Remember what is due to me as your father."

"I beg your pardon, my lord," said Gorton, raising his hat.

He fell back, and then they turned homeward, and went to Feverton Court without exchanging a word.

As they rode into the courtyard they heard sounds of conversation in the hall, the main entrance to the house.

Some fellow with a rough voice was lifting it up in a manner more vigorous than polite.

Gorton knew that voice, and turned pale.

"That ruffian here!" he muttered. "How dare he?"

As he rode up with the earl two grooms appeared to assist them to dismount and take charge of the horses.

Gorton threw himself from the saddle, and hurried into the hall, where he found Muzzle, the worse for drink, in altercation with three or four gorgeous flunkies who were trying to get him out.

But Muzzle had armed himself with a sword, snatched from some armour on the walls, and, thanks to the drink, was defying them in the old stage style.

"Come on, the lot of you," he was crying; "the British sailor may be outnumbered and slain, but he never yields. Arm yourselves and come at me like men, and I'll make bacon of you, you over-fed swine!"

"Muzzle!" cried Gorton.

"What chere, young Fontenay!" cried Muzzle, as he faced about him. "I say, these fellows won't give me anything to drink; they say I'm an impostor, and don't know you."

"Who is this man?" asked the earl, who now entered the hall.

"A worthy servant of mine on board the Cyclops," replied Gorton; "he is rough but honest, and seems to have let drink get the better of him."

"Drink be bothered!" cried Muzzle; "it never got the better of me yet, nor will you. As for being your servant, that's humbug. We were pals on board the Cyclops—confidential, too, in that Stornaway affair—"

"Muzzle," said Gorton, "that will do. Come in here; I want to reason with you."

"There's plenty of time to reason," returned Muzzle, "as I've come here to stop a week. I've left my bag at the pub in the village, and you had better send one of these chaps for it. Let that long 'un with the pimple on his nose go. High feeding and want of exercise is doing him no good. He wants exercise, and if he don't he's been the most cheeky to me. Let him go, I say."

"Whatever your relations with my son may be," said the earl, "you can't stop here."

Muzzle stared hard at him with drunken scorn before replying.

"And who may you be?" he said.

"I am the Earl of Staunton," was the answer.

"The very old cock I want to see," said Muzzle. "Look here!—but this isn't the place to talk in. There's too many flunkies around, and it's no affair o' theirs anyway. All they've got to do is to be humble, and eat, and sleep, and take their wages, just like well-dressed pigs."

"Gorton," said the earl, harshly, "this man must be

put out.

"Let me reason with him," urged Gorton.

"Reason with a ruffian like that!" cried the earl. "Here, you fellows! thrust him out. You are big enough to do it. If he doesn't go away, beat him."

"Beat me!" roared Muzzle. "I'd like to see it done. Fontenoy, are you going to stop this? If you don't, it will be the worse for you."

But the flunkies, in obedience to an imperative sign from the earl, were upon him, and, having given one an ugly chop across the head with his sword, he was disarmed.

Then they tried to put him out, and a desperate struggle took place.

Drink stimulated him, and the nature of his reception half-maddened him, and he fought like a fury.

The earl, with a haughty air, strode away, and Gorton Fontenoy was left a spectator of the scene.

He knew it was useless to interfere, as the servants would be sure to obey the commands of the earl. All he could do was to await the issue of the struggle.

The servants were very roughly handled, and two footmen were put *hors de combat*, but, others coming to their aid, Muzzle, with his clothes in rags, was dragged to the door, and thrust out.

He fell, panting and exhausted on the ground, and one of the men, in an excess of zeal, kicked him.

Gorton Fontenoy angrily bade him desist.

"You have half-murdered him," he said. "Isn't that enough?"

"And you've not interfered to save an old pal," gasped Muzzle. "But you'll be sorry for it. I swear I'll never forgive it, and whatever comes to me I'll drag you down into the mire."

Then Gorton Fontenoy, with a face deadly pale, was turning away, when a thought occurred to him, and, facing about again, he said—

"Why don't you put him out of the park? Kick him—kill him, if you like—only get him out!"

Then the servitors, smarting under the blows they had received, fell upon Muzzle again, and began to drag him down the path towards the gate.

Half-way down he seemed to get a second wind, and with desperate fury renewed the battle.

At length, with torn clothes and utterly exhausted, he was dragged down to the lodge gates and thrown into the road.

CHAPTER XXXVIII.

AFTER THE STRUGGLE.

SINCE he had been in England Muzzle had been doing little else but drink and "enj'y himself," and this course, following a very heavy time on board ship, had undermined his constitution.

He was very far from being fit to undergo the terrific struggle in which he had just taken part.

The treatment of the wretched man had been merciless, for his assailants did not hold themselves responsible.

They only obeyed orders.

So they wrenched and twisted him about, at the same time administering blows and kicks, their blood being raised by the resistance he offered.

They left him in the road, white as death, lying almost prostrate, and with a hand to his side.

Groans and sobs burst from his lips.

In all his experience of suffering he had never borne anything like this.

After awhile he tried to rise, but found himself unable to do so.

All the bones of his body seemed to be dislocated.

"I'm done for," he gasped; "and through that Fontenoy chap, too—him as I've risked so much for! Lord, let me live to make some amends for my many sins!"

He groaned and made another futile effort to rise; then he looked about for somebody to give him a helping hand.

The only living person in sight was a woman, who was walking quickly towards him.

It was Dick's mother, who came almost up to Muzzle ere she saw him.

She was startled, but not in any sense alarmed.

Instead of running away, as some might have done, she

went up to him and said—

"My poor man, what is the matter with you?"

Her handsome face and kindly manner acted like a charm.

He felt as if an angel had laid a soothing hand upon him.

"I've been knocked and kicked about," he gasped, "in there," with a feeble motion of his hand towards the park. "I reckon it was done to get rid of me; I know too much."

"Who and what are you?" she asked. "But never mind that now. I must get some help for you. There are some men working in a field not far from here; they will assist to convey you to the inn. I will get a doctor for you."

"Heaven bless you! marm, whoever you may be, said Muzzle.

She left him, and was away for about a quarter of an hour.

It was a long time to him, but no one came to his assistance from the court.

"They cast me out and left me here to die!" he muttered; "but I shall live long enough to be even with 'em."

He lay back and closed his eyes tightly, as people do when they endeavour to bear pain without moaning.

Presently he heard voices, and raising his head he saw some men bearing a hurdle running towards him.

They were agricultural labourers, and when they came up to him had little to say in the way of sympathy.

But their actions were better than words.

They raised him gently and placed him on the hurdle on the coats, which they took off to make a soft resting-place for him.

They they bore him away, keeping step together by softly speaking—

"One—two; one—two. All now. One—two."

It was kind and thoughtful of them, and he appreciated it.

"I didn't think there was much kindness in this world," he muttered; "but I'm beginning to find out that there is. Too late—too late!"

The inn was a roadside one, half-a-mile away. It faced the park, and bore the sign of the Staunton Arms.

Dick's mother was there making arrangements for the injured man's comfort.

Two messengers had been despatched—one for the doctor and the other for an officer.

The doctor came first, and before enquiring into the cause of the accident he examined Muzzle's injuries.

He said nothing, but his face showed that he considered them very serious.

"He will want good nursing, in the first place," he said.

"I can be his nurse for a few days," replied Dick's mother.

"What !" exclaimed Muzzle. "You, a lady, and nurse a man like me ?"

"I'm not a lady in the eyes of the world," she answered, with a faint smile that made her look more beautiful than ever. "I'm only the daughter of a poor man."

"I shouldn't have thought it," said Muzzle ; "but whoever's daughter you may be, you ain't far short of being a angel."

The doctor removed Muzzle's clothing, and with the aid of the landlord—a kind-hearted, feeling man—got Muzzle into bed.

Dick's mother meanwhile went downstairs to write a letter or two—one to Dick, and another to a lawyer who had taken up his case.

There was a third addressed to Captain Harrison, of II.M.S. Thunderbolt.

While these things were being done, one of the policemen arrived—a village constable—and he was told by the doctor that for a day at least Muzzle had nothing to say about his injuries.

The doctor, however, knew something about the affair, which he did not then choose to speak of.

Dick's mother took her place by Muzzle's side, and as the day sped on delirium set in, and he raved the whole night through.

She heard of things which had been done, and in an

indirect way got at facts of which she had only learnt a little from Dick.

What Muzzle cried out in his fevered dreams was like separate links of a chain of guilt, and she had good cause to hate the man now left to her tender care.

But she did not hate him.

In Muzzle she only saw the tool of a designing and more guilty man.

By morning the fever had abated, and he fell into a deep sleep, which lasted until noon.

Then he awoke in a strangely calm state of mind—fully conscious of the past and aware of his present peril.

"I take it kindly of you, marm, to do what you've done," he said. "I didn't think that a livin' person would do so much for such a worthless chap as I am. I can do nothing for you in return."

"You can do much," she said.

"How—what?"

"Shall I tell you who I am?"

He stared hard at her, and then something in her face let him into the secret of her identity.

"You are Dick Stornaway's mother?" he gasped.

"Hush!" she said. "Do not agitate yourself."

It seemed as though the discovery would be too much for him; but in a few moments he became calm again.

"It's all right," he said; "I'm not going to break down. But I'd better have what I've got to say put down in writing and signed. I'm sorry for what I've done—mortal sorry—and if anything I can do will help your son to punish them as have done their best to ruin him, I'll die happy."

"I hope you won't die," she replied; "rather live and strive to be a better man."

The tears trickled down his cheek, and he raised his feeble hand to brush them away.

"Fancy old Muzzle blubbering!" he said; "but I've cause to do so now, marm. Don't you lose no time, but just go and get the right parties to take down what I've got to say—I think it ought to be a magistrate. I've got to make a clean breast of it afore I die."

CHAPTER XXXIX.

THE RESULT OF THE COURT-MARTIAL—GORTON AND HIS FATHER—FINAL.

MONTH had elapsed since the events previously recorded, when one morning the Earl of Staunton sat in his library opening a heap of letters before him. The main part were letters of no moment, which he rapidly scanned and put aside. A few were on business of importance, and one he laid aside to be perused at the finish.

At length he came to it, and slowly breaking the seal, read its contents.

It was from Gorton, his son, and it acquainted him with the result of the court-martial.

The opening paragraphs will serve to give our readers an idea of the bearing of it:

"You were right—I ought never to have appeared in this trial at all, but, as you suggested, conveniently suffered in health and gone abroad. All is lost. I am ruined. Muzzle was brought in as a witness to complete my ruin. You remember he had been ill for a time in the village, and then went away, we hoped for good. We believed we had terrified him out of the way, but, alas! he has been only kept in reserve to deal me a blow that shatters all my plans.

"It was the mother of my successful foe who nursed Muzzle, and he in gratitude has told all. Gratitude! What a word!

"Father mine—all who we charged have come out of the court-martial with *honour*, while I—well, I am to be charged with conspiracy and what not. There is a warrant out for my arrest. By the time this reaches you I shall either be in a prison cell or abroad, a fugitive from justice. Father, look to yourself. You are no longer Earl of Staunton, and you are in *peril of your life.* Jecks is here to witness against you, even if it leads himself to the scaffold. Fly—take all you can lay your hands on. The family jewels will enable us to live in some far-off spot. I think Constantinople would be the safest place for the present for us both. They are sure to look for us in Spain.

"The evidence of the marriage of your brother to the settler's daughter is here. I burnt the church, but the day previous the old clerk took home the register of marriages to do some slight repairs to the binding. So you see it is all up. Ruin, shame, and ignominy are ours, and if we would live we must fly."

There was a good deal more in the letter, but it was merely an elaboration of what is here set down. The usurper earl read it all through, and then leant back in his chair to think.

What was life to him now? All that he had sinned for was torn from him. Was it worth his while to accentuate his wrong doing and become a petty thief?

"No," he said, "it is not. Gorton has only himself to thank for the terrible fix he is in. Henceforth he must see to his own affairs."

He rang the bell, and a gorgeous servant in livery promptly appeared.

"Benson," said the usurper earl, "I shall be busy all this morning. Please see that I am not disturbed until noon. Then bring in some wine."

"Yes, my lord," the servant replied, and vanished.

His master was busy the next hour in writing a full confession of all the wrong he had done, which when completed he put into an envelope, sealed, and addressed:

"To the Rightful Heir of Staunton."

That done he opened a drawer in his escritoire, and took out a small bottle.

He held it up to the light for a moment, then drew the cork and placed the bottle to his lips.

Precisely at the hour of noon Benson opened the library

door.

"Wine, my lord !" he said.

My lord was lying back in his chair as if sound asleep. Benson approached the table and put down the tray.

"Wine, my lord !" he said, again.

No answer. Not a movement. And Benson glanced at the still face. A tremour ran through his frame, and he bent over the motionless form. One earnest look sufficed.

"Merciful Heaven !" he exclaimed, "my lord is dead."

.   .   .   .

It was not until a year had elapsed that Dick came to take possession of his home as Earl of Staunton.

There was much to prove ere he could establish himself as the rightful heir—so many legal forms to go through that half the time expired ere a judge declared him to be so.

Then again, Dick—we cannot change the old familiar name, it is hardly worth while—desired certain changes to be made.

The library was in the west wing, and he had it pulled down, and another erected in its place.

"Let everything of the wretched past be blotted out," he said. "I wish even to forget my foes."

At length there was a home-coming, and, it was, indeed, a time to be long remembered by those who shared in it.

A whole week of merriment and hospitality introduced now the dawn of better times for the tenants and all around.

All Dick's friends shared in that merry time.

Seaforth and half-a-score members of his family, including his father, who, in spite of his pride, proved to be a very genial old gentleman; Ned Dawson, Dandy Banks, Tartub, Tokoa Fay, and Tu-tu.

The latter were in Melton suits, bran new, and wore tall, shiny hats, and very proud they were of their appearance.

And Muzzle, too, was there, in a bath chair, an invalid still and for many months to come, a softened and a better man, grateful for the kindness shown to him.

And Dick, Earl of Staunton, so handsome, looking worthy of his title. How proud was he to lead his mother by the hand and introduce her as a Countess of Staunton, but soon to be dowager countess, for there was a sister of Seaforth's in the throng of youth and beauty assembled to give the young earl welcome, who was destined to become his bride.

> Oh! happy hours; oh! precious prime,
> And affluence of love and time.

What a glorious out-coming of a time of suffering, and what a contrast to the fate of his unhappy cousin, a wanderer in a far-off land, fated to perish alone in a dismal lodging in the East, with no living being to help him in his agony.

Let us drop the curtain over such a scene, and draw it also on the old man Jecks, who wandered about awhile bereft of reason, and finally died in a casual ward, raving of the dreadful past.

Loved and honoured as landlord, husband, father, and friend, Dick lives on, with all who were faithful to him well cared for, and one old foe at least, Muzzle by name, is a grateful recipient of his bounty.

"A hero in spite of his foes," and doubly and trebly so, because he set forth on this mission not for himself, but to restore the honour of his mother, who, daughter of a settler though she be, bears the high honour which has fallen to her lot becomingly.

All things must end, and this story closes. For further record of Dick's life those who desire it must go to the broad lands which he calls his own, and ask the yeomen and the villagers and the poor what there they think of their lord and—no, not lord and master, but lord and friend.

THE END.

THE "BEST FOR BOYS" LIBRARY

(CHING CHING'S OWN).

Declared by Untold Thousands of Readers to be the most entertaining and mirth-provoking books ever written for Boys.

COMPLETE VOLUMES, PRICE 3d. each.

THE WILD ADVENTURES OF EDDARD AND JAM JOSSER ABROAD.

THE SLAPCRASH BOYS. A LIVELY SCHOOL STORY.

THE WILD ADVENTURES OF EDDARD AND JAM JOSSER AT HOME.

THE BRAND OF THE BLACK STAR.

VALIANT ROY; OR, THE PIRATES' SCOURGE.

COMPLETE VOLUMES, PRICE 6d. each.

JACK OF THE GOLDEN BELT; OR, STIRRING ADVENTURES IN THE GREAT SWAMPS OF CUBA.

YOUNG CHING AT SCHOOL; OR, HIGH OLD TIMES FOR THE SLAPCRASHERS.

OUR BOYS ABROAD; OR, THE BLACK BANDITS OF THE RHINE.

THE VEILED CAPTAIN; OR, THE HERO OF EAGLE CRAIG.

GALLANT HAL; OR, THE CRUISE OF THE SILVER STAR.

DICK STORNAWAY; OR, A HERO IN SPITE OF HIS FOES.

CHING CHING AND HIS CHUMS; A MOST MIRTHFUL, MOVING, AND MYSTERIOUS STORY.

DARING CHING CHING. A WONDROUS TALE.

COMPLETE VOLUMES, PRICE 1s. each.

TOM TARTAR AT SCHOOL. VOLS. I. AND II.

HANDSOME HARRY OF THE FIGHTING BELVEDERE. VOLS. I. AND II.

YOUNG CHING CHING. VOLS. I. AND II.

CHEERFUL CHING CHING.

WONDERFUL CHING CHING.

COMPLETE VOLUMES, PRICE 2s. each.

HANDSOME HARRY OF THE FIGHTING BELVEDERE.

TOM TARTAR AT SCHOOL; OR, TRUE FRIEND AND NOBLE FOE.

YOUNG CHING CHING. ANOTHER WONDROUS TALE.

www.ingramcontent.com/pod-product-compliance
Lightning Source LLC
Chambersburg PA
CBHW080733250626
47170CB00010B/2810